When Happily Ever After Fails

When Happily Ever After Fails

A Novel

Courtney Deane

Published by SparkPress, a BookSparks imprint,
A division of SparkPoint Studio, LLC
Phoenix, Arizona, USA, 85007
www.gosparkpress.com

Published 2024
Printed in the United States of America
Print ISBN: 978-1-68463-240-4
E-ISBN: 978-1-68463-241-1
Library of Congress Control Number: 2023921750

Interior design by Stacey Aaronson

When Happily Ever After Fails

Table of Contents

1

Rumors of My Virality
Have Been Greatly Exaggerated

This commute was not as easy as Abigail Gardner thought. Well, she never thought it would be *easy*, exactly. Nothing that involved five blocks, four subway stops, and two more blocks, with a heavy box of art supplies occupying both hands and a portfolio tucked under your now-sweaty left pit, could be easy.

But here she was. Panting in front of the wrought-iron gate that displayed "EP" in shiny, loopy gold letters. Her second chance at being a full-time art teacher just steps away. Sadly, those steps were up a monstrous-looking hill that welcomed all peons onto the pristine campus that was Excelsior Primm, one of Philadelphia's oldest and most prestigious preparatory academies.

Abigail took a big breath. The steamy late July heat filled her lungs as she stalled for one more second before conquering this hill and the doubts swimming in her brain. Though the email she'd received last week was a welcome respite during a particularly rowdy wine-and-paint class she was leading, Abigail was still a little skeptical that any school would consider her for another art teacher job. Especially since her last pupils—the high schoolers she'd abandoned in the middle of the day—were housed across the formal lawn at Excelsior Sanctum.

If she squinted really hard, Abigail was sure she could still see that room full of sophomores (well, juniors now), hooting and hollering as her pencil skirt split right as she was demonstrating the graceful, yet powerful maneuvers exhibited by the wildlife of the Serengeti. It was a particularly ill-timed art lesson—one the newly-pubescent pupils chose to capitalize on, much like the lion descending on the wildebeest in her now-viral art demonstration. Abigail shuddered as a vision of her nude-colored Spanx—which were mistaken for bare ass cheeks—and her spot-on impression of *The Scream* came into full view.

The heat boiled under her skin as she averted her eyes and made her way inside the only slightly less intimidating kindergarten through eighth grade academy. She comforted herself with the notion that her late father—one of the most noted Victorian literature minds ever to grace the academic circuit—tutored middle schoolers when he was a lowly grad student awaiting his big break.

Abigail steadied her breathing as she walked down the stark white hallway that smelled of bleach, marveling at how deathly silent her ballet flats were on the shiny marble floor, especially considering the weighty box she was carrying.

It was ten fifty-eight when Abigail crept into the doorway that displayed "Headmistress Evelyn Updike-Montgomery" on a nameplate that was too small for the twelve-syllable abomination to its left.

"Ms. Gardner," the headmistress said without looking up from the notepad her right hand was furiously attacking with a pen. "I see you're not a member of the 'on time is late' club, eh?"

Abigail stammered to say something but feared saying the

wrong thing. Her brain became fuzzy as all the blood in her body seemed to flow into her feet, which felt cauterized to the stone-cold floor. After what seemed like eight uncomfortable millennia, Headmistress Evelyn Updike-Montgomery broke the silence once more.

"Ms. Gardner, as my assistant's email noted, we have a last-minute vacancy on the staff. Our faculty summit is only two weeks away and the students return one week after that. Naturally, we try to avoid these kinds of situations, but unfortunately from time-to-time Excelsior Primm has to suffer for the . . . rash . . . decisions of others. Which leads me to you."

The headmistress slammed her pen down with a thwack before eyeing her wobbly prey. Her eyes were grey and steely, displaying none of the warmth that exuded from Excelsior Sanctum's headmistress during Abigail's interview for that position, just across the formal lawn. It was one of the reasons Abigail felt so confident taking on those older students, even though her art education emphasis was elementary school.

'Course, we know how that turned out . . .

Abigail gulped, swallowing her inherent desire to pre-judge this headmistress along with the tiny bit of saliva left in her increasingly dry mouth. After all, just because this woman—who held the key to her only teaching prospect, possibly ever—looked like a taller, boxier version of the school marm from *Uncle Buck* (minus the wart), that didn't mean she embodied her shit-kicking spirit, right?

I'm sure she's a perfectly nice woman, even if she gives off that whole "a house might fall on me at any second" vibe.

"Right, of course," Abigail squeaked. She took this as her cue to put down her supply box. Her eyes darted around the small room, searching for an appropriate space. Since every inch of floor seemed to be consumed by fake, waxy plants, she opted to use one of the guest chairs. Abigail stacked her portfolio on top of the box before shakily retrieving her résumé.

Holding up her palm, the headmistress said, "That won't be necessary."

"What? I mean, I'm sorry?"

"Your résumé or writing sample or whatever you've got there. It's not necessary."

"O-oh, but I'm very qualified for the job." Abigail cast the portfolio aside and began to place a sample of the art supplies she planned to use this semester on the headmistress' desk, feeling the opportunity was somehow slipping away. Abigail rarely encountered people who accumulated such disdain for her so quickly. She usually required a little time to disappoint.

"Ms. Gardner, tell me something," the headmistress said, flicking one of the markers that was rolling toward her. "What's your favorite book?"

"My favorite . . . book?" Abigail furrowed her brow and cocked her head like a dog. A raised eyebrow from the headmistress made her instantly shake this asinine expression off her face. "My favorite *book*. I guess that would be *Alice's Adventures in Wonderland*. I think we all can relate to feeling out of place and living in a world where nothing is as it seems."

She was certainly living in one now.

Why does she want to know my favorite book?

Determined to redirect the subject toward her actual specialty, Abigail added, "Plus, what's there not to love about all the various *Alice* illustrations over the decades? Centuries, really. There's the hand illustrations, Art Deco style many have used to display the Queen and her court and, of course, the beautiful color palette Disney used to—"

"Funny," the headmistress interrupted, turning her attention back toward the previously abused notepad. "I can hear your father's voice echoing those same sentiments, though in his British accent, of course. I attended a few of his keynotes at Bryn Mawr, you know. He wasn't just a literary mind. He was excellent at grabbing and keeping the students' attention."

"I . . . um . . . I didn't know that—that you knew him, that is, but thank you for the kind words." It was an autopilot phrase Abigail adopted in the early years after ALS had claimed her dad. Everyone always had something to say. Some way they knew him. Felt they had some part of him they could bestow on her like a fat cat doling out porridge to a hungry orphan.

What they didn't know was that these little displays of "generosity" never made Abigail feel any better. They couldn't tell her anything about her father she didn't already know, despite only having fourteen years with him.

Updike banished more of Abigail's art materials from her vicinity, found her pen and began maniacally scribbling once more. "Between the weight of your surname and your references from Temple University—quite a few of our pupils end up there, you know—I'm confident you can do the job. You'll be teaching sixth graders."

Abigail's eyes lit up as her heart leapt into her throat. "Oh, that's wonderful!" she exclaimed, clasping her hands together.

Never in a million years did I think this would be that easy.

"Plus, we're late in the game, I'm out of time, and there are more pressing matters I need to attend to before those golden gates swing open in twenty-four days. Which reminds me . . ." The headmistress reached for her office phone, batting at a violet-colored pencil that was near the receiver. "Mad-a-leen, please tell Mitch to report to my office with his pruning shears. That is all," she chirped before the phone was anywhere near her ear.

The headmistress glanced up, startled to see Abigail still standing there. An awkward silence lingered between them.

"Well, I won't take up any more of your time, Headmistress. I'll collect the paperwork from your secretary and be ready to go at the faculty summit." Abigail swiped the supplies back into the box and placed her portfolio under her arm as an act of good faith. "If you could just tell me which classroom I'm in, I'll be out of your hair at once."

"Good. Fine. Room twenty-three. Liberal Arts Building."

"Room twenty-three. Got it." She turned to leave before stopping in her tracks. "Wait, did you say *Liberal* Arts Building?"

The headmistress narrowed her eyes.

"Yes, the literature classrooms are housed in the Liberal Arts Building. One would think you knew that, given your pedigree."

Abigail stared back in disbelief.

"I—I—I. Miss—Headmistress, I'm an art—art teacher? Not a liberal arts teacher. My degree is in art education. My focus was visual art with an emphasis on three-dimensional storytelling." Abigail looked like she was playing with an imaginary Rubik's Cube as she rotated her hands in front of her, trying to illustrate her point.

"I know all of this, Ms. Gardner. I also know about your lit essay—the one on magic versus fate in seventeenth-century fairy tales—that made quite the rounds on the northeast academia circuit."

That was a stupid paper I had to write for a general-ed requirement. Ugh, when will people let that go?

"Now, if you'll excuse me, there are some bushes in the south wing that need my attention. The job is teaching sixth-grade literature."

"But the email didn't say anything about teaching literature." This *had* to be a misunderstanding. Perhaps the headmistress had simply mixed up her open positions and any minute now a librarian-looking type in big-rimmed glasses with a penchant for cats would walk through that same intimidating doorway declaring, "I'm here for the lit teacher opening." She pleaded, begged, bargained with the larger universe for this to be the case, though she also knew any requests to outside forces seemed to fall on deaf ears.

The email also didn't say anything about teaching art. Fuck.

"Look, I'm sure you're a lovely young woman, but I'm losing my patience," the headmistress said through gritted teeth. "Our appointment started late, you seem to need more hand holding than I can give you and your supplies are inappropriate for your classroom—Room twenty-three, in the *Liberal* Arts Building. My offer stands for exactly eight seconds. After that, you can go back to answering want ads or painting with a pilsner or whatever it is you do with your free time."

The left corner of her mouth upturned as the headmistress added, "Of course, you could always try your hand across the lawn again," a knowing expression filling her face.

Abigail's throat sank to her stomach, as it did every time this "incident" was brought up, which was more often than one would assume. Though her close friends knew not to tease her about it, acquaintances, paint-and-wine participants and even a couple Tinder dates referenced the video occasionally. To add insult to injury, there was a rumor going around that a local Catholic school was using the video as a teaching tool . . . on the pitfalls of wearing tight clothing that was not within the faculty dress code.

"Personally, I think your father would be proud—you are taking a page out of his metaphorical book and all."

More talk of her father brought Abigail out of the teenaged Serengeti and back to the current lion's den. "You know you have a talent for literature, thanks to that wonderful, wonderful man and his unquenchable thirst for knowledge. Now, *he* was a teacher. Top-notch, unprecedented. Anyway, you've got me off subject and now I'm very late. Take it or leave it. Right now."

Abigail's heart felt heavy. Her head felt heavy. Even her shoulders felt heavy. But she knew this woman was right. About everything. Literature may not have been her subject of choice, but there was no denying she was intimately familiar with every classic and most soon-to-be classics. Her father required it. As hard as that little girl fought against the old, tattered pages of leatherbound books that were heavier than any toy she ever owned, they both knew she had a talent for understanding complex characters. For teasing out themes. Seeing into the author's mind.

"Miss *Gardner!*"

"Of course," she yelped, as the paint brushes rattled around in her box, just as startled as she was.

"'Of course,' what?"

"Of course . . . I want the job." Abigail tried to sound excited and not the least bit dejected, which was exactly how she felt.

The headmistress stood up, grabbed her notebook and proceeded to shimmy between her desk and faux forest without so much as a glance upward at the exasperated girl standing outside her office walls. "Good. Fine. Room twenty-three. Liberal Arts Building."

"Thank you. You won't regret this," she promised as the woman passed by.

Abigail silently exhaled. She finally allowed her shoulders to relax a pinch just as the bottom of her box gave out, unleashing all the creativity that had been dying to escape mere minutes ago.

2

It Didn't Go Lightly

Sighing, Abigail yanked a small corner of blanket from under Brutus, a Spuds McKenzie–looking rescue who was more than happy to indulge her binge-watching habit that provided a small reprieve from reality that night. If she weren't so desperate to prove herself—and, well, climb out of the debt that came with an education you hadn't yet been able to use—Abigail could've stayed with the "Mommy Juice" crowd at Cup + Canvas. That would've given her some time to figure out how her life plan got so derailed.

How, again, did I become a lit teacher?

At times most intrusive the question would pop into her head like another round of pinball. Just as the last ball escaped through the gap between the two flippers, another would appear, ready to be launched and volleyed about for a good, long while.

All that time spent on visual arts—life sculpture, drawing with ink, concept design—was it all for nothing? Were the kids at Sanctum right? Could they smell a phony art teacher a mile away? Was my father right? Is literature in my blood? Doomed to haunt me until I give it the proper respect, like my own Tell-Tale Heart?

Determined to distract herself before another ball was

launched, Abigail hopped off the couch to grab a kombucha. She almost made it back to her favorite movie in peace when she caught the glow of her phone, which had been banished to silent mode. "Mathilda" flashed across the lit screen, along with a photo of Abigail and her BFF, arms around each other, standing in waist-deep turquoise water at Doctor's Cave Beach in Jamaica, Mathilda's birthplace.

Abigail let out a high-pitched groan that made Brutus come running. He sat at her feet, tilting his head in confusion, much like Abigail had a few hours earlier. It was Mathilda's third call of the day. Abigail knew if she didn't pick up, this newbie detective was certain to dispatch the CSI unit by midnight. She rolled her eyes once more before tapping the green icon, wishing there was a way to stave off inquiries from the outside world until she figured out the new mess that was her life.

"Hey, Mathilda. Listen, I'm kinda busy. Can we save it for Sophie's bachelorette on Saturday?" The two friends had recently canceled on their former co-worker from their college bartending days a total of five times (official score—Abigail: two, Mathilda: three), but seeing as how they were in her wedding, Saturday was pretty much a sure bet.

"What? What do you mean? You go on the biggest interview of your life, and you want to *save* it?" Though this wasn't a FaceTime, Abigail could've described Mathilda's face perfectly: a furrowed brow that consisted of two angry vertical lines and three horizontal ones, a scrunched nose and an indignant upturn that extended from the right corner of her full pout all the way to the scar by Mathilda's eye, an early injury from the police academy.

"Yeah, I'm just—I'm really tired. And I think Brutus might be coming down with something . . . ate some plastic maybe. The trash looked a little disturbed when I got home."

"Okay. Brutus? The trash? Stop stalling. It went horribly, then?"

Despite the earnest detective's best interrogation techniques, Abigail didn't budge. Netflix, on the other hand, gave up the smoking gun.

"Are you watching that movie again?" Mathilda's tone changed from concerned to accusatory in zero seconds flat.

"What movie?" Abigail feigned. She lowered her laptop screen as gently as she could to not arouse any further suspicion.

"I can hear that goddamn Audrey Hepburn in the background. Now I know something's up. What happened?"

Abigail had a history of trying to disappear into old movies when something was bothering her. At first her friends thought it was a quirky interest, maybe a way to escape all the pressures of young adulthood. But then they noticed a pattern. After ALS took her father's ability to speak, Abigail started watching Disney classics like *Pollyanna* and *The Apple Dumpling Gang*.

When her mother, Grace, suddenly passed six years later from a completely preventable complication due to diabetes, Abigail was consumed with the *Road to* series with Bob Hope and Bing Crosby. Even though she was studying the art of French masculine and feminine creation in North Philly, she often found herself on a journey to Morocco, Bali, Singapore, or Rio. She'd go wherever Hope would take her.

The Hepburn phase began when she failed to secure a gallery-girl internship in New York the summer before her senior year of college. This was the time when real-world immersion would really start to matter—at least in her mind. A dejected Abigail had passed the famed Tiffany's on the way back to the train station when her eyes fell on the enchanting storefront. Its big city displays showcased the dreams and envies of every small-town Lulamae who wished herself a Holly. She suddenly understood why that slight girl sought out the retailer when she was feeling down. It seemed much more attractive to fight a case of the reds with a little Tiffany Blue.

Now, back in Philadelphia at a career crossroads, Holly Golightly had Tiffany's, and Abigail Gardner had *Breakfast at Tiffany's*.

"It's not that movie . . . it's chatter from the street, I just . . . Mathilda, I love you, but I need to get back to Brutus." The dog farted right on cue. "I think he needs to go out. I'll fill you in on Saturday."

"If you use your dog as an excuse *one more time*, I swear I'm feeding him the credit card you use for Netflix," Mathilda said, only half-joking as the beast did have an affinity for plastic. "*Breakfast at Tiffany's* will become breakfast for Brutus."

Defeated, Abigail finally caved. She filled her lifelong partner in crime in on the long commute, the difficult AF headmistress, and the plot twist that was the teaching subject. Like the cooperative witness she was, she left nothing out.

"And the bottom of my art supplies box chose that exact moment to give way."

"Nuh-*uh!*" Mathilda bellowed. "So, what did you *do?*" Her tone was a mix of fascination and mortification, confirming that this situation was, in fact, as bad as it seemed. It was a familiar confirmation, one that was issued repeatedly whenever anyone brought up the "Full Moon Over the Sanctum Serengeti" video.

"I shut my eyes. When I opened them, she was still standing there. Staring at me. I swear I heard a muffled growl. I couldn't even tell if that was from her or the old janitor who showed up right on cue." She threw her head back as her heart raced. Clearly, PTSD was already kicking in. "Ugh, the whole thing was awful. It looked like a Pride parade threw up on her floor. And one of the

yellow acrylic paint tubes broke upon impact and started dribbling in the cracks, toward her shoes."

"Were they cute shoes?"

"Of course they weren't cute shoes. They looked like they
were from 1692 but that's not the point," Abigail lamented,
throwing her free hand in the air. "This is supposed to be my
new *boss*. And after she'd just given me that speech about what an
opportunity this was and how qualified I am and how much my
father would be pleased. Oh, God, my father would have *died*."

"If it makes you feel any better, I would've died, too."

"Ugh, I feel nauseous even thinking about it."

"If this is your way of saying you're too sick for Saturday, forget
about it," Mathilda warned. "You're not leaving me with that
bridezilla and her gaggle of Italian cousins."

"I just don't know what I've gotten myself into." Abigail
sighed as the weight of the situation she'd been trying to avoid
finally sunk in. "If this job is anything like that interview, I may
never feel well enough to hang with someone's large Italian family
ever again."

Mathilda cackled and slapped her hands together before
declaring, "RIP Abigail Gardner's dating life."

3

You Ain't Just Whistlin' Trixie

Abigail adjusted her shiny blue bob. She did a quick spin in her bodycon dress, making sure she sparkled head to toe after a thorough glitter spraying. Though she was much too depressed for a Saturday night on the town, she was trying to rally her fun, vibrant persona. Well, *somebody's* fun, vibrant persona, anyway.

Abigail normally loved a good bachelorette, but not for the reasons most girls do. She liked to adopt fake identities. Abigail always put her character-development skills to great use at these shindigs, creating people out of thin air with family histories, job complaints, and even regional dialects. These personalities were big hits with her girlfriends. It was always fun to see who showed up that night, and downright hilarious to watch the men respond to a person who didn't exist. In a way, it was Abigail's own form of "ghosting."

It was also where she got her thrill. These identities allowed self-conscious Abigail to cut loose, sans judgement. She didn't have to worry about her friends egging her on to take a shot out of some random dude's belly button or whether the whole place would boo her if she refused to dance on the bar with the rest of the bridal party. Abigail was already doing these activities, except it wasn't her—it was Peregrine from Augusta who was a save-the-whales naturalist. Or Masie who was the fourth employee at We-Work and was destined to be a millionaire until it all came crashing down. Thanks to her natural talents, she created these people in no time flat.

Lacing up her knee-high boots, Abigail had to concede this look was over the top, even for one of her characters. But tonight, they were going to Tākō, a drag queen supper club, on "Sass Me Saturday." Abigail found this theme particularly fun and un-inhibiting. Strike that—*Trixie*, the Southern belle from Tennessee—found tonight's Sass Me session particularly fun and uninhibiting.

The pandemonium began as soon as the bachelorette wagon pulled up to her stoop.

"Woooooo. Hot stuff—yeeeeeoooow," the cronies screamed as the party bus's door whooshed open.

"Oh, my God. Oh, my God. Who are you?" Sophie cackled and snorted as Abigail tried her best to get up the steps in five-inch heels without exposing her undersides. With all the bags and booze littering the floor, it was a challenge not to collapse onto the bride, who sloppily sat with her knees apart, already exposing her undersides.

"Why lil ol' me?" Abigail drawled, resting her fingertips on her glittery chest in feigned exasperation. "Uh, shug, you should know . . . I'm Trixie from Tennessee, y'all." More hoots and gaggles filled the bus, along with the strong aroma of Fireball. Abigail settled in, silently vowing to put all thoughts of tragic novels and curtailed career aspirations out of her head. This wasn't that hard to do as the Fireball came in more than just aroma form.

The group was deposited in front of their favorite downtown spot before she had time to settle on Trixie's backstory. Being regulars, the party easily secured the coveted front-row booth, known as Resting Bitch Place, next to the catwalk. This booth also made them instant RBP VIPs, which had its own perks, including a hostess, or Head Bitch in Charge. Theirs was named Jordanne, who sported a purple mohawk, rainbow blush, and mile-long lash extensions.

"Where's dat Tanqweray and tawnic, shugs?" Abigail purred slowly, obnoxiously, as she settled into the booth.

"Right here, you little Southern sluuuuuut." Sophie poured the drink like it was second nature, which it probably was since she was a career bartender. A pro pourer but sloppy drunk, Sophie spilled some of the contents on her own neon-green mini dress before handing it over.

The party was in full swing before long. Abigail surveyed the scene and caught wind of Mathilda, who'd been dancing and grabbing just about anyone who would let her since they'd arrived. Though she'd undoubtedly deposit herself on the doorstep of the thrice-divorced, middle-aged detective she was banging once the night was over, Mathilda's preference for "keeping things casual" meant she was free to do whatever she wanted. To whomever she wanted. Whenever she wanted. Having this type of freedom was her own version of "self-love," Mathilda would profess every time someone seemed to bat an eye at her flirty ways.

Her current prospect was the tallest beauty Abigail had ever seen. At least seven feet tall, she reckoned.

I wonder if Trixie knew very many queens growing up in the good ol' South.

Abigail loved the queens' passion for beauty. Being an arts major, it was something they had in common. Mathilda returned from her twerkathon soon enough, and after Sophie was "forced" by the emcee to perform a lap dance on one of the queens, the tiny booth was once again full.

By the time the commotion had settled, and all approved clips had been uploaded to social media, Abigail's bladder had become a four-alarm emergency. She popped up and sprinted over to the restroom, thankful most guests wouldn't dream of missing the *Lady Marmalade* routine that was up next.

Standing at the sink, a sense of relief washed over her as she turned on the faucet and cleaned up her smudged lower eyeliner, peeling a few blue strands off her glistening forehead.

She was just cooling down when a man with mesmerizing hazel eyes, broad shoulders, and an adorable chin dimple that made Abigail bite her bottom lip emerged from one of the stalls. Her gaze followed him over to the sink next to her. He rolled up the sleeves of his unbuttoned brown flannel shirt and turned on the faucet. The man glanced at her in the mirror, causing Abigail to shake off whatever alcohol-induced lust she was feeling. If that hadn't done it, the t-shirt poking out under the flannel, which featured Animal from *The Muppets* doing a drum solo, would have.

"Umm, excuse me, shug," she said, trying to stay in character. "But y'all are in the girls' room."

He seemed unfazed by the fish-netted, blue-haired girl who was staring at him through the bathroom mirror.

"I know," he said, reaching for a paper towel without missing a beat. "I'm literate. I'm also fluent in stick-figure bathroom door art."

Abigail straightened her wig and brushed glitter off her shoulders as she took in this sight. "You know, this club has a few gender-neutral restrooms down the hall if that's what you're looking for . . . unless, oooh," she slurred before quieting down and turning back to her own sink.

The man looked at her once more in the mirror, but she simply re-wet her hands as a few more seconds passed.

"'Oooh,' what . . . ?"

"Hmm?" Abigail hummed, looking up and catching her own droopy daze staring back at her.

"You said 'oooh.' I imagine you have some great theory as to why I'm using the women's restroom?" He turned to face her, resting his hip on the side of the sink as he folded his arms. She assumed he must've been pulling his lip into his teeth, as his dimple intensified.

"Oh, it's nuthin'. None of my business if ya'll are transitionin' or somethin'. I don't know your story, but whatever you're into, I'm all for it. You gotta set your soul free, you know?"

"Or it could be that there's a flood in the men's room and the line for the single bathrooms is already twelve deep. This one was empty when I came in and my friend was supposed to keep watch. I guess he got distracted. Some of these outfits will do that to you, you know." The man gave her a quick once-over, raising an eyebrow. "So. Tell me your story. You in a state of transition?"

"No," she said, a little too loudly before turning off her faucet. She refused to acknowledge that her life actually *was* in a state of transition.

"My bad. It's just the wig. And the fake eyelashes. And the fishnets. And we *are* in drag country," he said with all the confidence in the world that his argument would hold up in court. Abigail was getting ready to retort when something caught her attention.

"Are you just gonna lit the water run like that?" she said, pointing to his sink.

He glanced at the faucet and flashed her an annoyingly perfect smile. "Why? Is it bothering you?"

"W'll, yeah. Don't *waste* it like that."

"Because then the poor queens in China won't have any water to wash out their wigs?"

All right.

Even drunk, Abigail knew when she was being pulled into a dumb conversation. The kids at Sanctum did it all the time. She could never figure out if they wanted to wind down the clock or to make her flustered, but she didn't appreciate it then, and she certainly didn't appreciate it now.

The man stood there, near the running sink, waiting for a comeback as a barrage of thoughts floated through her head. Her face went from annoyed to confused to smug all while remaining perfectly silent. When she failed to produce a comeback, he turned off the water. The final insult came when he threw her his best "I didn't think so" stare as he exited the bathroom.

Sensing her opportunity for one last comeback, Abigail yelled, "Next time don't waste so much water," though her voice had diminished to a whisper by the time she finished the sentence. Abigail walked back to Resting Bitch Place hugging both shoulders, her eyes pointed at the sticky floor.

"What is this? What's going on here?" Sophie demanded, circling her sharply manicured fingernail around Abigail's glum mug. As much as she was great at adopting other personas, disappointment always registered on the face that officially belonged to Abigail Gardner.

"Oh, it's nothing . . . stupid stuff. I'll be fine."

"You better slap that sadness right off before I do it for you." Sophie waved her lime green talon inches from Abigail's nose. "And I can tonight. It's my bachelorette. You all have to do what I say."

"You're right, you're right," Abigail relented, thankful to Sophie for breaking the tension within her own body.

"And right now, I say have some liquid courage." Sophie poured some vodka in a glass. She added a splash of club soda and squeezed the life out of a lemon wedge before passing the concoction off to Abigail.

"Yes, ma'am," Abigail agreed, trying her best to disappear and re-emerge as the fun persona. The one people wanted to see when you're supposed to be having a good time.

"Hens, peckers, stags and all you other animals . . . it's yo'-time to get up here and DANCE!" yelled a Lady Gaga lookalike who had just finished a raucous rendition of *Radio Gaga*. Feeling her confidence returning with her blood alcohol level, Abigail led the party pack. She played with the boas, lip synched with the boys, and even did an only slightly naughty lap dance for Sophie, who was loving the fact that one of her girls was outshining the members of the other parties on stage.

Abigail's head began to spin as she was exiting the stage. She looked around their booth for some water but found all the clear containers empty.

"Soph? Hey, Soph, I'm going to grab some water and get your Bitch to refill the carafes," she said, pointing at the empties.

"We're out of alcohol?" Sophie squealed, stunned even though eight girls had been there for two hours with numerous guys and queens coming in to congratulate the bride and grab a drink or a seat, whichever presented itself.

"You guys are the worst," she snapped at her party. "You didn't even leave the last drink for me."

"Relax, shug," Abigail quickly added as she deposited Sophie into the booth. "You let lil ol' Trixie handle this. Why, I'll be faster than a cheetah on roller skates."

"Oh, my God, I love you, Trixie," Sophie said, all the tension dissolving immediately. "You're the best. I wish you were around more often."

Abigail tried not to take that personally as she released herself from Sophie's strong grip, promising to find Jordanne. She briefly scanned the crowd for the purple mohawk but didn't see the harm in getting some water for herself first.

Sitting at the bar for a few minutes, Abigail sucked the last bit of water out of the paper straw and held the now all-ice cup to her forehead. Cautious not to disappear for too long—lest she be labeled a lazy bridesmaid or, worse, a bad friend—Abigail took in one more Zen-like breath before executing a quarter spin on her barstool.

"Oh, hello. Again."

That stupid smirk.

God!

"You. What are you?" Abigail said before realizing she'd abandoned Southern hospitality in favor of East Coast glib in her anger and surprise. "I mean, what're y'all doin' here?"

"It's a bar," he stated. His bemused expression enraged her. The man with *The Muppet* shirt on was staring at her like *she* was a petulant child.

"I know it's a bar. Listen, if y'all don't have nothin' nice to say, then just git outta my way."

"I should get out of *your* way? Seems like I can't turn around without running into that Smurf 'do." He pointed at her wig as Abigail blew a few sweat-soaked strands out of her eyes. "Although colored hair pieces seem to be in abundance. It kind of looks like there's a *Trolls* reunion in here tonight."

Abigail clenched her jaw, pleading with her brain to say something clever. When that failed, she settled on a swift exit.

Abigail stepped off the barstool, ready to walk back to the booth with her dignity intact, but life had other plans. The tip of her right platform boot hooked the footrest as all her weight headed toward the stranger.

Christ, can't I even get a small win here?

She looked up at the smug man who was the only thing standing between her face and a floor covered in confetti. Abigail met his wide grin with a half-hearted nod before releasing his solid forearms. Regaining her footing, she began shuffling away once more.

"Hey, look," he said, stepping in front of her. His eyes had changed slightly, displaying a warmth that had been missing earlier. Or maybe it was the strobe lights and alcohol. Abigail couldn't tell. "If you're going to hate me and go back to your little hen party over there to spill all the details on how you met some pompous prick in the women's bathroom, then you might as well know who you're hating. I'm Nate." He wiped his hand that was now covered in body glitter on his distressed black denim before extending it to her.

Just smile and nod politely, and this guy will be out of your blue hair in no time.

Abigail looked around the club, somehow hoping to find reassurance in the crowd. That's when her eyes suddenly caught sight of an uncovered vagina that came out to play after its owner lifted her hands over her head as she bounced to a remix of Britney's *Piece of Me* atop one of the tables.

"I'm Trampie . . . Trixie! Damn," Abigail said, stomping her foot as her hand involuntarily went to her forehead, displacing her wig in the process.

"Your name's Trampie?" Nate asked, pulling back his hand. "Now I *know* you're a queen."

"It's not. It's Trixie. From Tennessee. Oh, forget it. Have a nice life and . . . have a nice life." She beelined it for the sanctuary that had become Resting Bitch Place. Knowing she wasn't getting out of there anytime soon; Abigail did what any level-headed girl named Trampie would.

She drank and danced her ass off.

4

First Things First

A bigail stood in her small walk-in closet, feeling completely naked and exposed, despite being fully dressed for her big day. Not only was she starting at a new school, but she couldn't hide behind her armor of art supplies.

Her paintbrushes and colorful acrylics had been replaced with the most depressing reading list she'd ever encountered. She had no idea whether titles like *With Every Drop of Blood*, *The Yearling*, and *Romeo and Juliet* were assigned to her class by Updike or if it was the universe continuing its sick joke, but either way, they ensured Abigail would remain attached to the themes of death and destruction.

At least for the next nine months.

She couldn't even console herself with the lame "but I'm a good teacher" argument, lest the internet or seventeen fifteen-year-olds from the neighboring campus prove her wrong.

But she had her syllabus, her summit training—which mostly consisted of Updike chiding the teachers on everything from incorporating participation into their grades to the lack of after-school involvement—and a(nother) shot at a respectable, stable income for the first time in her life.

Abigail was increasingly aware of the latter after her credit card got denied when she tried to purchase a first-day-of-school ensemble at the new boutique on Market. A quick check of her account told her what she already knew: spending three hundred and twenty-seven dollars at an overpriced supper club to drink away a maddening encounter with a man was the kind of activity reserved for those who already received their paychecks via direct deposit.

Yes, today was sink or swim. She was either going to emerge a bona fide Excelsior Primm faculty member, or she was going to spend the year chasing down substitute teacher positions in Amish Country.

Exhaling, she reviewed her look for any imperfections. The second-hand shop hadn't been her first choice, but since quitting Cup + Canvas to focus on the summit training, it was the best she could do. The place had turned up a pale pink blouse that was not too low cut and light cream pants that were neither too tight nor too transparent. She knew this because she spent a good five minutes bending, twisting, and squatting in the dressing room to be sure another Sanctus shitshow wasn't imminent.

Abigail nervously thumbed the cursive "A" that hung from a delicate gold chain around her neck. It was a gift Charles had given Grace on her thirty-fifth birthday, the year she was pregnant with Abigail. The pair didn't share the same first initial, but they shared the necklace until it became the sole possession of Abigail by default. While it might have been nice to rely on the college fund her dad always talked about, or even a bit of the life insurance payout her mom used to reference from time to time before she eventually dropped the subject entirely, Grace's penchant for spending ensured neither were available now. Instead, Abigail basked in the few possessions she did have. This included

Charles's vast book collection, along with the necklace and a few other trinkets that didn't have to be sold off to cover Grace's credit card debts upon her death.

She watched as the charm's angles caught the fluorescent light. Abigail looked . . . presentable. She had prepared well for this fresh start and had managed to pull off a decent first-day look.

The preparation she'd put into the reading list was even more impressive. Abigail vowed she'd do whatever it took to avoid the panic she'd felt at Excelsior Sanctum. For her, that meant re-reading, researching and analyzing four books in three weeks. Yes, it was overkill (Mathilda's favorite word—and form of death), but as her dad used to say, "Knowledge is the source of all power, Abigail. It's like a garden: if it isn't nurtured, it cannot grow. And what are we?"

The proper response was "We are Gardners."

She fingered the necklace once more as she swallowed hard, trying to stave off the sadness that was creeping over her. She thought about her parents and all the comments she'd received recently about how proud they would have been of her. She was following in her father's footsteps, after all, whether she liked it or not.

Abigail knew these remarks were meant to be encouraging. Distant relatives took it upon themselves to remind her how thrilled Grace and Charles would have been whenever something good happened to her. Like they were supernatural ambassadors who were assigned to convey a special message from beyond the grave. Like the pair simply couldn't get to a phone or were stuck in a foreign land.

No parents on the first day of school.

It was a childish thought, she knew. She was the *teacher* now. She was the adult.

Mercifully, her phone pinged. It was Quinn, Abigail's close friend from her own prep-school days. He'd been a savior during their respective single-sex schools' freshmen welcome week dance, coming into her life at a time when she needed someone the most. Just eight months after her father had passed.

I know you don't need it, but I wanted to wish you good luck today. "May your troubles be less, and your blessings be more, and may nothing but happiness come through your (classroom) door."

Pretty slick, huh? Can't wait to hear about it tonight! Just remember to smile and you'll be fine. The Kellys are pulling for ya! ☺

Abigail's heart warmed. If there were ever a dysfunctional family to love, it was the Kellys. She had become the fifth wheel in their foursome. Pre-college summers were spent at their Martha's Vineyard cottage where the Kellys entertained. Nights typically ended with Mr. Kelly playing piano as Mrs. Kelly—a once-prominent Manhattan lounge singer who settled into a supporting role as The Professor's Wife—sang the sweetest renditions of hits by Billie Holiday and Etta James. Quinn and Abigail spent most of their time at the beach, with his then-sister, Avery, often tagging along.

See? There are people who believe in you. Who know you can do this. You know you can do this.

"I can do this," Abigail said to Brutus, her voice a little wobbly. She grabbed her bag, and she was off. Taking her first steps as Ms. Gardner, literature teacher at Excelsior Primm. Striding into the sunrise on the first day of school.

✳

Abigail's hands shook as the mass of newly minted sixth graders filed into her classroom—a space she'd filled with colorful sketches from some of their reading list's most noteworthy scenes. She pressed her palms into the desk, hoping no one would notice her knuckles whitening as she tried to stop the tremble.

She was immediately struck by how young these kids looked. Their baby faces were such a drastic departure from the sophomores, the last kids to issue her blank stares and eye rolls. Most hadn't entered their awkward phase yet and still resembled the cherubic children their parents would always remember them as.

"Good morning, class," she began, trying to steady her voice. "My name is Ms. Gardner and I'm your literature teacher. You certainly have some wonderful and challenging reading ahead of you, but I'm sure you can handle it. You're quite advanced to be reading books typically assigned to junior high or even high schoolers, I should know."

She silently chided herself for that last personal tidbit, but no one seemed to notice.

"I'm really looking forward to getting to know you, and I hope you'll enjoy the exciting work we're going to jump into. So, let's start with attendance."

The sheet in front of her looked more like a Scrabble scorecard than a list of East Philly kids' names. She was struck by the number of inherited family monikers. *Long*-held family monikers. There was a John, a Henry, a John Henry Prichard III. They were joined by a George Stephen III, Marshall Franklin III, and William Benjamin IV, who wanted to go by Willy BJ, which she quickly shot down.

Good to see the patriarchy is alive and well.

Then there were the modern names that sounded more like descriptions and feelings than children.

"Peace?"

"Here."

"Birdie?"

"Here."

"Honor?"

"Yup."

"Dieter? Dieter?"

"He's not here," one of the legacy kids pointed out. A double-check of the day's absentee list confirmed this fact.

Absent on the first day of school? How odd. A European vacation must've run long or something.

"I thought we'd start the year off with a real classic, Shakespeare's *Romeo and Juliet*." Abigail held her copy up like a poor man's Vanna White. The suggestion was instantly met with groans and seat shifting. "Now, *Romeo and Juliet* is an interesting play—a tragedy, really—because we know from the beginning how it's going to end."

"I know how it's going to end," John Henry III said as he fidgeted with the cuff on his uniform blazer. "I saw the movie."

He looks like he's literally trying to unhook himself from Shakespeare.

"It's kind of a crazy story," added Reese, Birdie's obviously identical twin sister. "The whole time you're waiting for these two people to get together but they can't because they die."

More groans ensued as a boy in the back dramatically slammed his forehead onto his copy.

"Relax, everyone, Reese didn't ruin anything. The Chorus actually tells you that these two will meet their demise in the Prologue, the opening of the book." Abigail made her way to the boy and patted him on the shoulder. "That's what I was alluding to. This play is very different from many others because they tell us the ending up front."

"Why would they do that?" Marshall inquired, flipping through the play like an answer would suddenly reveal itself. "Who wants to read a book if they already know how it ends?"

"Because the play isn't about plot twists and turns. It's about two people who are fighting a losing, yet valiant, battle against societal norms and . . . fate."

It was so quiet Abigail swore she could hear the kink in the front lawn sprinkler that was causing a dry patch. This was a famous dry patch, as Abigail had learned at the faculty summit when she overheard Updike berating the head custodian about it.

"Listen, these two teenagers, they want to be happy and do their own thing, like every teenager. And like other teens, they're pretty sure their parents are ruining their lives. So they rebel. This rebellion just had more consequences in 1590s Verona than it would today."

She noticed a handful of students were following her with their heads as she walked up and down the classroom's aisles. A few were even making eye contact.

"So, whaddaya say? You're about to become teenagers. Let's see how similar, yet different, your lives are from these two."

Most of the kids took this cue to crack their books, though a few stragglers sat staring blankly.

"Or we could always read *Old Yeller*."

"No!" the class echoed as the holdouts quickly found the first page.

"Okay, then. Like a true Chorus, we'll read the Prologue together. Then John Henry, you play Sampson. Marshall, you'll be Gregory."

"Who's going to be Juliet?" Reese asked, blinking her eyes rapidly. It was more of a sales pitch than a genuine inquiry.

"She doesn't speak until Scene Three, but there is a Lady Montague. And a Lady Capulet. Reese, Birdie, wanna take those parts?"

The other roles were soon doled out, with the children showing an interest in "playing the parts" rather than simply reading long blocks of text aloud. They began, in unison . . .

Two households, both alike in dignity,

In fair Verona, where we lay our scene . . .

5

Cheers to New Beginnings

A few hours later Abigail pulled her wavy, dirty-blonde hair into her best messy side braid. She didn't normally wear her hair like this, but she felt a little too conservative for Manayunk's cool arts scene, which was where she was headed to meet Quinn and celebrate her first day back in action.

All in all, it went well. The kids' protests over their reading material weren't too dramatic, and all clothes remained firmly in place, which Abigail was particularly proud of.

As she approached, she marveled at how effortless it was to pick Quinn out of a crowd. No matter how many other so-called artists occupied the area with their token messy brown hair, nicotine habits, and smartphone addictions, Quinn's penchant for hunching over the table and anxiously scratching his head as if he were trying to defuse a bomb made him so easy to spot.

"Hiyeee," she said, tapping Quinn on the shoulder as she rounded the other side of the white picket patio divider. It was a familiar routine, one they did at least once a week at Killian's, the same sticky Irish pub where Quinn ordered the same dry meatloaf sandwich night after night when he wasn't working. Which was often, these days.

"Hey," he replied, clearly startled that someone had broken the concentration he'd bestowed upon the new graffiti littering the table.

Abigail plopped her quilted Zara backpack onto the cigarette-laden floor and settled into the aluminum armchair. No matter how many times she did this, she was always startled by how rough the chair was. She was sure one of these days she'd emerge with a bruised fat ass.

"So, how'd it go? I already ordered your bottle of rosé," Quinn said, pointing to the stainless-steel bucket sitting between them that held her favorite drink. Well, her favorite alcoholic drink, anyway.

Abigail grinned and rolled her eyes in feigned bemusement. Quinn was the only friend who voluntarily indulged her rosé habit. The poor man was six-foot-four and a semi-celebrity among the East Coast hipster scene, thanks to his viral documentary that chronicled the many musical talents of America's unhoused population. He seemed to pay in major street cred every time he was seen out with Abigail drinking rosé or, God forbid, frosé in his neck of the woods while his comrades opted for a pint from Evil Genius.

"I went with a sparkling this time since, you know, we're celebrating." He handed her a delicate flute. "Tell me everything."

Half a bottle and two cigarettes (for Quinn) later, Abigail took a big, smoke-filled breath and became quiet for the first time since she sat down.

"Well, if you ask me, it all sounds great." Abigail involuntarily scrunched her nose, which seemingly motivated Quinn to up his cheerleading game. "I mean, I know you'd rather be teaching art, but literature isn't a bad second, right? Not for someone like you who's such a natural at it, not to mention a legacy and all."

He extended his glass toward her to cheers.

"It is. It's great," Abigail reflexively shot back, making herself sound defensive as she raised her flute halfway up before setting it back down. "It's just that . . ."

"What? Is the pay shit? You know us Kellys are always willing to help you out. If that's the case, say no more . . ."

"No, it's not that. It's just . . . it's me. And teaching. Kids. Again. After everything." She gestured around wildly like her hands could whip up another Sanctum storm.

"Hey," Quinn interjected, banging his palm on the table. "Those teens were shits, okay? *Anyone* would've run for their life if a group of high schoolers laughed, pointed, and recorded when their ass cheeks were on display."

"It wasn't my bare ass," she corrected. "The Spanx were unfortunately a little too close to my skin color for anyone to know that."

Abigail appreciated Quinn's attempt to deflect the blame. To make her the unwitting victim and the kids the sole source of her early career's demise. It would be a convenient narrative, to be sure—one that, if told correctly, might even elicit sympathy. She could say they bullied her. That she felt threatened—sexually and physically. That the rip triggered something deep inside that caused her to flee in terror. But it wouldn't be true.

The students had been annoying and perhaps inappropriate, yes. But they were *teenagers*. She was the adult, and she was the one who ran for the hills, abandoning an entire class in the middle of a school day. As if no other teacher had ever suffered a humiliation in front of their pupils . . .

"I wonder if I'll ever be able to move past this," she said, staring through the mesh metal table at the butts below. "I know I handled myself poorly—I *know* I did—but I feel like I can never escape these ghosts of mine. Whether it's a viral video or popular lit essay or even the deaths of my parents. These ghosts seem to follow me and define who I am before I can even speak for myself."

Abigail blew air out the right side of her mouth like a deflating balloon. She shoved the tip of her finger into the table's mesh before adding, "I'm tired of my reputation preceding me, good or bad. I can't live up to the good and I can't escape the bad. No matter how hard I try."

"Look, screw that." It was Quinn's go-to advice when he didn't like what he was hearing. Deny. Avoid. Renounce. What he failed to add was that he most likely knew how she felt. Quinn's documentary-making career started off strong before a flop, and then a project that hit too close to home, threatened to take him out of the scene for good. He even had his own viral video. One that involved him getting nose to nose with an influencer who called him a "no-talent ass clown" in front of a popular gyro food truck last year.

"These sixth graders are like, what, eleven?" Quinn continued. Abigail nodded. "They're young kids. Shit, they probably still play with dolls. Your specialty was elementary education, right? Well, it's about time you put all that schooling to good use."

He raised his flute once more, but Abigail failed to notice. She solemnly rubbed the stem of her glass, moving it down the lengths of her index and middle fingers. Always getting a little emotional when she drank, Abigail was miles away, determining how this next chapter might play out and what kind of heartache she was in for. It seemed to be a fact of life.

"Ab, you'll be fine," Quinn encouraged. His dark brown eyes moved mechanically from left to right, scanning her face. "You're a perfectly wonderful teacher. You're friendly and you're patient. Kind and empathetic. I mean, shit, you put up with a dickhead like me."

To many people, Quinn was a lot of things: an asshole, a sell-out, a self-important shit, an entitled little rich kid, a has-been, a never-was. But Abigail and Avery (now Everest) knew that, above all else, Quinn was the person you wanted in your corner when the chips were down, the stakes were up, and your life seemed all but over.

"You're extremely relatable. Easy to talk to and amazing with kids." He spoke with a gentleness Abigail wished he'd show the rest of the world. "Minus that *ooooone leeeetle* incident at Excelsior Sanctum."

Finally. She smiled. Quinn beamed ear to ear, gulping a big sip of bubbly that he'd been saving for their toast.

Abigail looked around before leaning across the table. Quinn followed her lead, meeting her halfway and bracing for whatever might come next. In an ever-so-hushed voice, like it would destroy society if someone heard, she whispered, "I don't always feel that normal, you know? And I'm afraid I won't know how to relate to kids with normal problems."

Quinn shook off the close encounter, falling back into his chair with a thud.

"Okay, first of all, fuck normal," he said, giving the table another whack. "Number one, none of us are normal. Number two, if you ever find one of these people who are supposedly normal, go running in the other direction. They're either a serial killer or they'll be so painfully boring that you'll want to turn into one yourself."

Abigail emitted the same awkward laugh that first revealed itself at that fateful freshman dance under the boys' championship banners. She took a sip of rosé, wiping her mouth and running her tongue over her teeth to remove the excess liquid that was seconds away from dribbling out. For this very moment, at least, Abigail knew she was exactly where she was supposed to be, inhaling smoke, drinking bad rosé, and sharing a big, fuzzy moment with a big, fuzzy friend.

"Seriously, Ab," Quinn said, picking up his glass as she did the same. "You'll be fine. It's what you were born to do."

6

The First Day Getting Schooled

One place completely devoid of warm fuzzies was the faculty lounge, where all the teachers sat as Updike chided them during their first staff meeting of the school year.

"The lackluster commitment to creating well-rounded students through the engagement in extracurricular activities is appalling at this institution," the headmistress lamented as she walked around the lounge, hands clasped behind her back, prison-warden style.

"I'm not asking you academic-minded to lead our crew team to victory," she continued to a room full of snickering, "but I'm sure many of you could fill supporting roles both on and off the field. And there is absolutely no excuse as to why Excelsior Primm has one of the lowest non–language club turnouts of any prep school in the Lower Delaware Valley."

The room fell silent as the teachers guiltily focused on the floor, a ploy they had almost certainly learned from their students. Mrs. Chang, the biology teacher, had warned Abigail that the parents' extreme drive to take home only the top spots—which was encouraged by none other than Updike—had caused many teachers to shy away from the extra-curricular arena.

"Now, there are competitions in chess, math, science, and computer programming." Updike narrowed her eyes, thrusting a judgmental stare in each teacher's direction. "Surely you can find a use for your talents somewhere. Hmm?"

Cursed with a full bladder and a butt that went numb six minutes ago, Abigail shifted in her seat.

"Ms. Gardner?"

Crap.

"Yes?" she squeaked, while trying to act as though she had absolutely no idea what this woman wanted.

"How about you?"

"As you know, Headmistress, my specialty is art and, well, you mentioned you don't have a use for my . . . talents . . . here?"

A few chuckles were met with a death stare from the headmistress.

"Ms. Gardner, we are not one-dimensional people at Excelsior Primm. If you believe this is true, then this is not the place for you. I'm sure you have *something* you can contribute to these growing minds. That is, aside from the little drawings you hung on your classroom's walls. I guess it takes real talent to color within the lines. I especially love what you did with the *nude*-colored pencil."

Laughter erupted as Abigail stopped shifting and met her boss's stare.

"Stick to the curriculum, Ms. Gardner. If you want a place to channel your inner passion, pick a pre approved activity and start there."

"I have to go to the bathroom," was her genius response.

"This is not a classroom, and you are not a student," Updike rebuked. "If you have to go to the bathroom, go to the bathroom."

"Right," Abigail said. To the contrary, they were assembled

in a former classroom that had been converted into a teacher's lounge. And Updike was lecturing at the front of the room as the others sat in rows of chairs and tried not to make eye contact, lest they be forced to participate. And furthermore, if she wasn't a student, then why was she just reprimanded in a room full of her peers?

She stood to walk.

"Of course, Mrs. Vangundy could use some help reviving the drama club." The headmistress stopped behind a chair that held a wrinkly, translucent-colored woman who sat on two pillows and smiled kindly. Though she was sure the smile was genuine, Abigail was less confident that this woman was following the conversation. From her vantage point, Mrs. Vangundy simply seemed to be pleased all eyes were on her for once.

"Yes, sure," Abigail quipped. It was a reflex, really. "If you'll excuse me."

She quickly made her way out the door and threw herself against the impeccably white, shiny wall. Abigail was just beginning to calm down when she heard the door open again. Mrs. Chang's black bob swung left, then right where she caught sight of Abigail, who appeared to be stuck to the wall like fly paper.

"Don't pay attention," Mrs. Chang commanded.

"What?"

"You heard me," the diminutive woman said as she stood toe to toe with Abigail. "That headmistress, she's a bitch and she knows it."

Abigail let out a gasp. She'd never witnessed anyone stand up to Updike—even behind her back.

"Now, don't get too carried away with that. She may be a turd, but she knows what she's doing, so you have to respect her. But you *don't* have to let her walk all over you."

Mrs. Chang held her gaze as she spoke. Her eyes were dark and felt somewhat invasive, but Abigail could sense a warmth, albeit a tough-love kind of warmth, behind them. "Don't worry," she said, looking Abigail up and down. "You'll find your way. There's a quiet strength in you. I can see it."

"There is?"

"There is. You know it. I know it. That one?" Mrs. Chang pointed toward the lounge. "She may not know it. But that's okay. Updike . . . more like Uptight. That woman needs to get laid."

Mrs. Chang shook her head, her hair whipping against her cheekbones, as she turned to head back into the lounge. "And you should think about the drama club. Vangundy's as old as a bat. She can't relate to these kids anymore—or their keen sense of hearing."

Now it was Abigail's turn to shake her head in disbelief over this little fireball. She wished she'd had someone like this at Excelsior Sanctum. Maybe it would have made a difference.

"You'll be okay. You gotta make this school your bitch," the elder teacher said right before she cracked the door.

Abigail stood there for a few more seconds, though she was no longer glued to the wall. Rather than risk running into another faculty member who might not be as empathetic, Abigail opted to use the girl's bathroom down the hall. A few minutes later, she found herself in front of the mirror, her usual place of shame, judgment, and general self-loathing.

I'm sure they're gossiping about this right now. "Is she always so squirrely?" "Some people just have that fight-or-flight nature, and she definitely takes flight." "Not everyone is cut out to be a teacher. I can see not hacking it at the high school level, but here? Please. And do you know who her father is?"

Abigail felt a pressure well up behind her eyes. She turned

on the faucet and splashed cool water on her neck, which had grown blotchy. Not half a second later, the door opened.

"No. No, no, no, no, no, no."

"Oh, God. I didn't know . . . it's late in the day . . . no one's *ever* in here after class on a Friday," Nate stuttered. His '90s grunge look might have been replaced by a sweat band and compression pants, but that voice. She'd recognize that deep, enticing voice anywhere.

"No . . . what . . . what are you doing here?" She pounded on the porcelain sink, causing the water to leap a few inches in the process.

"I'm sorry." He held his hands in front of him as he sprinted to the dispenser. "I ran in here to get some paper towels. I can't find Mitch, the custodian. It's four o'clock, so I figured he'd be in here. We need him in the boys' bathroom. One of the new soccer players puked all over the floor from running drills and . . ."

"And you just seem to find yourself drawn to girls' restrooms, don't you?" She cocked her head and gave him her best "this better be good" expression, refusing to let his charm or flirty dimple soften her.

Nate placed a hand over his eyes as he snatched a huge wad of paper towels. "I totally get how this looks, but this bathroom is never in use after school hours. The only girls on campus right now are the volleyball team, and they're practicing in the gym, over in the South Wing."

"How do you know that? And why are you *here*? On school property, in this bathroom, in *my life* again? Huh? Why?"

"Oh, I'm in *your life*?" Nate said with a chuckle that exposed his annoyingly straight bottom teeth. Anyone could have exquisite upper incisors, Abigail surmised, but only those truly committed to dental aesthetics made sure their less-pronounced bottom teeth were as straight and white as their upstairs neighbors. "Tell me, have you been subbing at this school for three years before finally being offered a full-time position? And was it you who helped Coach Kay get the soccer team to the State Cup last year?"

As if on cue, a brawny man in a baseball hat with a whistle around his neck poked his head into the bathroom.

"Nate, we found Mitch. We're all good," the giant head yelled as the door swung open and shut in one swift motion.

"See? We're all good." Nate started to unfurl the crumpled paper towels in his hand, flattening each one as he laid them down meticulously on the counter near Abigail's sink. "You know, I almost didn't recognize you without your wig."

She stared at him in disbelief, her eyes as wide as silver dollars.

"Your blue hair?" He puffed his hands around his head like he was coiffing his own 'do. "No wonder you wear that out. Wouldn't want anyone to find out that a faculty member is moonlighting as a stage dancer at Tākō."

"Are you kidding? I wasn't moonlighting as anything. I was there with my girlfriends. For a bachelorette party."

"Oh, I definitely saw some moonlighting going on," he said, making air quotes around "moon." "And your fishnets? Those were a nice touch." He threw her a wink as he tended to his stack.

"Are you really a teacher here?" she shot back. "If so, why weren't you at the faculty summit? And why aren't you in the meeting downstairs?"

"I jumped on board full-time yesterday. Apparently, Mr. Parker—the history teacher who's like eighty-something? I've been subbing for him for a while, and I guess he had a heart attack after the first day of school. As I mentioned, I also help with the soccer team when I can. I've been mentoring a few of the new kids on the team, including the kid who puked. Alex barely made the cut—he's a little heavy, hasn't really lost the baby weight and all. Anyway, these running drills are killing him. As I'm sure you noticed, it was unseasonably humid today."

"Yes, I noticed." She pulled her arms in tighter. It *had* been unseasonably warm, and Abigail had yet to do a pit check as she had been focused on the professional lashing she was giving her reflection. Before she was unceremoniously interrupted, that is.

"Alex didn't feel well, and I thought I could get him into a stall before the rest of the team saw him embarrass himself. He missed the toilet by a mile, but at least no one else was there. Well, aside from me and Coach Kay. And now Mitch, who is probably in there right now swearing up a storm."

Abigail stared at Nate as she processed his story. He stared right back, with a slight grin on his face.

"Say, aren't you the water preservationist?" Nate nodded his head toward her still-running faucet. She had forgotten to turn it off in all the chaos surrounding puke, soccer, heart attacks, and men in women's restrooms.

Damn!

"I am. Wasting water is such a . . . waste. Now, if you'll excuse me." She turned the faucet off and tried to push past him, though they both knew there was plenty of room on either side of him for her to maneuver.

"And brush up on your stick-figure bathroom art," she said as she swung the door open, turning her head back to look at him. "I don't want to find you in the women's room again." Nate through his hands up in a "guilty as charged" gesture.

Abigail exited the lavatory with a little extra pep in her step, turning back around to carry out her victory walk when she ran right into Mitch's cleaning cart.

7

Family Matters

As bad as it was going for Abigail, Romeo was faring even worse.

"But he doesn't have to leave," Honor argued, kicking her legs wildly under her desk. "They could throw him in jail. Then he'd be punished but he could still write to Juliet. Maybe Juliet could even stand outside the prison, like he did under her balcony, and they could talk."

Abigail issued a tight-lipped smile. She appreciated Honor's fight for Romeo. And for love. There was a part of her that admired the young girl's naïveté, thinking it would be so easy to convince a patriarchal Elizabethan society to simply lock Romeo away after he killed Tybalt.

"That's a nice thought, Honor, and one that may very well take place today, but I'm afraid they weren't as . . . understanding . . . back then."

"My grandpa was sentenced to prison," John Henry suddenly added. "He said it wasn't going to be that bad. Because he was in the white one."

"The 'white one'? They don't separate prisoners by race, John Henry."

"No. By color. Shirt color, right?" He fiddled with the drawstring in his Navy zip-up sweater as he spoke.

"Oh, *collar* you mean. As in white collar . . . crime?"

John Henry shrugged, blowing his penny-colored hair out of his face. "I guess so, if that's the white one."

"And was it? As bad as your grandfather thought it would be?" The exchange made Abigail's heart pound. She unconsciously drummed her fingers on her chest. "Do you think Romeo and Juliet's love could have survived if Romeo were cellmates with your grandfather?"

"Oh, dunno. He died before he ever went to jail. My grandmother seemed pretty mad at him though, so I'm not sure Juliet would've stuck by his side."

Abigail stood there dumbfounded at this revelation. She'd never seen someone so young divulge such personal information, and with such ambivalence. Her family was firmly in the "stiff upper lip" club, thanks, in part, to her dad's British upbringing. There were never any talks of sickness or death—at least none outside of the literary realm.

Her father would've rather disintegrated on the spot than uttered even one word about his ailment in a work setting or any other environment. In fact, he took a leave of absence as soon as the ALS diagnosis was confirmed. Though his speech was one of the last things to go, Charles couldn't stomach "the indignity of teaching from a wheelchair. I am *not* goddamn Stephen Hawking," she heard him shout to Grace one day early on in his illness, before anyone but the two of them even knew something was wrong.

"If you have questions about jail, you can ask Dieter when he comes back," Marshall said, referring to his often-absent classmate. Dieter seemed to be able to string four or five school days together, but not much more than that.

"You mean, Dieter's been to jail?" The words flew out of her mouth before Abigail had the chance to consider the ramifications of her question.

A few kids chuckled, while Honor rolled her eyes and put her palm on her face, clearly astonished at how little this teacher knew.

"No," Reese clarified as she colored a heart on her sister's hand. "His brother, Deacon. He's been in jail a whole bunch of times."

"It's not jail, it's juvie," John Henry explained, sitting up a little taller and clasping his hands together. "That's the kid's jail."

"You would know, since you come from a long line of criminals." Birdie scrunched her nose at him before turning back to her sister.

"That's enough," Abigail squashed the sarcasm but not the stares. "I shouldn't have to tell you how wildly inappropriate this conversation is. It is never okay to name-call and it's never okay to talk about someone who isn't here. Now, let's continue with our read. Hit it, Nurse."

A low moan rose from the crowd, but Honor found her place and continued aloud. Abigail sat at her desk and stared blankly at the pages in the play. She assumed kids like these led cushy little existences. Even though she'd technically been one of them, she'd always felt like an outsider.

The other kids watched Nickelodeon, escaped to vacation homes, and got manicures with their mothers. Charles, meanwhile, believed in books, not TV, and Grace, ever the insecure homebody, wasn't one for long summer vacations, or even leaving the state, save for visiting family in Massachusetts. She certainly wouldn't have been caught dead doing something as extravagant as a mother-daughter spa day. A quick glance around the classroom revealed what Abigail already suspected: all the girls had perfectly buffed and polished fingernails.

Now, as Abigail contemplated tales of delinquent brothers and felon grandfathers, she wondered if she'd maybe made some unfair assumptions about life for these kids and their families.

"If all else fail, myself have power to die," Birdie read as Juliet.

The kids had reached the end of Act Three, Scene Five, and the first signs of the lovers' intended suicide were beginning to reveal themselves.

As the period ended, Abigail was at a loss for how to end such a heavy read. She looked up right before the bell rang, leaving them with, "What can I say? I never promised you a happy ending."

Abigail tried to shake off that morning's discussion, to no avail. Though she didn't know what was going on in Dieter's home, she couldn't help him if she remained in the dark. This caused her to wind up in a very unfortunate place after school.

"Headmistress?" She poked her head into her boss's office cautiously, as if arrows might dart out at any minute. "I—um— wanted to talk to you. About one of my students?"

"Having problems already, are we?" The woman shimmied in her chair but her eyes remained firmly fixed to the papers in front of her.

"Not exactly. It's just . . . Dieter was absent today. And yester-day. And had a few no-shows before that. Some of the children had mentioned his brother might be having . . . emotional problems?"

"If by 'emotional problems' you mean a raging drug habit, then yes, I guess you could say Deacon Ebbisham has been feeling a little emotional lately." She reached into a ripped-open bag of Milano cookies and bit one in half, producing a loud snap.

Again with the nonchalance. Isn't anything sacred or . . . private . . . to people anymore?

"As much as I don't want to pry, don't you think I, as Dieter's teacher, should know if something's going on? He's practically gone more than he's here. It feels like that, anyway. I debated asking him about it, but I didn't want to make him feel bad. Now that the other kids are talking, though, I'm not sure I can ignore it."

When this failed to elicit a reaction, Abigail cleared her throat. Loudly.

The headmistress finally tore her eyes away from her reading materials to scowl at Abigail. "It seems you are requiring something more of me, Ms. Gardner. Either spit it out or kindly remove yourself from my office. I have other things to attend to."

"I just—if there are any special circumstances or hardships my students may be facing I'd really like to be aware of them."

She secretly felt like a hypocrite. Being her father's daughter, Abigail had hated when teachers pulled her aside to tell her they knew all about her "situation." That they were there if she needed them, whether it be for a hug or a deadline extension. These pep talks were followed by awkward shoulder pats and a creeping sensation that Abigail needed to close herself off even further.

She wanted *less* attention, not more. Why didn't they understand that she wanted to be viewed as a normal kid and not as some pity party or pet project?

Yet, thirteen years later, here she was. It felt strange on the other side of the coin . . .

"You want the dirt on your first-period students? Fine." The woman dusted cookie crumbs off her fingers before continuing. "Birdie and Reese's mother moonlights as a high-end escort. She doesn't need the money but likes the excitement. John Henry's grandfather—the original John Henry—jumped off a skyscraper in New York after he lost all his clients' money in an investment scheme. Honor's father walked out on their family about a year ago. Left the mom with very little money. She didn't want to sell Honor's horse, knowing how much the animal meant to her, so she downgraded her boarding to some fly-by-night facility. Next thing you know some lunatic sets fire to it and the girl's lost her best friend. Dieter's brother is an eighteen-year-old crackhead who occasionally dabbles in fentanyl. Mrs. Ebbisham likes to keep Dieter close by when she's feeling particularly insecure about Deacon's whereabouts, or his health status. Are we all caught up now?"

"Yes," Abigail uttered, booking it out of there as quickly as she could. She walked to her train terminal at a furious pace, reeling from this recent enlightenment.

How could I have been so naïve? These kids aren't new to tragedy. Their lives are full of hardships . . . and they're not even teenagers.

She hated the idea of adding to that load by immersing them in these heartbreaking reading assignments. Abigail even began to worry that these plots might put ideas in their heads as they embodied characters who faced the same young-adult issues that could one day be on their plates.

Young love. Families at war. What is the cost of happiness, and is it worth risking it all? Is it even really happiness if you must risk it all? Can you make this sort of a sizable wager at the age of fourteen?

Abigail laid on her couch like the stereotypical psychiatric patient, feeling both enlightened and more entrenched. She had to find a way to implement these dark literary lessons without bogging the children down in the negative. Thinking back over the past decade or so, she was ashamed to admit how she'd let unpleasant situations of all kinds hold her back. How she curled into a protective ball in their presence, shutting down to preserve what she had, unwilling to risk that in favor of possibly achieving something more.

No wonder those sophomores didn't respect me.

Abigail stared at the books that lined her entertainment unit, silently pleading for a solution that could conquer her greatest weakness. Brutus leaned against her, his furrowed brow producing a worried look.

For God's sake, even your dog is named after one of the most tragic characters of all time.

Feeling thoroughly defeated, Abigail walked into her closet and threw off her work sweater in favor of a babydoll tee with a honey badger on it. "Wish I was more like the honey badger #hedontcare," she hastily captioned from her window seat as her tragic dog laid below. She looked around her apartment noticing, for the first time, how barren her walls were.

Some art enthusiast you are.

Her eyes eventually settled on the slim wall that separated her bathroom from her living room. That held the only thing she'd bothered to hang in the past three years. And wouldn't you know it—it wasn't art at all. It was a quote.

"If I'm honest, I have to tell you I still read fairy-tales and I like them best of all."

—AUDREY HEPBURN

8

I Read the News Today, Oh Bother

"I'm telling you, Quinn, this school is going to be harder than high school," Abigail lamented as she slouched in the booth at Killian's that Thursday night. A dart whizzed past her head as two bros sporting Drexel sweatshirts tried to one-up each other.

"And all this is over spilt paint and a crack about you liking to sketch?" he said, scratching his scalp. His fingers instantly became entwined in his unkempt 'do. Just then Keleigh arrived with his dry, dependable brick of a meatloaf sandwich.

"It's not just that," Abigail said after exchanging niceties with the waitress. "The other teachers seem to think I'm a joke— oh, and I'm a *literal* walking, talking punchline to this douchebag history teacher who seems to have this school all figured out, despite the fact that he's newer than me."

She crumbled a corner of meatloaf off his sandwich and popped it into her mouth, a decision she instantly regretted. Much like taking the job at Excelsior Primm.

"Oh, did I mention the head custodian? He's not real fond of me, either. Not after I rammed his janitor's cart and almost ended

up face first in that bright yellow trash can." Abigail sat up, dropping her head to her hands. "What am I going to do? I already
quit Cup + Canvas. I can't . . . I mean, I don't think I should . . ."

"Hey," Quinn said, banging his fork against his plate. The
frat boys looked over at him before returning to whatever viral
video was producing their Beavis and Butthead laughter.

*Please don't let it be mine, please don't let it be mine, please don't
let it be mine.*

"Did you get into teaching to make 'friends'?" Quinn pointed
his fork at her as she shook her head. "Does it matter one fucking
iota what these other hacks think of you? What about your students? Aren't *they* the reason you're there?"

Quinn was right—he was always right—at least when it came
to doling out advice for anyone but himself. She wasn't there for
peer approval. Abigail became a teacher to try and impart just a
little bit of the magic her dad bestowed upon his pupils, but in
her own way. This next chapter may not have been unfolding the
way she pictured it, but the one complaint she didn't have was
her kids. Abigail might have loathed that downer of a reading list,
but if these kids had to be introduced to such heavy works, then
she figured her early brushes with tragedy made her an expert on
the subject.

Abigail looked up at Quinn, scrunching her lips.

"I need to give this a chance, don't I?" An audible sigh escaped
her lips. It was one part relief and one part terror, but it was the
breath she needed to get ahold of herself and put things in per-
spective.

The kids. You're there to be a teacher to these kids.

"I think you know the answer to that," Quinn shot back,
signaling Keleigh for the check. "And I think you also know that
if we don't get going now, we're going to be late to *Beatfest with*

the Beatles, and you definitely know how pissy I get if I miss the early years."

Three hours later, Abigail and Quinn poured themselves into her apartment. Quinn was singing "Birthday" in his best raspy voice, strumming an air-guitar. His performance was more reminiscent of the geek from *Sixteen Candles* than John or Paul, at least in her eyes. Quinn hummed through the kitchen as Abigail dug deep in the back of her fridge for that last bottle of coconut water that she was sure she still had.

"Du, nuh, nuh, nuh, nuh, nuh," he sang as he bounced around her. Brutus, obviously wanting in on the action, quickly began bouncing around him. Soon the small strip of yellow kitchen was quite crowded.

"Quinn, stop it." Abigail giggled, despite her best attempts to sound serious.

"What's the problem, babe?" he said in his best Bea'les accent as he danced behind her.

"I—I'm trying to find this bottle of water and you're not helping." She gave her hip a powerful thrust in his direction as she continued her search.

"But I think I is, me love. The world needs music, don't it? An' that's what I'm doing, you see. I'm givin' the people what they wants. An' for free. I'm a regular Fadder Christmas, I am . . . says I."

"I can't tell if that's British or pirate, but either way could you kindly move? You two are going to make me drop something." She rummaged around the fridge as far as she could without winding up elbow-deep in last night's spaghetti.

"Aw, 'tis not me an' the beast. 'Tis that luscious arse of yers that's gittin' in yer way." Quinn put his hands around Abigail's waist and pulled her closer. "Here. Let me lend a hand. You pull

the pesky jug, I'll pull the pesky lady, Brutus will just . . . be . . .
pesky, an' we'll be outta this poppycock in no time."

He pulled, then she pulled as the two tumbled onto the hexa-
gon-tiled floor with what turned out to be an old, sour-smelling
bottle of kombucha. Abigail turned over on her stomach to get
her bearings. And found herself face to face with Quinn.

"Well, hello," he said as he placed his hands behind his
head, his accent vanishing as quickly as it arrived. Quinn stared
at Abigail, a bemused half-smirk on his face. She could tell he
was waiting for her to react. After more than a decade and a
handful of failed attempts, it was clear Quinn—as confident as he
could be—wasn't going to make the first move.

"Now see, what did I tell you? It's all fun and pirate accents
until someone winds up on the floor with a bruised fat ass and an
old bottle of bacteria," she said, trying to soften the blow while
simultaneously pretending there was nothing to soften in the
first place. Quinn was also trying to recover. He stood up and
brushed himself off after Abigail quickly hopped over him, putrid
bottle in hand.

"Hey." He patted the back pocket of his Levi's. "I think I'm
out of cigarettes."

"Well, you should be. You were handing them out like you
were the freakin' Maharishi."

"What does that even mean?" He shook his head as he made
his way to the front door.

"I don't know. I'm drunk. And I have Beatles on the brain."

"Right. Why don't you . . . work on that . . . while I run to Sal's
to get some more."

"I could really use a coconut water," Abigail called from the
closet as she determined which pair of pajama pants was the least
attractive. "Ooh, or coconut milk. *Chocolate* coconut milk, kay?"

"Chocolate coconut milk? Seriously?" Receiving no response, he continued. "Hey, tell Alexa to crank up *Meet the Beatles* for when I return, Yoko."

Abigail was already halfway into her ugliest bottoms—turquoise-colored with photos of polar bears, a present from Charles's sister years ago—when Quinn closed the door. She pulled one of her old Temple shirts over her bra, noting the sacrilege of leaving this straitjacket on with such a comfy outfit.

Flopping onto her beige sofa, she grabbed her laptop. Abigail was browsing through videos of dogs seeing snow for the first time when a news alert flashed across her phone.

BREAKING NEWS: Local Teens Jump to their Deaths from Ben Franklin Bridge

She instantly closed out the screen that featured a golden retriever with white powder on his nose and went straight to her Google News feed. A couple clicks later, there it was. A young boy and girl had walked hand in hand on the bridge in dark hoodies around seven p.m., according to the driver who stopped to call police. He described seeing the pair hug, and the male hoisting the female over the railing before he hopped over himself. Police assumed the pair landed on the high-speed rail line below, where they made their final descent into the Delaware River. Neither survived. They were fourteen.

"Hug your loved ones tight tonight and be thankful for the life you got," the witness was quoted as saying. "There are families out there that will never be the same. Those two, they were just kids."

"I'm back, babe," Quinn said as he burst through the door, reeking of smoke and bad accents. He turned to march into the living room when Abigail's droopy face stopped him in his tracks. "What the hell? What's all this then?"

"Double teen suicide," Abigail said, looking up from her screen. "Less than two miles from here."

"Jesus." Quinn headed into the kitchen with two bags on his wrists. She could hear the plastic crinkling as he placed a few glass bottles on her laminate table.

Abigail filled him in on the details she knew. Scrolling past a banner ad, she took in the last few lines of the story.

"Ugh, it gets worse," she called.

"How can it get worse?" Quinn was taking a particularly long time in the kitchen, though Abigail was pretty sure she knew why. She was starting to think she should've hidden this news from him.

"They found the female victim's body," she said as she tried to steady her voice, "stuck on the RiverLink Ferry dock in Jersey. Steps from the Camden Children's Garden. God."

Quinn emerged, holding two red solo cups filled with chocolate coconut milk. "Come on," he said, nodding toward her front door. "Put that shit away. Now I need a cigarette."

Grabbing her imitation Uggs and a blanket, the trio headed outside. Abigail sat with her back against the building's entrance while Quinn puffed away, and Brutus lay on his side nearby. The potbellied pooch wasn't sure whether to be excited that he was included or annoyed that his night didn't end two hours ago.

"So, speaking of teen suicide . . ."

"Quinn, stop it," she ordered. This, Abigail would not have. "Don't talk about your sis—don't talk about them that way."

"Sorry," he said, turning to make eye contact. Abigail was happy to see he seemed sincere. "You know I specialize in bad jokes and poor timing."

She did know this. She also knew it was a cover for a deeper cut, one that would scab over but refused to heal. Quinn might have found Insta Success with his first film, thanks mostly to a viral clip involving a transient woman in Louisiana singing *The Devil Went Down to Georgia* backwards, but his second film had consequences he never could've predicted when Hulu agreed to fund a documentary on eating disorders.

The Tone of Hunger took an up-close look at an inpatient facility for the ultra-wealthy that utilized music as healing therapy. While his film was getting panned across the board, Quinn had no idea his own little sister, Avery, was struggling with identity and body-image issues.

Her fellow students at Fashion & Merchandising Academy were even harsher than Quinn's critics when the film debuted last year. They called Avery a heretic and accused her of using her classroom connections to give her brother an inside look at the fashion industry's dirty little secret. All this was too much for the then-nineteen-year-old. She tripled her usual Xanax dose, chugged as much vodka as she could and swiftly called her mom, crying.

Avery only emerged from her rehab facility two months ago, sober, with a rekindled love for reiki. Upon their return home, they declared they wanted to be called Everest. That they identi-fied as nonbinary for now, but that they reserved the right to change their mind—and their identity—at any time.

"How are they adjusting?" Abigail asked, picking at the curly faux fur in her seafoam green blanket, one of the zany gifts her mom ordered years ago.

"They're okay. I think part of the adjustment period is getting used to my mom hovering twenty-four-seven, but I guess they have reiki to cope with that now."

A bouncer yelled "All right, clear out," from across the street, eliciting groans from the crowd.

"They will find their way," Abigail offered. "It's just horrible to think there are this many young people dealing with problems so heavy that they don't see an alternative solution. And it's not just Everest. The kids in that news story were fourteen. Fourteen! You know who else was fourteen when they took their own lives? Romeo and Juliet."

"Yeah, that shit's heavy," Quinn said. "Who knows? Another pill, no response from my mom, a few more cruel DMs and Ev's story might've had a different ending. It might still have a different ending. That's what scares the shit out of me."

Quinn and Abigail watched as the passersby poured out of the last open bars. One particularly rowdy gentleman leaned against the large bulb attached to her building's front banister, eliciting a guttural bark from Brutus. She wrapped the blanket around her and the beast as a gust of wind blew by.

"What scares me is that Everest was a kid playing with their Pooh bear, like, yesterday," she said. "It's like the kids in my class. One minute, they're reading stories about talking animals and carnivals and their introduction to death is through a spider who's well-loved and lived a long, happy life. The next minute, it's—BAM—double teen suicide."

Quinn shook his head as he scratched at the peeling black paint on the banister.

"I mean, how do we get from pigtails and Winnie the Pooh to drugs and suicide?" Abigail pondered this as "I Wanna Hold Your Hand" wafted from her second-story window. "I wonder how the Beatles wrote so many innocent, upbeat songs in the early days."

"Speaking of drugs . . ." Quinn chuckled.

"You think so?"

"I know so."

"Quinn, I think I'm drunk," she said, cuddling up with

Brutus and tapping on Quinn's hunched-over back with her boots.

"You think so?"

"I know so."

The two sat there in silence, taking in the fresh, crisp air now that his smoke had cleared. A large crow landed in a golden rain tree near the group, instantly catching Brutus' attention. It looked agitated as it shuffled from claw to claw, flapping its wings as it settled and uttered a huge caw.

"Huh," Abigail mused, holding onto Brutus's collar. "I guess black birds really do sing in the dead of night."

9

Buried Skeletons

By first period, the end had finally come. The children would face a very tough subject that was all too real for today's youth. Abigail felt ill qualified to lead this lesson, despite her up close and personal view of death. It was a lesson that should perhaps be left to a better educator. A more experienced one.

Where's Dad when you need him?

Abigail took a breath. She knew she was being absurd. *Romeo and Juliet* was not going to break these kids. Most had survived some bad encounters already. A seemingly prehistoric tragedy—even one that ended in a double teen suicide—wasn't going to shatter their lives.

Still . . .

"So, what did you think of the play?" She glanced around the room, which was unusually quiet this late in the period. "How was it knowing all along that the characters you're getting to know—that you're embodying in class—were never going to make it in the end?"

"A little . . . haunting, I guess?" Honor said as she rubbed her arm. "It's funny that you know they're going to die, but you don't know how. And in a way, because you know they're going to die, you almost don't want to care what happens to them or even bother to keep reading because, what's it all going to matter anyway? They're gonna be dead in a little bit."

Yep, Abigail was not prepared for that.

She couldn't help but think of her father and whether her own interactions, her opinions of him, would've changed if she knew he was dying. Being so young when he was first diagnosed, Abigail never fully grasped the severity of his illness. Grace and Charles knew he had about three to five years, but Abigail? She assumed he'd die in his old age, maybe just a little weaker than the other seniors.

"Thanks, Honor," she said, feeling a bit weaker herself. "Do the rest of you feel this way? Are the characters *worthless* because we know they're going to die?"

"No," John Henry said. "I don't think about it that way. Everyone dies. So what? What I don't like is that they didn't have to. There were so many times where this whole thing could've been prevented."

"So, what if *you* were Romeo and Juliet, what would you guys have done differently?" Abigail leaned on her desk as a few hands went up.

"They could've had the Nurse and Friar John talk to their parents." William tapped his fingers on his desk. "Or maybe they could have all gone to counseling or that thing where everyone talks and you can't leave the room until you all agree."

"Meditation," John Henry offered.

"I think you mean *mediation*," Abigail corrected.

"Our parents and their lawyers did that." Abigail looked over to see the twins shaking their heads in unison.

"What else could they have done?"

"They could've run away," Dieter said, clearly familiar with the subject.

"Joined the circus."

"Moved to Ireland."

"They should've had Romeo dress up as Paris and marry Juliet in front of the whole kingdom," Marshall said, flashing an excited grin.

"Yeah!" Birdie added. "They could've done a masquerade-themed wedding. Older people always throw parties like that. And then? After they married? Romeo could've shown his face when he kissed the bride and sealed the deal."

"But wouldn't the two families be furious?" Abigail was heartened by their level of enthusiasm.

"Only for a minute," Birdie continued. "Then they'd realize it was still their daughter's wedding day and she obviously loved Romeo a lot to go through all that trouble and I don't think people got divorced back then, so they'd just have to live with it."

"Besides," John Henry said, "that's what they wanted their kids to do anyway—just live with it—so it would be like a taste of their own medicine."

Abigail had to hand it to them. The room was teeming with creativity.

"Okay, kids. How about this? Rewrite the ending to *Romeo and Juliet*. You can either expand upon the ideas we've thrown out here or work your ending in a new direction."

"I know exactly what I'm gonna do," Honor said, raising her pen in the air.

"I can totally picture Juliet's wedding dress."

"You do the wedding outfits, I wanna design the masks," Birdie said to her sister.

Just then there was a knock at the door. Abigail hated to interrupt the creative flow. She secretly hoped they'd continue their lively discussion, though she didn't want to encourage them to get too loud.

God knows who's on the other side.

Opening the door, she stopped dead in the middle of the entryway.

"What . . . what could you *possibly* want right now? I'm in the middle of class," she said as the door swung closed, bumping Abigail's butt and nudging her a bit closer to Nate. So close she could smell his Old City Coffee breath. Though there was plenty of java in the faculty lounge, she'd noticed that Nate checked his staff cubby every morning around seven forty-five with that tan-and-red coffee cup in hand. He'd issue a nod, wink, or perfect smile to any fellow co-workers before making his way to Room seventeen in the Liberal Arts Building.

Not that Abigail knew his morning routine or anything. It was simply impossible to overlook such obvious patterns when they happened five days a week and the subject sported that fresh-out-of-the-shower look and smell. Minus the coffee breath . . .

"I thought you might want these back," Nate said, holding up Abigail's apartment keys. Her keychain featuring a self-portrait of a one-eared Van Gogh dangled from his index and middle fingers.

"How did you get those?" She snatched them out of his hands and shoved them into her knitted open-front cardigan's pocket.

"You dropped them on your way into the building. When you stopped to adjust your skirt? I tried calling after you, but you didn't hear me. Well, I kind of think you heard me, but you didn't want to *hear* me, if you know what I mean."

She knew what he meant. Abigail remembered the morning

quite clearly. The second she paused to pull up her gypsy skirt, she could've sworn she heard Nate calling after her. Unwilling to face another wardrobe malfunction—or, worse yet, be reminded of one—she grabbed her skirt at the waistband and quickly made her way into the building.

"Thank you," she said, her cheeks warming a bit as she realized her overreaction. "You could've put them in my faculty mailbox, but I appreciate you picking them up."

"So, how are you?" His smiley eyes revealed he didn't have a care in the world.

"Are you kidding? My class is in session." She peeped through the small vertical window in her door to see the kids still in full conversation over the play's new ending. John Henry seemed to be leading the pack, as he kneeled on his seat and gestured wildly with his hands.

"Sorry, it's my off period," he said as she turned back around, making eye contact once more. "I just figured you'd have a hell of a time getting home without these. Guess I could've put them in your cubby, but I only see you in there during the morning, so I figured why risk it?"

Nate shrugged as a half-smile brought his right cheek up to his eye, revealing his late-twenties laugh lines. Abigail watched them materialize, wondering for a second about what joys created them before getting back to the task at hand.

"Well, thanks again for the keys," she said, conscious of her own mid-twenties wrinkles as she issued a tight smile. "I really should be getting back."

She executed a full one-eighty-degree turn on her kitten heel as she strode back into her classroom. "All right, class," she said with a simultaneous clap.

Abigail noticed Nate linger by the door's window. She could

see his head out of the corner of her eye but forbade herself from looking in that direction.

Instead, she did her best to play the role of confident, in-control teacher as they continued their discussion. The kids were eager to tell her they had talked and wanted to run with the same ending. A bait-and-switch groom it was.

Abigail laid in bed later that night, recycling the day's events. Though she was physically tired, the children's excitement over their new project, which she'd assigned in all her classes, had energized her. If she were going to be fresh for tomorrow's plot rewrite, however, she needed to get some sleep. She checked her phone one last time before turning in, the sounds from the street below floating through her window.

There was a text from Quinn about Thursday night's plan and one from Sophie about the upcoming bridesmaid dress fitting. A third text was from an unfamiliar local number.

> Hey! I got your number from the faculty directory. Hope you don't mind but I figured I should probably have it on hand in case you ever drop your keys and decide to flee in the opposite direction again. Have a good night. :-)

Abigail banged her fist on her pixel plaid duvet, rolling her eyes at her own idiocy before switching out of text and into email.

Crap. The headmistress.

Updike made it clear that a firm commitment to the drama club was expected after she returned from the bathroom during the faculty meeting. Or the following Monday. Or pretty much any time before tonight. Because now the headmistress was losing her patience (her words), and demanded to hear a plan to turn around this shaky club "post-haste."

Abigail bolted upright. Pulling on a sweatshirt, she headed to her window seat and began to jot down some thoughts in her spiral notebook.

To reinvigorate the drama club, we could . . .
bring in more guest speakers
enter a film festival
recreate some famous scenes and monologues from movies
just do what normal drama clubs do and act?

Abigail sketched a woman shrugging next to that last suggestion. "Ugh. This is all wrong." She flung her No. 2 pencil onto the cushion, causing it to bounce to the floor.

For God's sake, you can write a viral lit essay and you can't compose a few club suggestions?

She sat at the window with her ankles crossed, wondering how to tackle this new role just as she was settling into her first one. The commotion on the street below was finally starting to die down as the crowds headed home.

There was one bar, a dueling-piano lounge across the street, that was still going strong. From her position, Abigail could barely make out a rendition of "Don't Stop Believin'" sung by about fifty or so drunken Philadelphians. She grinned, knowing that was one of those songs you couldn't help but belt out after a long day and a couple drinks.

Abigail leaned closer to her window, letting her eyes fully adjust to the soft glow of the streetlights. She sighed as her gaze wandered upward, beyond her neighborhood to the sky that was lit up by a harvest moon. Staring through the backlit bald trees and building silhouettes, Abigail wondered how she got here, where she was going, and what she would think one day when she looked back.

An encouraging word from a father or sympathetic hug from a mother would've been nice right about now, but there were none to be had. Instead, she walked over to the entertainment unit. She ran her hands along the books' bindings, unable to see which work she was touching until she pulled one at random. *Paradise Lost*. Abigail had never grown particularly fond of this poem, but there was one quote she believed captured the human psyche quite well. It was perhaps Milton's most famous—or at least his most accurate:

The mind is its own place, and in itself
Can make a heav'n of hell, a hell of heav'n

It was a sentiment Abigail tried to keep in mind when outside circumstances stood to threaten her well-being. Even when she couldn't quite summon the strength to change her own attitude, she knew Milton's words were true. Just as they were true now as she thought of her students, who had every opportunity and material possession afforded to them but were not spared from heartache even at a young age. And of their parents, most of whom had more money, power, and status than the majority of people in Greater Philly could ever hope for, yet couldn't master the primal instinct bonds that brought parent to child, husband to wife.

The same could be said for the Kellys and their children, who could choose any path they desired, yet seemed to wander aimlessly in the world searching for some unidentifiable thing to make them whole. And of the Deckers, whose home should've been overflowing with love, though you wouldn't know it from the middle daughter who sought it out in the arms of a jaded, much older man.

Then there was Abigail. She tried to see the silver linings in life, but the happier she attempted to look and feel, the further the goalpost seemed to move. She wanted to turn everything around for everyone, including herself.

Placing Milton back on the shelf, she returned to her window seat to watch the remaining stragglers stumble on their journeys home. She wondered how many of them were out that night trying to drink their problems away. Burning off some steam from work, hiding from loved ones, or perhaps not wanting to return to an empty apartment where no one cared how late they were out—or whether they came home at all.

Abigail wondered all these things and stared. Though these people were not her people and their problems not her problems, she bore their weight anyway. Abigail turned as she heard Brutus give a disgruntled sigh from the other room, no doubt bothered that his spooning partner had taken her warmth with her when she got up. As she turned to leave the light of the window for the darkness of the bed, a pair of high beams reflected brightly off her lonely little Hepburn frame.

Suddenly she knew just what to do.

10

An Indecent Proposal

bigail walked with purpose up Excelsior Primm's torturously uphill driveway as she made her way to school earlier than usual. She'd dressed with intention that morning, putting on her navy slacks and tying a cute scarf around her neck that featured the Cambridge coat of arms, her dad's alma mater. She was trying to strike the right balance between revered faculty member and creative extraordinaire. Though she didn't know much about business, she assumed businesspeople dressed to the nines when they had something to pitch.

Wiping the moist morning off, she made her way down the hall with her head held high, ready to wow Updike with the idea that had kept her up all night. There was just one problem. The woman wasn't in her office.

"Damn," Abigail exclaimed as she stepped into the doorway. She'd wanted to nab the headmistress at her freshest, before the day inevitably erupted into chaos and Updike turned from your garden-variety grump into Cruella De Ville.

Abigail's stomach churned as she considered how irritated Updike would undoubtedly be when she did finally reach her.

She hadn't responded to the headmistress's email, opting to deliver her idea for the drama club in person. She figured it would have a more "dramatic effect" that way. If she wasn't going to achieve that before, Abigail certainly would now. Updike was not one to be ignored on email or on any other platform.

She crept into the office and began writing Updike a note, careful to ensure her penmanship was impeccable.

"Hey, what're you doing here?" Mrs. Chang was known to arrive early on the days she held her Mandarin club meetings.

Abigail jumped as the pen retreated off the envelope, creating a huge, annoying line that extended onto another important-looking document on Updike's desk.

Shit.

"You . . . okay?"

"Yes," Abigail said, taking a breath. "Yes, I'm fine. Just leaving a note for Updike."

She let out a little laugh, self-conscious about the level of panic she'd displayed. Hadn't she wanted Updike to walk through that door? Wasn't that why she awoke early, threw an irritated Brutus outside in the freezing cold and banged her right hip—hard—against that railing she didn't see because it was still dark when she'd left for work?

The older woman gave her a once over as if she could visually diagnose what was going on here. "You feeling sick or something?"

"Not exactly. I was hoping I could catch Updike to tell her about my plans for the drama club."

Mrs. Chang opened her mouth in surprise and nodded. "So, what's your plan?"

"I haven't told anybody yet." Abigail scratched at her blazer's inner sleeve and tugged on her scarf before swallowing hard. She'd been bursting to talk about her big idea. But after little sleep, a hurried commute, and no Updike, the wind seemed to have left her sails—or at least her sales pitch.

"Um, I was thinking we could start putting on plays again. Like they used to do in the late 2000s when the Kraemers' three girls attended Excelsior Primm . . . and when Mrs. Vangundy had more energy."

The Kraemers were local celebrities. The husband-and-wife duo met at Excelsior Primm before taking their talents to Broadway. Their youngest daughter had even made it to the semi-finals of *The Voice*. Abigail knew this because there was a photo of her and Adam Levine on the wall of "Primmpressions," the school's cutesy way of honoring notable alumni.

"I guess that could be one way to revive the program," Mrs. Chang said. "What play do you wanna do?"

"That's the thing." Abigail bit her lip as she stared at the mess of papers on Updike's desk. "I was thinking we could do our *own* play—or at least our own revised version of a play." She searched Mrs. Chang's face for any response, but having a husband whose main hobby was Texas Hold'Em, Abigail couldn't read her.

"You see, my first-period students, we were talking the other day and we felt like a lot of their reading material is really . . . heavy?" she continued. "I mean, if you look at their reading list . . . the whole thing is full of tragic literature. And it's not that they can't handle it. They actually empathize with these characters and see how they could've made smarter choices to better their outcomes. At least that's how it was with *Romeo and Juliet*. So, we've decided to write an alternate ending to the play. We're going to work out the new dialogue in class today."

Mrs. Chang looked at her, a large vertical crease appearing on her forehead. "And that's what you want to put on?"

"Yes. When you really think about it, it's the students' own work. And we wouldn't be exclusive. Instead, we'd form a club—I guess it would be the drama club, though I thought I'd call this endeavor 'Happily Ever After Productions'—and open it up to other students. That way, the kids in my class who don't want to be a part of this don't have to be, and the ones who do can."

"Huh."

Abigail prayed Mrs. Chang liked her pitch. She wasn't sure she could present it to Updike if it received early criticism. She wondered how her dad found the courage to submit grant proposals and new class ideas at the rate he did. He always seemed to have something new to pitch that was enthusiastically received, or at least that's what she gleaned from her little nook in his study where she did homework on Tuesdays and Thursdays during office hours.

"And your students? They really like this idea?" Mrs. Chang asked, studying Abigail's face.

"Oh, you should've seen the way they were shouting with ideas and excitement and—not shouting but, you know, really passionate about this assignment. And when I went into the hall to talk to Nate . . ."

Mrs. Chang's mouth formed a long "O," though she didn't say anything.

"Uh, Mr. Carter. Anyway, by the time I got back inside they'd settled on a new ending and were mapping out how to get there," Abigail said before adding, "not that I was gone that long. It may *seem* like I was because they came up with such great ideas, but that's because they're smart students. Not because I was in the hallway too long."

Shut up, Abigail.

The short woman stared at the ground, giving Abigail a front-row view of her salt-and-pepper hair. "I like it."

"You do?"

"Yeah, I like it," Mrs. Chang said, a thin, red-lipped smile spreading across her face. "It's creative. And new. We need that around here. Too much tradition. And stuffiness. But be careful. Updike isn't one for change. If it were up to her, she'd be happy to keep sending students to these theater festivals and calling that a drama department. You've got a good idea, but she's got the power. Really think about it before you say anything to her, because once she says no, that's it. Kaput. You got me?"

"I got you." Abigail crumpled her note, gave Mrs. Chang a light squeeze and bounded off to her classroom.

"And say hi to that Nate for me, will ya?" Mrs. Chang yelled after her, adding an extra emphasis to his name. Abigail pretended not to hear that last part. Walking down the hall, she hoped no one else heard it either.

It's Mr. Carter.

She silently scolded herself for calling him by his first name. *So unprofessional.*

No matter now. She couldn't wait to get to her kids.

Abigail was happy to find their enthusiasm hadn't diminished. They traded ideas all morning, writing a rough outline on the board and creating what was turning into a bona fide, modified version of a Shakespearean classic. She was very pleased with their work by the period's end, though she knew her work was just beginning. She decided to write Updike a proposal during her off period.

Abigail swung by her boss's office again that afternoon, knowing Updike usually lingered around campus until around four o'clock. Rumor had it she avoided going home as long as possible. Abigail didn't know Updike's husband, but she sure felt sorry for the poor sucker.

She was pleased to catch sight of the woman's abnormally

large head and broad shoulders as she rounded the corner. She was also pleased that the yellow tint was finally fading from the floor, shuddering to think about the workload that must have added to the janitorial crew.

Abigail stopped once she got to the doorway. She tipped the door open a little wider with her hand as she waited to be acknowledged. The mahogany slab instantly creaked to life.

"Yeeees?"

"Good afternoon, Headmistress." When this failed to elicit a response, Abigail continued. "I—um—I know you've been waiting for my reply about the drama club. I received your email and was going to send you one back, but . . ."

"But what? In this day and age, I thought all of you had mobile devices sewn to your palms."

"Oh, we do, yes," Abigail stammered, realizing she wasn't helping her case. She smoothed out her pants before continuing. "It's just that I wanted to talk to you in person. I had some great ideas and I thought it might be better if we went over them. Together?"

Updike humored her for once. She closed the laptop and put on her reading glasses, motioning for Abigail to hand her the paper currently absorbing her palm sweat.

"You see, I was thinking . . ."

"I'm reading."

"Right. Sorry." Abigail sat quietly with her hands in her lap. She prayed she had done an okay job emulating one of her dad's grant proposals, which had fallen out of Milton's classic work when she was placing it back on the shelf.

"I see. Ms. Gardner, wouldn't we all be happier if you simply assisted Mrs. Vangundy with the drama competition entries?"

"Oh, but I was hoping we could get the kids a bit more . . .

involved?" Updike raised her eyebrow at this notion. "I realize the students actually *competing* are already involved in the drama program, but I thought this might be a nice way to bring everyone together. Everyone who wants to be a part of this play, that is. And the first-period students are *so* excited about crafting an alternate ending."

Updike stared at the paper for another minute.

"Plus, if the play's any good we can enter it into competitions. In the original works category. Maybe this could be a new tradition at Excelsior Primm—and every semester or year the kids could take a different play and reinvent it."

The stare moved toward her. Abigail could feel Updike searching her face for something, though she had no idea what it was.

Couldn't be fear—that's too evidently displayed.

"I know Marshal Struthers is already hard at work on a production of *Our Town*."

"Ugh, that school is so out of touch." The headmistress smacked her lips together as if she'd tasted something sour. "*Our Town*? Really? It is the *most* tired play you could possibly choose." The disdainful words flew out of Updike's mouth at a record pace.

"Yeah. Boring, right?" Updike's eyes said, "go on," though her mouth remained silent. "I mean, come *on*. 'Oooooh, it's 1938 and we're doing a play-within-a-play,'" Abigail mimicked while rolling her eyes.

This produced a sound Abigail had never heard before. Not quite a cackle, not quite a howl—and definitely part rooster crow. It was an entirely unpleasant sound, and yet not, as it was Updike laughing.

Abigail saw her opening and decided to take it.

"That's why we hit back at them with a revamped, student-created version of *Romeo and Juliet*," she said, moving to the edge of her seat. "Even if it's horrible—which it won't be—what criticism could anyone possibly have? The entire production will be student-run. And just think of the compliments we'll get on the maturity level of these kids. That they tackled a subject as heady as teen suicide and found a better solution."

"The local papers would have to cover it," Updike said, a glimmer in her eye. "And they're not going to rip apart a play written by a bunch of kids. They'll have to applaud them. They'll have to applaud . . . *me*."

She glanced at the proposal one more time before setting it on her desk where it was instantly absorbed by a sea of papers.

"I see you have a budget here of twelve hundred dollars."

"Yes, for costume and set materials. I'll provide the art supplies for the poster boards and most of the set design if the school can just —"

"Five hundred."

"Done!" This program might send her to the poor house—or poorer house—but Abigail was on the cusp of her first actual, artistic professional endeavor. "Can I ask one more thing?"

Updike raised her other eyebrow.

"Could we use the Little Theatre?" Abigail saw her eyebrow, and raised her one crinkled face.

"The theater has been used as a storage facility for the past decade or so, but that's Mitch's department." Updike looked at her watch and gathered her things. "You'll need to talk to him."

Abigail shot up as soon as the headmistress stood. She scrambled to push in the chair and clear the doorway before the woman made her way over. As Updike turned down the solemn hallway, Abigail yelled out, "Thanks so much, Headmistress. You won't regret this. It's going to be great."

"Oh, I won't be the one regretting anything." The headmistress' deep voice bellowed through the sterile corridor. "But you might. Pull this production off and we may be able to carve out some art classes for you next year."

Abigail gasped as she pulled her hands into her chest.

"Fail and, well, let's just say we may not have a place for someone with such untraditional, out-of-the-box thinking. Good luck, Ms. Gardner."

She swallowed hard, feeling the air from her initial excitement travel down her system in one massive bubble. A mix of doubt, dread and a little drama.

Abigail tried to carry the same confidence she brought into Updike's office with her as she headed to the Little Theatre. She circled the Fine Arts Building numerous times, but Mitch was nowhere to be found. Abigail was hanging onto the rough brick border of the theater's transom windows, stretched out on her tiptoes, when Nate ran by.

"Hey," he called out. She stumbled back from the wall, observing the concrete crumbles that had embedded into her fingertips before taking in his sight. Nate stood for a second in his black basketball shorts and a Philadelphia Eagles muscle shirt before his heavy breathing forced his hands onto his thighs. Abigail had never liked that look, though her eyes didn't currently mind it much.

"What're you up to?" His sweat pooled below him as he craned his neck up at her.

"I'm looking for Mitch."

"Oh, yeah? What d'you need ol' Mitch for? Out of whiskey? Although I seem to remember your drink of choice being vodka-soda with, what was it? Lime?"

It was well known that the cantankerous custodian had a penchant for whiskey. Updike overlooked this fondness as long as he only drank after four o'clock and kept his flask out of sight. Abigail suspected his stash was in the Little Theatre, where his office was.

"Lemon," she smiled, wishing her memory of that night was as good as his. "And no. I need to ask him something."

"What's that?" Nate straightened out, placing his hands behind his head. Abigail tried not to notice the muscle definition that had previously been hidden beneath his infamous layered look. He was pale for how involved he was in soccer, but his work on the field was clearly displayed in his trim physique.

"I've been in talks to help Mrs. Vangundy with the drama club, and I want to put on a play. I need to convince Mitch to let us use the Little Theatre."

Nate let out a surprised cackle that once again left him breathless. A tall, gangly man brandishing a leaf-blower backpack marched briskly behind him as he bent over once more.

"Mitch! Excuse me, Mitch?" Abigail sprinted to catch up with him.

The man gave his bald head a quarter turn before muttering a barely audible "Whad'ya want?" through his thick Scottish accent.

Nate trailed them for a few steps before positioning himself near the theater's side door for a front-row view.

"I was wondering if—you see, the thing is I'm going to be putting on a play—and I was hoping we could use the Little Theatre?"

"No." He picked up his pace, inserting earplugs and walking toward the line of shrubs that separated the Fine Arts Building from the Liberal Arts Building.

Abigail tried to round the side of Mitch, but the wily gardener engaged the blower down by his hip. Her pleated skirt instantly blew up, producing an encore Spanx performance—except these were rainbow colored—as she flailed around in a hail of wind, leaves, and indignity.

Oblivious to her plight, Mitch wielded his blower in all directions. Abigail matted down her hair, collar, and skirt once the initial shock wore off. She was just about to turn her attention to the debris in her mouth when she remembered they weren't alone.

Abigail shot her head toward the red brick building, where Nate was leaning forward. She had no idea whether he was catching his breath again or trying to camouflage muffled laughter. In either case, she was relieved that he seemed to be the only other human in sight. And that he wasn't holding up a phone. She quickly looked in the direction of Excelsior Sanctum, despite the fact that there was no possible way anyone could see the high school from this vantage point.

That's one way to make your debut in visual arts, you idiot. Fuck.

Not wanting to face further humiliation, Abigail made her way out of the school, hastily pulling pieces of stems and leaves from her hair and clothes as she lumbered toward the train station. She didn't even attempt to compose herself until she was fully seated on her way home.

It was then that she pulled out her phone, only to find a few texts.

Hey. Don't forget to put an audition flyer in cubby two zero four. Trust me, you're going to want my kids. The way they try to get out of their homework and tests . . . they can act.

Still too mortified to say anything—but grateful that Nate didn't bring up the incident—she tapped the text and selected the thumbs-up response. Catching her first moment of peace after a particularly long, trying day, Abigail placed her head against the train's window. She figured the grimy surface was no match for the icky things already swimming figuratively and literally around her head.

And that's when she felt the buzz of a second text.

Also, very cheeky performance earlier. Just as I remember you that night at Tākō.

11

There Art Romeo

Abigail peeked through the small windows of the double classroom she'd reserved, confirming that the poster announcing "AN R+J LOVE STORY—AUDITIONS HELD HERE TODAY AT THREE P.M." was still securely fastened.

She had been thrilled to finally put her art skills to good use, having spent the past two weeks crafting colorful posters advertising her new club and the play's audition. She worked on both endeavors from the time she got home until she got up for school the next day.

Thankfully, she had some assistance. Quinn agreed to swap their weekly outing for an at-home Photoshop session as he assisted with digital flyers. Mathilda, meanwhile, gladly traded in their Sunday morning aerial yoga class—or "circus freak shit," as she called it—for plot analysis and fact checking.

Though Abigail definitely felt the pressure from Updike's latest threat, she found the time spent working on these materials to be quite fun. It was cathartic to finally channel some of her energy into her first love, even if it was only middle-school marketing materials. She was also soaking up the QT with Quinn and Mathilda.

"I think he's taking too many cues from his horn dog soccer team," Mathilda had advised Abigail about Nate that Sunday as her red pen ran rampant through the scene where R&J hatch their big wedding plan. "I hate 'pull-the-pigtails' kinds of guys. Unless it's in bed. And I'm playing Britney Spears."

Abigail was grateful to hear that work was still busy, just how Mathilda liked it. Her romps with Detective Santos also seemed to be going well after they hit a rough patch, when his latest ex-wife filed a motion to move their kids out of state.

"It was great at first," Mathilda said, waving her pen in the air as she spoke. "Everyone likes an anger bang. But then it turned into phone calls asking for parenting advice on this and that. And then he started to get jaded about women, complaining we're all heartless bitches. It was like 'umm, you were *in* this heartless bitch five minutes ago, can we talk about something else? For once?' I almost took up coke just to drive him away."

Quinn's love life was equally messy. He'd begun dating a former reality star who had settled in the area. He wasn't sure, but he thought she'd said she was on *The Bachelor* or "one of those desperate-for-fame and ratings shows." The series didn't matter to Quinn. He didn't care what she did as long as she was doing him.

Ever the world traveler, he was planning a January trip to Reykjavík to assist one of Mrs. Kelly's friends with a pet project—literally. It was good money and easy work, particularly as Quinn suspected this woman was only interested in ordering a younger man around. Still, it was hard to escape the fact that documenting global winter pet wear trends wasn't exactly thrilling to him.

"Should our furry friends wear fur?" he'd lamented with fake indignation as he clicked away on his Macbook, making the audition flyer's font grow larger and more angular. "Give me a fucking break."

All this conversation left Abigail feeling refreshed and, ironically, exhausted by the time the actual audition rolled around. Her heart pounded and her stomach flipped as she listened to the low but strong chatter building outside those two doors.

Though she couldn't tell exactly how many students were in the hall, the turnout for the informational session had produced forty-five kids between the ages of eleven (the minimum) and fourteen. The kids had asked some great questions and, luckily, Abigail was able to answer most of them with little thought or additional research.

The only question that plagued her was whether they would get to use the Little Theatre. This dusty space apparently held quite the allure around campus. Some students thought it was haunted. Others assumed Mitch lived there. But most just really, really wanted to see what the thing looked like inside.

She tugged at the waistband of her skirt, knocking her father's nearly five-pound *Complete Works of Shakespeare* off the desk with her elbow. The hardcover landed with an ominous thud as all the outside noise hushed. Abigail began to reconsider whether this book would bring the good luck she was hoping for when she'd lugged it all the way from her apartment that morning. Having realized how silent the hallway remained, she had no choice but to take this as her cue to begin auditions.

No turning back now.

She placed the book back on her desk and headed to the doors, swinging them open like Ebenezer Scrooge on Christmas morning. A sea of startled faces greeted her.

"Welcome, kids. Let the auditions begin." She threw her fist in the air as she tried to muster a level of excitement that would carry them through the rest of the afternoon.

The kids shuffled in, placing permission slips on her desk.

She was heartened to see a good amount of her first-period kids, who had inspired this idea. This included Reese and Birdie, who made it very clear they were only there for the role of Juliet—even if it meant taking down their genetic clone. Though the twins' auditions fell flat, Abigail was particularly impressed by the performance of a seventh grader, who sported thick glasses and deep red, curly hair.

"I'm Kennedy. My favorite subjects are history and English," the freckled girl said as part of her required introduction. "I'm only here because my parents insist I take an extracurricular and I hate sports. And math."

"Okay, fair enough," Abigail responded, fighting the urge to tell Kennedy that she, too, was forced here by a superior.

Maybe she'll grow to like it well enough. Hopefully we both will.

As the afternoon progressed, Abigail was getting a pretty good vision of the cast. All except one. Romeo.

John Henry had given a decent reading, and an eighth-grade boy had mastered the dialect well, though Abigail thought he came off a little too unlikeable to play the lovelorn teen the audience was supposed to root for.

One of them will have to do.

Abigail stood to wrap just as she heard the handle on one of the classroom's doors. A somewhat awkward student with poor posture and a wrinkled uniform entered on what didn't seem to be his own volition. This was soon confirmed as she noticed the toned, sleeveless arm nudging the boy forward.

"I hope we're not too late," Nate said as he continued to direct the burly kid into the room.

"I was about to dismiss everyone," Abigail said, trying to quash her visible annoyance.

"I'm sure you are—and I'm sorry—but maybe you could fit in

one last audition? For Alex?" Nate contorted his face in much the same way Abigail had when asking the headmistress for permission, or for just about anything.

Her pride wanted to tell him no—that he knew exactly what time auditions were held, especially since she made sure that flyer made it into cubbyhole two zero four. But her eyes caught the boy's. That quiet boy, whose back was pressed against the tips of Nate's fingers like a gun to a hostage, made her think twice. There was something about this child's face, a mix of self-consciousness and optimism. She had to relent.

"As I was saying, we *were* just finishing up, but since we're still a few minutes from four thirty, I'll let him have a go." She flashed the boy a big smile, hoping to put his somewhat pathetic-looking self at ease. Her mouth stiffened when she got to Nate, though she held a warm admiration for his advocacy efforts.

"What part did you want to read for?" she asked, breaking eye contact with her fellow teacher.

"R-Romeo." Sweat beads appeared on his forehead the second the word was out of his mouth.

"What's that?" Nate said from behind the boy. He pulled Alex's pumpkin-shaped head closer as he added, "You gotta speak up—loud and clear—if you want to be on stage. Isn't that right, Ms. Gardner?"

She caught a glimpse of those annoyingly perfect teeth as Nate gave the student a few pats on the shoulder.

"Y-Yes," she mumbled, clearing her throat and realizing the irony of her tone. "Yes, that's right. So . . . Romeo? Okay, here's your scene. You can begin whenever you're ready."

She handed Alex the audition monologue and returned to her seat. Nate gave him one last fist bump before grabbing a desk-chair combo and sliding it right next to hers.

"But, soft?" Alex choked out, taking a huge breath before continuing. "What light through your window breaks—umm, it's in the east and Juliet is the sun . . ."

"Cut," Nate proclaimed, leaping to his feet. He put his hand around the boy's dejected frame. "Alex, man, it's just like we practiced in the hallway." Nate turned toward Abigail, who wore a stunned expression as her audition had clearly been hijacked. "I'm sorry, Ms. Gardner. Can we take five?"

The room erupted into groans. Kennedy muttered "Unbelievable" under her breath, while John Henry blurted out, "C'mon, man." Alex sheepishly hunched, causing what little neck he had to disappear.

"You know what, we don't even need five," Nate said. "I'm sure you—I'm sure *everyone*—would like to go home. If we could get maybe one minute?"

"Fine. One minute." Abigail turned to face the audience. "Thank you all for your patience. We're almost done."

Abigail tried to busy herself with her notes to give them some privacy. She silently waved at the others to do the same. Most obliged, though Kennedy stared at the duo with a look of indignation, or perhaps moral outrage, slapped across her face.

"Alex, you've got this, you're a great actor," she could hear Nate say. "You've got to believe in yourself. Remember to project and emote with your face. Like you were doing earlier. And yesterday."

The two returned to the center of the classroom.

"Take it away, my man." Nate presented Alex to the audience, shuffling to the side of the room like an over-the-top ringleader. The man-child looked to Abigail for assurance that he could begin once the muffled laughter faded.

"Go ahead, Alex. And don't be nervous. We're all friends

here." She turned to see Nate staring at her as she finished that last sentence, causing her voice to heighten a little.

Alex folded the monologue prompt and placed it in his uniform shirt pocket before beginning again. Abigail listened, enraptured, to a seemingly different child. She watched as Alex paced back and forth, making full use of the floor.

"She speaks yet she says nothing: what of that?" he asked, tensing his brow and waving both palms in front of him.

Nate gave Abigail a quick poke in the ribs, though neither took their eyes off the boy.

"Stop it," she whisper-hissed as Alex's star performance came to a close.

"O, that I were a glove upon that hand," he lamented. "That I might touch that cheek!" Alex reached his hand longingly out to touch an imaginary Juliet, a pained expression overtaking his face.

The boy ended his audition by bowing his head. When he raised it back up, his face beamed with pride. This quickly faded as he looked around and saw that no one was moving. Abigail immediately began clapping, hoping it would urge the others to do the same.

"Alex, I *knew* you could do it," Nate exclaimed. He made his way over to the still-heaving boy, lifting him off his feet.

A broad smile instantly overtook Alex's face. It wasn't quite as perfect as Nate's but it was equally as adorable. Abigail was thrilled to see a child so proud of himself. Especially one whose efforts produced this amount of sweat.

"Was that great or what?" Nate placed Alex back on his feet and turned toward Abigail.

"It was very good, Alex," she said, consciously remaining calm and professional. Nate playfully narrowed his eyes and shook his head, letting her know he'd seen right through her poker face.

There was no denying it. They both knew Abigail had found her Romeo.

12

Spilt Tea

"You should have seen it, Mathilda, this kid was on *fire*," Abigail exclaimed as they browsed around Kendra Scott that Saturday. Having emerged from Sophie's bridesmaid dress fitting, they were on strict orders to buy dangling earrings and a complementary necklace.

"Not a *matching* necklace, not like a *set*," Sophie had barked an hour earlier as each girl stood under the bright fitting-room spotlights, trying their best not to scratch at the irritating material they were entombed in. Well, Abigail and two other maids tried not to scratch. Mathilda openly dragged her chipped fingernails across her chest, creating a horrible sandpaper sound with the tulle and purple marks across her upper half.

Standing near the digital custom-jewelry display now, the young detective's patience with this day didn't seem to be replenishing. Abigail knew her jaded friend well enough to sense this was the case, but she'd been bursting at the seams (no pun intended) to tell her about the play's auditions.

"He completely killed it," Abigail continued, comparing a pair of rose gold hoop earrings to crystal-studded ones. "From the minute Alex started—the second time, that is—he just . . ."

An audible exhale coming from Mathilda's direction inter-rupted her. Abigail turned and found her weary friend leaning against the screen, massaging her glabella with her thumb and forefinger. Mathilda looked up to see Abigail standing there. Staring at her. Silent for the first time in minutes.

Mathilda swallowed hard and slapped a tight smile onto her face. "So, he was that phenomenal, huh?"

"Yes . . . no. Wait, who are you talking about?" Abigail was suddenly confused about the subject of the matter.

"Your new 'star,'" Mathilda said, resting her palms on a jewelry counter.

Abigail looked at her sideways.

"Hello. Your new Romeo?"

"What? Oh, my God, don't be so immature, Mathilda. I don't *have* a new Romeo." Abigail rolled her eyes at the ridiculousness of this.

"Huh? I thought you were doing *Romeo and Juliet*. Didn't you cast Romeo? Alan whoever?"

"Alex," she quickly responded. Abigail internally reprimanded herself. She knew this shouldn't have been a question that needed answering.

"I'm glad the club's coming along," Mathilda said as she fingered a pair of ear jackets with pointy spikes.

Abigail gave a high-pitched "Mm, hm" without looking up from the sparkly display in front of her. She had her eyes fixed on a pair of platinum tear drops with aquamarine stones in the center.

"Say, have you heard about the string of burglaries happening at the old folks' homes?" Mathilda asked as she held the jackets' card up to her ear.

Abigail swiftly marched over, grabbing the biker-chic acces-sory from Mathilda's fingers and replacing it with a pair of chain thread drop earrings. "What? I told you I'm allergic to all things wedding."

Abigail rolled her eyes before jumping on the opportunity to change the subject. "They're called assisted- and independent-living facilities," she corrected. "And no, I haven't heard anything. I've been a little busy lately."

"If you consider Serenity Nouveau, Standing Strong Philadelphia, and Poppy Grove a form of 'independence,' then I stand corrected."

"Oh, you can't be serious," Abigail said, slapping her palm onto the shiny white counter and causing the earrings to jump to life. "They hit Poppy Grove?"

Abigail had visited Poppy Grove every Mother's Day since 2018, when she realized that she had zero plans on this holiday. That she would never really have plans on this day again unless she married or had kids of her own. With this gigantic factor in mind, she began to micromanage all the holidays to prevent any semblance of loneliness or orphanhood from overtaking her well-being when she least expected it.

Thanksgiving was spent in Boston with her dad's sister and her family. Christmas was celebrated in King of Prussia with Grace's extended brood. The summer holidays were enjoyed at either the Kellys' cottage or in whatever seedy bar where she and Mathilda managed to maintain employment through college. Easter . . . well, no one seemed to care much for Easter anymore. Abigail found that holiday particularly easy to avoid. All these dates were planned to a tee. She had learned to minimize sadness by maximizing distraction.

While Abigail was happy to see her relatives, the parental holidays held a special place in her heart. Many of Poppy Grove's residents were also without company on these days. The saddest cases were the ones like Mrs. Sheridan, who had an adult son and daughter. Rather than spending the day with the mom who raised them, the siblings chose to celebrate with their "own" families. Rounds of golf, brunches, spa days—whatever the event, they never included Mrs. Sheridan.

"And why would I be included?" the old woman with foggy eyes had posed to Abigail two Mother's Days ago. "They're the ones doing the active mothering now. They should get the privilege of celebrating the holiday."

Abigail was touched by the woman's grace and poise, but she couldn't understand why her kids wouldn't want to visit with her. Mrs. Sheridan was a perfectly chirpy senior with the sweetest disposition.

The parentless daughter would've given anything to visit her parents on their respective holidays, both now and in the future. To have them watch her grow up and have kids of her own. To have the privilege of pulling into a nice senior home like Poppy Grove with a bouquet in her hands and a silly Mylar balloon that said "#1 Mom!" trailing behind her in the wind.

Abigail also would've given anything to be those grandkids. To have a mom who actually took her on social outings. Rounds of golf. Brunches. Spa days. How her heart ached when she heard about these types of events through friends when she was growing up. Even when her mom was alive, such activities were out of the question for someone as reclusive as Grace.

After she'd met Mrs. Sheridan, Abigail had wondered whether for each peppy girl who showed up to school that following Monday a bit tanner or with newly painted toes—there was an elderly one who sat by a phone that never rang that day.

The thought of someone robbing Mrs. Sheridan and the poor other "tucked away" residents of Poppy Grove made Abigail nauseous. She was hoping some fresh air and hot tea might help.

"So, how's your man's custody thing going?" Abigail asked as she and Mathilda strolled the few blocks to Penn Roasters.

"Eh, fine," she answered, playing a virtual game of hopscotch as she avoided the small puddles. "Oh, Santos wants to get married."

"What?!" Abigail spun around on the ball of her right foot to block Mathilda's path.

"It's not a big deal," she responded, pulling an errant leaf out of her braided hair. Mathilda attempted to keep walking, but Abigail's body failed to move. Her face, on the other hand, was another story. Her eyes had gone wide, mouth agape.

"What?" Mathilda shrugged. "I said no. Naturally."

"*Mathilda*, what the hell?" Abigail said with a stomp of her foot that sent water flying everywhere.

Rolling her eyes, Mathilda explained, "He thought it might help his custody case if he showed the judge he could provide a stable family environment for his kids."

"Oh." Abigail began to soften. "So, it wouldn't have been for love? I can appreciate him wanting to do what he can to see his kids as much as possible, but a fake marriage? No wonder you said no."

"Aw, hell, no. He knows better than to ask me to marry him out of *love*," Mathilda said. Her face was so contorted she looked like she'd eaten a bug. "It would've been a business arrangement. I could stay at the house whenever I wanted, drive his spare car, and have access to a joint account that held money for incidentals. He, in turn, would have a better case to present to the judge."

Mathilda stepped around her newly befuddled friend and began walking. Abigail followed quietly behind. This news worked wonders on her nausea. She was now too focused on her thudding heart to worry about the potential threat of vomit.

"I still can't believe he would ask that of you," she finally offered, shaking her head.

"I thought about it. The arrangement certainly had its perks, but it's not worth the hassle. My parents would flip," Mathilda said, opening the door to the coffee house.

"Yeah, I suppose," Abigail agreed as she caught the door. "Is . . . that the only reason, though? Why you wouldn't go through with it?"

Mathilda was almost at the counter when she turned back to see Abigail still holding the large glass door. Half of her body was inside the quaint little establishment, while half was still out on the street. She looked wedged into the glass, like the building's frame had enveloped her and refused to let go. Mathilda let out a terse exhale before turning back to retrieve her friend from whatever was swallowing her whole.

"I'm simply saying," Abigail began, trying not to sound judgmental after they were seated with drinks in hand: a green tea for her and a dark roast coffee, black, for Mathilda. "It's a very different . . . stance . . . you have from the rest of us. That you would be willing to marry out of convenience—as a formal business arrangement—and not out of love." Her porcelain cup pinged against its saucer.

"Love?" Mathilda guffawed, throwing her hands in the air. "Abigail, c'mon. Who marries for love? Okay, maybe people *think* they're marrying out of love, but they're not. It's loneliness or narcissism or pure sadomasochism that masks itself as this so-called warm emotion we know as love."

"You don't believe love exists . . . at all?" Abigail was still wary of this whole discussion, but had to participate when such wild claims were being thrown around. "I mean, seriously. I know you love your siblings. And your nieces and nephews. And your parents. And me."

"I *do* love you—all of you—but I'm not going to sign a piece of paper legally binding me to any of you for the rest of my life. And parents. You want to talk about parents? Mine have been married for thirty-two years and they're miserable."

"Okay, they're not *miserable*."

"Oh, yes, they are," Mathilda said, slamming her mug and spewing its contents across the table. A few patrons turned to stare. "You can feel it when you're around them. The way they're always moving about, avoiding each other as they play a lifelong game of musical chairs."

"That doesn't mean they're miserable. They see a lot of each other, I'm sure, since they're both home so much. They probably need their space every now and then. I bet they don't even know they're doing it."

"Ha. Yeah. That would be great." Mathilda applied the same manic force to wiping up the coffee as she had to spilling it. "Except that's not the case. My mom even told me once. It was during one of her chardonnay afternoons when she was out back watching the twins play. I sat down next to her at the picnic table, and she said 'Mathilda, don't ever get married or have kids. They're the two worst mistakes I ever made.'"

Abigail was swiftly forming a comeback for whatever Mathilda was going to say when this truth bomb stunned her into submission. "I—I—I'm sorry, Mathilda. I had no idea."

"Well, now you do." She sat back in her chair, granting the table a reprieve as she clasped her fingers so tight her knuckles lightened. "But it's not just my parents. My brother-in-law is screwing around on my sister. He confided in my younger brother and swore him to secrecy, which the kid agreed to. Though I don't count, naturally."

Abigail's head pounded harder with every revelation.

"And Santos. You look through his bottom right drawer and you'll find a bottle of scotch. Under that scotch is a mountain of picture frames he used to have on his desk of his family. He and his wife and their kids and you know what? They look like the happiest goddamn people on Earth. If you were to walk up to the people in those photos and say 'Hey, did you know that in less than three years you're going to hate each other so much that you'll be throwing lawyers at one another for fun? Just to cause them a certain amount of inconvenience and an even larger amount of money? Just so you can revel in how much that must piss the other one off?' If you said that then to that family, do you know what they'd tell you? They'd say, 'fuck you.'"

Abigail understood Mathilda's point, she really did. The rate of divorce and infidelity and even the unreported number of couples who stayed married for God knows what reasons even though they were miserable were all hard to dispute.

But so was love.

People didn't move across countries, donate organs, or spend two months' salaries on seemingly irrelevant gemstones from Sierra Leone because love didn't exist. They didn't quit the dangerous hobbies they adored, get "real jobs," or cohabitate with cats because love didn't exist. They didn't contort their too-large bodies around hospital beds, throw themselves in front of live ammunition, or reach for their phones during their seemingly last few minutes in this universe because love didn't fucking exist.

Sure, hate, anger, resentment, and even ambivalence were powerful forces, but so was love. It might not conquer everything, but it sure as hell is a useful companion to have in your corner when the battle, whatever form it may take, begins.

"Yes, people are miserable sometimes and, of course, love isn't guaranteed to last," Abigail finally responded after the initial shock wore off. She forced herself to meet Mathilda's stare. "But it does exist. And some people are happy. My aunt and uncle have been married twenty-seven years, and they seem to be stronger than ever. Even after losing a son, they're still together and they're still happy."

Mathilda gave her hair a quick shake. She looked like she was ready to jump out of her skin. "I'm sure they are. They're united in their grief. I've seen it a million times at the station. Tragedy either breaks you or it unites you. Sickness and death are hard things. Some people need support during that period, others need solitude. And some get so bitter and angry with their whole situation that they consciously remove themselves from the rest of us to silently self-destruct, either because they think they brought that tragedy upon themselves, or they're royally pissed off at whatever they believe did that to them."

The girls sat silently for a second. Mathilda stared into her mug as if a genie would appear, one who could make this conversation vanish just as quickly as he could.

"You of all people should understand that," Mathilda added, wincing the second those words left her mouth.

Abigail focused on a crack in her cup, tapping her foot and clenching her arms tightly across her chest. She was not going to let whatever rage was building in her left foot travel up her body. Her straitjacket stance would prevent it from getting any farther than her heart.

Lame excuses were soon issued, along with promises to see each other later and to talk soon. On the walk home, Abigail thought about her own parents and what sickness and health and then sickness and death had done to their marriage. What it had done to her.

She often wondered what would have happened if her dad hadn't gotten sick, losing the ability to do anything for himself including, ultimately, breathing. Undoubtedly Grace would've taken better care of her own health, as the strength of one partner might have bolstered that of the other.

Aside from that, though, Abigail frequently wondered how their relationships would have unfolded. Would her mom and dad have beaten the odds and stayed married? They always seemed relatively happy. But sickness and death tended to paint a rosy gloss over everything. Once vulnerability and, later, mortality presented themselves, people became all good. So did relationships. And encounters. No one ever spoke ill of the ill. Or of the dead. At least not in any socially acceptable scenarios.

In her own head, though, where other people weren't allowed, Abigail wondered. Would the arguments she and Charles had over what book to read or how to spend an afternoon continue into adulthood? Would they have eventually seen eye to eye, laughing at all their petty encounters early on in her own life? Or would the fights have escalated as Abigail found her voice and Charles considered his own to be more important than ever?

Sometimes these thoughts were even comforting to Abigail. If given the choice between losing a hero or keeping an adversary, Abigail would choose the former. She believed most people would.

In times of sickness and death, people tend to look for the silver lining as a coping mechanism, but what about after the fact? Was Abigail herself sick for thinking she might be better off preserving her relatively happy memories? For thinking, in those dark and hazy moments before she fell asleep, that "maybe it's better this way"?

13

You're In

*A*bigail spent the rest of the uneasy weekend holed up in her apartment, doing the only thing that felt natural. She took a *Roman Holiday*. Sitting with her legs under her—a bottle of chocolate coconut milk in one hand and Brutus's sloped brow in the other—she vacantly watched the movie play out on the screen.

Left alone with her thoughts today, she felt hollow. It wasn't that she was lonely, though the still apartment didn't help. And it wasn't so much the fight with Mathilda, either.

Over time, the two had come to realize they were very different people. They had disagreed on many topics ranging from politics to relationships, fashion and, unsurprisingly, the criminal justice system. They never loved each other any less after these disagreements, though levels of patience waned from time to time during their more complex divergences.

Still, she couldn't shake the feeling that maybe her views of love, loss, and even everyday life were a little too Pollyanna-ish for the increasingly hardened detective. Perhaps if Abigail wasn't always running from negative situations, she would be better equipped not only to see the world more accurately but to deal with it in a healthier manner.

Abigail pondered this as her on-screen counterpart traipsed around the Colosseum, Trevi fountain, and Mouth of Truth. As the credits rolled, she felt better—and not just because Princess Ann's secret was safe with the hot reporter. Sure, these Hepburn movies wrapped up nicely, but Abigail was more pleased that these heroines hadn't found happiness; they made it happen for themselves. She knew, in some way, she had to do this, too.

Abigail carried this newfound determination with her—along with the final cast list—as she entered the faculty lounge that Monday morning. Today she would get a glimpse of how well pre-adolescents handle rejection.

Will they congratulate the students who nabbed the top roles? Will they cry? Will they buy my explanation that every part, no matter how small, is equally important? Even if that "part" is Stagehand Five?

Her thoughts were interrupted as Mrs. Chang shuffled into the room. Her slumped shoulders looked like they bore the weight of the world. Abigail winced at this sight. As stressful as her own weekend was, she could tell Mrs. Chang's was even worse. Abigail's mentor had experienced her own demotion in roles recently, as her youngest had fled the nest. He and his girlfriend were getting married, and Mrs. Chang had spent her Saturday watching him load his whole twenty-four years into a moving truck.

"Did it go well this weekend?" Abigail asked. She didn't really want to hear the answer but was committed to being a source of support for the woman who had been her EP hero.

"Yeah, yeah. It was fine," Mrs. Chang answered, her voice stumbling a bit as she fixed a cup of tea.

After an unusually long time, Mrs. Chang turned around, flashing Abigail a forced smile and joining her at the round table. While the woman's body language revealed disappointment as she said goodbye to her main role as caregiver to the last of her four children, her intentionally upturned mouth tried its best to convey her excitement in entering a more (albeit less) supportive role.

Abigail wondered whether her new drama club members would handle their own disappointments in the same manner. Looking across at the suddenly wilted woman, Abigail wasn't sure if she even wanted them to.

"I'm posting the final cast list this afternoon. I can't believe we're doing this. I mean, I don't think I would've had the confidence to approach Updike if you hadn't liked the idea to begin with."

Mrs. Chang quickly nodded before issuing an excuse about her allergies and moving once more to the coffee counter, where there was a tissue box.

Abigail wished she had some words of wisdom to impart. Ironically, the very nature of their current life situations had Abigail at a loss. What was a parentless twenty-something supposed to say to a parent who was losing their last twenty-something to adulthood?

"You know, your work as a mother isn't done," she said cautiously, making her way to the printer to copy the rehearsal schedule. "Your nurturing ways will always be needed—both here and at home."

As she organized her own stack of papers, Abigail felt disappointed she wasn't able to fill the role she felt Mrs. Chang needed her to play. She was placing her cast materials in a folder when a bony set of arms enveloped her lower half from behind. Mrs.

Chang's bangles clanked together as she settled in. The unexpected contact took Abigail's breath away, though she tried not to let it show. This became more difficult as tears welled up and she held her breath.

Abigail dispatched the quietest gasp she could, her chest shaking nevertheless. She felt a jolt behind her as Mrs. Chang's body did the same, except longer and a little more violently. Placing her hands on top of the older teacher's, she wondered if her own role as orphaned, newbie teacher had given this woman permission to take on the part that was dying to break out of her—that of a grieving mom whose child had not perished but had simply grown up.

By the time three o'clock rolled around, Abigail had her own lines to deliver. It would be her job to remind the students that people don't always get what they want. That sometimes they have to settle for what life hands them. That regardless of how well they did or didn't deal with their assigned roles, the play, much like life, would march on—so they might as well make the best of it.

Her little speech was met with suspicious eyes as she surveyed the double classroom. She wished their reactions left her more confident that they understood what she was trying to impart. Instead, she suspected they wanted her to shut up and post the damn list. Abigail took a page out of her own book, accepted that she wasn't going to get the reaction she was hoping for, and embraced her new titles as play director and stage mom.

She walked over to the mounted corkboard, taking a smooth, shallow breath as she drove a green thumbtack into her cast list.

"Nooooow!" she yelled as she whisked herself away like a pro matador.

The kids rushed the board as the occasional "Yes!" and "Aw, man!" filled the room for the next sixty seconds. The twins pouted at first, balking at their roles as Lady Capulet and Montague, though both took solace in the fact that neither was awarded the role of Juliet.

Abigail had her own misgivings about Dieter. She so badly wanted to give him the role of Tybalt after his excellent, if surprising, audition. But his attendance was still too inconsistent, and she knew she couldn't set the production up for failure. Her career depended on it. Instead, Dieter was awarded the front-row spot in the chorus and the role as "extra" in just about every scene.

"Hey! No fair! Why does Dieter get like six roles and I only have one?" John Henry argued, pointing to Dieter's name on the list.

"Excuse me," Abigail retorted. She had promised herself she would not allow diva-like behavior, especially on the first day. "Tybalt is one of the biggest, baddest guys in all of Verona. If you don't want to play him, I'm happy to give him to someone who's up for the challenge."

"No, no," he quickly backpedaled, waving his hands in front of him. "I—I was *congratulating* Dieter. Good job, D. That's, like, awesome. You're gonna be in all the scenes. That's so cool . . . for you."

Abigail was relatively confident this little show had quashed anyone else's objections to their roles. She had also done her best to flesh out even the smallest parts, placing colorful illustrations and glamorous or noble descriptions next to each character's name, hoping to buoy any deflated egos.

She ended the session by imploring them to go home, study their scripts, and come prepared to work the following Monday. Most of the kids happily grabbed a schedule and their things before fleeing the room, though one tall, scraggly haired boy remained.

"What can I do for you?" she inquired with a knowing smirk.

"Oh, nothing," the child stammered, his face beginning to flush. "You've done enough. I just wanted to say . . . thanks."

"You're quite welcome, Alex." She gave his broad shoulders a good squeeze. "You earned that role, you know. You're the perfect one for it."

The redness deepened, as did his pleased expression. "Well, thanks again, ma'am." Alex turned to walk out the door before adding, "I think Mr. Carter was right. I'm going to enjoy working with you."

Now it was her turn to blush. Truth be told, she was surprised Nate hadn't swung by for the big announcement. Being Alex's top supporter, she assumed he'd be there when the cast was unveiled. Or perhaps he'd be waiting outside the room to greet him with a big "How'd you do?"

She had one last glimmer of hope that maybe he was waiting for her in the lounge, not wanting to hear the news from anyone but her. Abigail swung the door open, just as she had that morning, but all that greeted her was a full recycling bin and the smell of stale coffee.

Abigail pressed her lips together and sighed, producing a horse-like noise as she placed the cast lists and supplemental information in each of the teachers' cubbyholes. A glint of light from her own mailbox caused her to turn, her spirits lifting immediately. She held the key up, examining its ridges and the red topper that had "Little Theatre" written in permanent marker.

She would get to use this space after all. Abigail couldn't wait to throw her arms around Mitch in a big bear hug of a thank you. Or perhaps a polite head tilt, which might be more to his liking.

Looking back into her mailbox, she saw a note under the hardware.

Glad the key made its way to you. The play will be a slamming success in the Little Theatre. Sorry I couldn't be there today for the unveiling. Family obligations . . .

Though the ripped piece of notebook paper wasn't signed, Nate's signature was written all over it. Abigail triumphantly placed the key in the zipper section of her canvas messenger bag and headed toward the train station. Sitting on the platform, she thought once more about the roles people play and how they must sometimes change. Doting mothers became grieving Empty Nesters. Beloved children turn into orphaned adults. Your biggest antagonist could someday become one of your top supporters. Fallible teachers could redeem themselves as play directors. And sometimes innocent middle-school students could remain as such for just a little bit longer as they wrote their own happy endings.

14

D'Oh, A Deer

*A*bigail power-walked down Main Street, silently lamenting the fact that all this bouncing was sure to pull her high ponytail down. She couldn't let up on the speed, though, as she was already twenty-five minutes late to meet Quinn.

It all started that afternoon when she ran into Mitch on her way out of school. Abigail was thrilled to finally see him. Despite the abysmal state of the Little Theatre—a fact she'd discovered earlier that week—she'd been wanting to thank him and assure him in person that she was going to take great care of this space.

"I don't wanna hear yer woman yappin'," he said as they stood in front of the theater doors. "That pretty boy got involved so I wouldn't hafta. Plus, he promised those soccer kids would stop usin' the second-floor bathrooms durin' practice. Don't they know I've already cleaned 'em by then? Big smelly lot o'em come in like a herda cows and muck it all up widdin' minutes. Disgustin'."

Abigail stared at her feet like she was one of the bovine boys who was actively being scolded.

"And you . . . *missy*." She immediately jumped to attention. "*You* better not get in there and screw with my stuff. You gotta put on a play? Fine. Place could use a good cleanin'. But stay away from my office, my desk, an' my booze."

She had managed to hand him a rehearsal schedule, complete with an invite to sit in whenever he liked, before she fled the scene in terror. Mitch instantly crumpled the paper, though Abigail took solace in the fact that instead of throwing it in the large, open-mouth trash can he wheeled across campus (or at her), he deposited it in his pocket.

She tried to shake off the surprising encounter, along with a few sweat beads, as she rounded the patio to Kill's.

"Hiyeee!" she called out as she lumbered to catch up with her words. Abigail cautiously eyed Quinn from the side, trying to determine if he was irritated with her or not. All these recent school commitments had done a number on her social life. Aside from the Photoshop session, she hadn't seen much of her friend lately.

Quinn's initial disappointment seemed to wear off when he met "the bachelorette," as they'd nicknamed her. It turned out she had a very flexible schedule, among other malleable parts. Abigail was equally delighted with this new girl. She didn't have to feel guilty anymore for canceling on her oldest friend—and she didn't have to feel guilty for not dating him.

"Hey, Ab," Quinn said from the corner of his mouth, lighting another cigarette. He threw his left hand over the patio gate as he hugged her, almost burning a passerby in the process.

"What's new?" He obligatorily poured her glass of rosé as she settled in.

That's all Abigail needed to be off and running. The kids. The play. The *drama*. She rehashed it all.

"I could not *believe* it when I saw he'd put that key in my cubby. It was seriously the greatest thing." Abigail smiled and released a wistful sigh as she transported herself back to that moment. That feeling. She took a large sip of wine, catching Quinn's dark eyes as she set the glass back down.

"Do you still need me to go with you to Sophie's wedding?" he asked without acknowledging anything she'd said. His left hand picked at the other's cuticles, like he could peel this encounter right off of him.

"Yeah, sure. I mean . . . of course." Abigail was trying to sound upbeat without betraying the fact that she didn't really need him to go with her. She'd felt obligated to ask after Sophie failed to invite him. The two had gotten to know each other relatively well whenever Quinn would pop into their bar for a free Yuengling draft or an incorrect order, which wound up in the trash if none of the staff wanted it.

Quinn probably would've kept scoring those meals, and an invite to Sophie's wedding, if it weren't for that unfortunate incident in summer 2019. Sitting on his barstool, eating someone else's fries, Quinn referred to Sophie's mid-forties investment banker then-boyfriend as "the short old guy with the Jew 'fro and too much gold jewelry." He happened to be standing right behind him at the time.

"You're obviously *welcome* to come to the wedding . . . if your girlfriend doesn't mind," Abigail teased.

"We actually broke up," he said, lighting another cigarette and engaging in his best ventriloquist act.

"Oh, I didn't know." This, of course, complicated matters. "I thought things were going well with you."

"Eh. It was okay. Sex was fine. Conversation was not." Quinn looked up from his cigarette. His furrowed brow and grimace quickly reversed when he saw the look of concern on Abigail's face. In reality, the look was one of frustration. She could never understand why he couldn't keep a relationship for more than six weeks.

Why does he have to be so hard to get along with? So contrary?

"But I thought you liked her."

"She's a reality-TV star," he said, throwing his arms up like her literal existence was a joke. "And not the trashy kind who throws down when you say they live in South Jersey but they're from Central Jersey. Those girls are hot. She's of the 'dress a two-pound dog up like an asshole and make the Sucker of the Week carry it under his arm because you can' variety. Because you were on *The Bachelor* and you wear nothing but pink and you have perfect fake Cs and you almost made it to the hometown dates but he gave your rose to that bitch Ashleigh C. because she's one of those classy North Jersey girls."

Exasperated, Abigail searched her brain for something that would lighten the mood.

"You could've at least used her on your next assignment." She threw one of Quinn's discarded matches at him, receiving a head tilt and a look that said *Really?* in return. "Hey, she's clearly an expert in pet wear. Girls like that are a rare breed, you know." Abigail banged the table and roared at her own joke.

Truth be told, she wasn't quite sure how to respond to this new—but not novel—relationship status. It wasn't that she loved the idea of this kind of girl for Quinn. She loved the idea of *any* girl for Quinn. Well, maybe not a murderer or a thief who targets seniors. Mathilda definitely would not approve of that. But a normal girl with a few of her own quirks, who could maybe inspire him to be a better person.

"I'm not saying she was the love of your life, Quinn, I'm just saying . . ." And then suddenly she realized she didn't know what she was saying. "I'm just saying . . . why didn't you tell me sooner?"

"You have been a little preoccupied lately," he said, looking at her.

This conversation wasn't getting any more comfortable.

"I have been, haven't I?" Abigail placed her hands under her thighs and squirmed in her seat. "I've been kind of a shitty friend lately. I'm really sorry."

Quinn blinked three times in rapid succession. He gave his scraggly hair a quick tousle as a grin broke out across his face. "It's fine. It's all been good, right? Things are working out for you. You're excited, you're busy. Nothing to be ashamed about."

"Really?" she asked, her shoulders loosening a bit.

"Really," Quinn said, signaling the waitress that they needed a refill on their wine.

"Speaking of your next documentary, when are you leaving for Iceland?" Just as Quinn began to speak, her phone chirped. His eyes glanced at the device, which lay screen-side down on the table.

"Ignore it," she politely demanded. "Okay . . . Iceland."

Quinn launched into the side research project he was planning while he was there. He figured if he was going to be dragged halfway around the world on a humiliating assignment, then he might as well work on something that actually interested him. This, for Quinn, was a profile on the Samtökcn '78, the country's LGBTQIA+ organization that was founded as a refuge for these identifying groups in 1978. Though Abigail knew Quinn was a huge equality advocate, she also knew this project had Ev written all over it. This would be his apology to them. His compensation for something he didn't do, but felt responsible for anyway.

Abigail nodded enthusiastically as he explained the group's origins. She was trying her best to listen intently, genuinely fascinated, except she couldn't follow what he was saying because her phone continued its cacophony.

"Why don't you check it?" he suggested, his jaw clenched. "Maybe it's something important."

Abigail used to be a fanatic when it came to picking up calls and texts, but that was when her mother was alive. Though she still fought the urge to answer every call with "What's wrong?" and reviewed most texts for imminent signs of death and destruction, her panic was somewhat allayed by the fact that she'd already experienced the worst.

What else can possibly happen? she used to think. Sure, Mathilda or Quinn could get hurt. Brutus could get sick. But after losing the two most pivotal people to her existence so early on, she felt like she'd bought herself a few passes. Like the Grim Reaper couldn't touch her anymore. At least not yet.

"I'm sure it's fine," she said. Quinn sat across from her, arms crossed, as his chin nodded toward her phone.

Finally, she decided to placate him.

HI.

It was from Nate. Abigail's heart leapt as she jostled the phone. She scrambled to maintain control of it as the device threatened to topple her wine glass. Embarrassed at her clumsiness, she looked at Quinn, who stared back at her wide-eyed. This reminded her to wipe the dopey smile off her face.

Mitch wasn't the only one Abigail had been looking for all week. She wasn't actively searching for Nate but sought out small moments—peeking in the lounge, lingering near the Fine Arts Building where he ran by that one time—so she could thank him for his help with the Little Theatre. And for introducing her to Alex. And for maybe putting forth more effort and patience than she deserved, considering how short she'd been with him.

Perhaps to get to know this fellow teacher better. She wasn't saying she wanted to *date* him or get to know him on an *intimate* level. No. That was absurd. She simply wondered what an actual conversation might look like if she weren't always so guarded . . .

"Ab? Your phone."

She shook off her daydream to find she had two new texts and an irritated happy-hour companion.

PRETTY DAY, ISN'T IT?
I LIKE YOUR HAIR PULLED BACK LIKE THAT. IT LOOKS NICE.

This last text confused her. Her head shot up and she looked around, scanning the patio and neighboring establishments for those pearly whites.

"What's wrong?" Quinn asked, trying to decipher her cranial bobs and weaves.

"Nothing." She cursed her poor low-light vision.

"Hey," a voice suddenly said from behind her right shoulder. She jumped once more, her knuckles knocking into the wine glass just as Quinn leapt out of his chair to stabilize it.

"Hi," Abigail screeched, standing to hug Nate over the gate. She failed to notice Quinn's act of heroism. Nate quickly enveloped her, pulling her lower half tight against the railing. He smelled so good. A mix of cedar and vanilla.

"Quinn, this is Nate," she added after a loud throat clearing came from his general direction. "I mean, Mr. Carter. He works with me. At Excelsior Primm. He's a teacher."

Real smooth.

"Hey, man. How's it going?" Nate threw his hand out and flashed his teeth.

"I'm good . . . 'man'," Quinn retorted, making a show of putting his cigarette down to shake this guy's hand. "Just having drinks with my oldest friend, *man*. Speaking of which . . ."

The waitress walked by with a new bottle of wine on her tray. She had resting bitch face and blatantly ignored a customer who tried to get her attention, but this woman looked like an angel to Abigail, nonetheless.

"Thank you," she stammered, hoping to divert attention away from the competition over who could utter that three-letter word with more emphasis.

"That's great. You do this every Thursday?" Nate waved his finger between the two glasses.

"Yes." Quinn moved the stemware away from the fence, out of Nate's finger firing range.

"Huh," Nate said, eyeing the bottle. "Rosé. In fall. At night. In forty-eight degree weather."

Quinn winced as he looked at Abigail, clearly unhappy.

"Oh, well, I like it," she sheepishly explained. "And the heaters here work really well." She glanced at the bottle's label, *All the Way Rosé,* internalizing how cheesy that was.

Fucking GOD.

"Rosé is her thing, man. She likes it," Quinn reiterated. He made a giant effort to pour hers just right, like the sommeliers did at the restaurants where the Kellys typically spent their Friday nights during summers on Martha's Vineyard. He reached across the table, victoriously placing Abigail's impeccably poured glass in front of her.

"Huh. I didn't know you were a wine drinker. Although evidently, you're not. You're drinking rosé." Nate gave her a friendly shoulder poke over the fence, eliciting an embarrassed squeal from Abigail and a stone-cold stare from Quinn.

"Nate. What the hell are you doing over there?" A high-pitched voice rang out from across the street. A young, willowy woman with jet-black hair and tight leather pants was hobbling her way over to the threesome like a baby deer. Abigail was about to return Nate's poke when she caught sight of this girl, instantly retracting her hand.

"Just chatting with some friends," Nate responded, his voice now devoid of sarcasm, as the woman approached in four-inch heels. She sported two of the iciest blue eyes Abigail had ever seen. She wasn't traditionally pretty—she had an extremely small nose and eyes set a little too close together—but her unique features assembled into a stunning face.

"Guys, this is Bethany," Nate offered with no further explanation.

"Hi," she said, looking about as pleased as Quinn had when Nate first showed up. "We should get going." Bethany stared at Abigail for a second too long—revealing that she'd seen their little finger play. Creating a thud, Bethany placed a forceful hand on Nate's cotton twill jacket as she began to direct him up the street.

"Yeah, I guess it's getting late," he relented. "Good seeing you, Ms. Gardner. Nice meeting you . . . *man.*"

Abigail watched his perfect head of light brown hair slowly transition away from her, thanks to a creature who seemed more qualified to navigate Santa's sleigh than her fellow teacher.

The friends found themselves alone once again. Abigail was pretty sure neither of them knew what to make of that encounter. Quinn quickly snubbed out the cigarette he'd been smoking when Nate arrived.

"That was the famous Nate, huh?"

"Guess you could say that." Abigail rested her chin on her fist. She suddenly didn't feel like drinking or socializing anymore.

"Huh," he repeated. They sat in awkward silence for a few more moments before he added, "And what the fuck was up with that chick?"

"Right?" Abigail quickly grabbed onto the subject, planting both palms on the table and leaning forward. She felt a small surge of energy return.

So what if Nate was dating someone? That was good for him. It's not like she wanted to repay him for the key with sexual favors, or anything. And clearly, he didn't want that, either. If tall, skinny, and icy was his type, well then, that was fine by her.

"Man, if anybody ever needed a good anger bang, it's her," Quinn continued, grabbing his chest. "I swear, she took one look at me and I could feel the cold wrath of hell wrapping around my shriveled soul."

"Nah, that's just lung cancer settling in."

"Oh, yeah?" Quinn playfully lobbed his now-empty pack across the table. They both laughed as she swiped pretend ashes off her violet micro-suede blazer. Abigail swirled a sip of wine in her mouth, looking at Quinn as they shook their heads in disapproval of Ms. Bethany.

15

Plot Twist

"If I knew you were going to drag me through shit today, I would've gone into work," Mathilda said from deep inside the bowels of the Little Theatre that Saturday morning. She wiped her hands on her black sweats, leaving a visible mark. If those pants had been logged into evidence, Mathilda would've likely surmised that the victim was dragged and pawed at by their assailant, which was a pretty accurate assessment of the current situation.

"But that's *why* I picked you," Abigail said in her most upbeat voice. "Who else is better at sifting through shit than Philly's finest up-and-coming detective?"

"Fuck you," Mathilda countered as she dropped a cardboard box, disturbing the two-inch layer of dust on top of it. "At least I solved one case today."

"Oh, yeah? What's that?" Abigail yelled from the modest room she'd stumbled upon backstage. It was bleak, with fake wood paneling and brown carpet. A roll-top desk and chair were the only discernible pieces of furniture in the space, which somehow looked both cluttered and empty, like a family had cleaned out their storage unit, taking all their important belongings but leaving a few insignificant items behind. It took Abigail a minute to realize this was likely Mitch's office. She wasn't planning to disobey his strict orders not to touch anything, though she saw no harm in sitting at the desk. Besides, that pushed-in chair seemed to be the only surface not covered in dust.

"Where that psycho hid his anthrax following the 2001 attacks." Mathilda laughed at herself, instantly triggering a coughing fit.

"Mathilda, really. Do you have to be so morbid?" Abigail gestured wildly with her hands, as if Mathilda could see her from her current position in the first row of seats. One of her right knuckles made contact with something square and glass. Abigail froze immediately, failing to move a muscle until she heard it. The ping.

Oh, thank God.

She blew air out of her mouth, knowing that blunt, yet beautiful little sound meant all was right with the world again. Sure enough, there on the floor was Mitch's whiskey bottle. Abigail had never been so happy to see worn-to-the-bone-but-still-softer-than-the-concrete-underneath-it carpet in all her life. She was also thankful that Mitch had been considerate enough to drink at least nine-tenths of the bottle before leaving it out in the open, where any old hapless drama coach was sure to bitch-slap it right off the desk she wasn't supposed to go near.

Abigail took her time placing the bottle back in its original position, lining it up perfectly with its dust outline. It was then that she noticed a drawer slightly ajar, with a long white envelope sticking out.

"I do. I really do have to be *that* morbid," Mathilda said in a jagged voice as her respiratory system settled.

"Wasn't someone convicted of those attacks?" Abigail asked, though her mouth and brain had already completely disconnected. She was focused on that white envelope.

Who's Jennifer Beaton of Egg Harbor City, New Jersey?

"No one was ever convicted."

"I thought they caught the guy," Abigail continued to goad her BFF on. Mathilda might not have had any connection to Mitch or the Little Theatre, but Abigail still didn't want anyone knowing she was slowly removing the contents of the unsealed envelope. Questions about a potential terrorist circa 2001 seemed like the perfect bait for a spry detective.

"It was Steven Jay Hatfill."

"Huh?" Abigail muttered, unfolding the letter.

"No, no. Anthrax . . . anthrax . . . it was . . . the mad scientist," Mathilda declared, poking her head into the office with a raised pointer finger. Abigail instantly threw her hands up as the letter slowly zig-zagged to the floor. "Bruce Edwards Ivins, the mad scientist. He was the prime anthrax attack suspect."

Mathilda slapped her hands together in a self-congratulatory fashion, turning to leave. "Damn. I should've known that right away."

"Yeah?" Abigail offered. She bent down to retrieve the letter. "Why do the worst offenders always go by three names?"

"Good question. See, the thing about that is . . ."

Abigail was too distracted to listen. Her eyes darted back and forth across the page.

Dear Jenny Girl,

It's been a while, huh? Might've taken some time for me to say it, but I miss you and Cadence. I hope I spelt that right.

*How is she anyway? How are you? I think about coming to
New Jersey sometimes, but I'm afraid you'll throw something
at me, and I'll deserve it.*

*I wish I were a better father, Jenny Girl. I really do. If I could
go back in time to that little white house in Albany during
those early years I would. Shoulda quit the bottle when
Grandmum passed. I know that now. Old habits die hard. I
also woulda been more understanding of your situation. Still
can't say I like that Kevin much—or the Irish that runs
through him—but it runs through my granddaughter, too,
and that shoulda been reason enough to like him. Or at least
tolerate him. I'm telling you, if I could go back, I'd do it
different.*

*But I guess there's no point in crying over spilt milk. Listen to
me, rambling on about the past like a blubbery Irishman.
Maybe Kevin and I have more in common than I thought.
Whatever the case, I'd like to find out. That's if you're willing
to have me.*

*I know I've let too much time go, but God willing we still got
plenty left. Especially that little one. Sometimes I look at the
kids 'round here and wonder if that one looks like her or if
this one sounds like her. Hell, even some of the teachers
'round here remind me of you in your day. Feisty, sensitive,
with plenty of girl problems to go around. Annoys the shit out
of me, but then I think of you, and I secretly get a kick outta
the whole frilly bunch. Damn. Rambling again.*

*Anyway, point is, I'd love to see you. Any of you. All of you.
Whatever you'd be willing to offer. If you wanna just send
Kevin to punch me in the face and call me a drunken sheep-*

shagger, that's okay, too. Long as he returns and tells you I
send my love. And yes, I said love. I'd come to Egg Harbor
anytime. Or you can come to Philly. Digs aren't that nice, but
they're cozy enough, though I'm sure Mum wouldn't have
approved. Not a framed cross-stitch in the whole place.

LOVE,
Pop
XOXXO

Abigail quietly folded the letter and placed it back in its envelope. She peeled her tongue off the roof of her mouth, swallowing
hard as she internalized her sympathy for the old man who wrote
it, and her own guilt over reading it.

There are some things you can't unsee. Abigail knew this was
one of them. How was she supposed to slip the letter—which was
clearly never sent—back into the drawer and pretend like none of
this ever happened?

It was the last thing in the world she wanted to do, but her
chest felt heavy as the violation of her offense really set in. There
was no other choice.

"What the hell do you mean, 'pick up my kids from soccer'?
I'm not your wife. *Or* your chauffeur." Getting back to the task at
hand, Abigail could hear Mathilda shouting into her phone
thanks to the theater's brilliant acoustics. If anything could rile
her, it was having to pick up the slack for Santos' ex-wife.

This was a particularly frustrating situation for Mathilda, as
she was just breaking free of her own familial obligations. In
fact, apartment hunting was the first thing she did after receiving
word she'd secured an entry-level detective position.

Unfortunately, Mathilda seemed to have spun right out of

one dysfunctional household and into another. "I cannot *believe* you," she screamed, slamming her thumb down on her phone screen. Abigail crept onto the stage and began sweeping incessantly. She tried not to notice anything was wrong.

"I'm so sorry, but that dick—strike that—that dick's *ex-wife* says she has a migraine and can't get out of bed to pick up their kids. He's stuck at work. Apparently, we have a new lead on that burglar, who the media nicknamed the 'the Boomer Bandit.'" Mathilda rolled her eyes, shaking her head at this last revelation.

"It's no problem, really," Abigail offered. She felt a lump in her throat as she tried to imagine how she would finish the rest of the cleaning job by the end of this weekend. "Look around, we're almost done."

It was true that they had made good progress. The piles were organized, the stage was (maniacally) swept, and all trust and sense of privacy had already been annihilated.

What else is there left to do, really? Except move the potential props backstage, carry the Goodwill boxes down to the bottom of the hill and take out the fifteen or so piles of trash, also near the bottom of the hill . . . Ugh.

Abigail smiled weakly, nodding her head.

"You're positive you're fine with this?" Mathilda was already retrieving her zip-up hoodie and silver-studded skull tote bag. "Because I said yes to you first. These aren't even my kids. Fuck, why am I always stuck with other people's kids?"

"Totally fine," Abigail reiterated, not wanting to add another pound of guilt to Mathilda's load. She was starting to suspect that pile was even heavier than the garbage bags sitting outside the theater's side entrance.

Abigail watched her friend storm up the aisle and out the heavy main double doors. She caught a sliver of natural light before they slammed shut. Though it was gray, she could tell the sun was fading. A quick glance at her phone confirmed this—it was nearly five o'clock.

She surveyed the room before deciding on what seemed like the easiest task: organizing the few viable props they'd found backstage. Abigail was conscious to avoid the perimeter near Mitch's office as she maneuvered in the low light. This worked for a while, until she slammed her left wrist, which happened to be attached to a very heavy mirror, into a wooden pillar.

"Ow, god *dammit!*" she screamed as her right palm scanned the back wall for a light switch. The one closest to her lit up the left side of the backstage area. The damage didn't seem too bad. A little redness, a few scrapes. The mirror held up fine. While examining this prop, Abigail caught sight of signatures that were scattered up and down the pillar like ants.

They appeared to be from 2003 to 2007, when EP's theater program would've been in full swing. And when Mrs. Vangundy would've been quite a bit younger. There were cast signatures under *Cinderella*, *Oliver Twist!*, *The Secret Garden*, and *The Wizard of Oz*.

Had a blast!
Drama Club '04 is the best!!!
Long live the orphans!
First stop . . . Excelsior Primm . . . next stop Hollywood!

The pronouncements energized and terrified her. Abigail now had confirmation that these plays had been a success—at least in the casts' eyes. She also knew they had more money, talent (*three Kraemer kids in the same* Wizard of Oz *production!*), and experience in the form of the not-so-decrepit Vangundy.

Sure, it was possible to pull off another success, but was it possible for her? Abigail ran her fingers up and down the wooden columns, studying the signatures and trying to decipher what the kids were like based on their penmanship. Then she heard it. A loud creak. Abigail let out a short gasp as she froze in place. Someone else was there.

But who could it be?

Few people even knew the Little Theatre had been unlocked. She immediately regretted turning on the backstage light.

Listening intently, Abigail could hear footsteps approaching the stage. Her eyes frantically scanned the area while her head remained completely immobile. She knew she wasn't going to find an answer in these pillars of positivity, so she grabbed a nearby shadeless lamp—the one thing Mathilda had successfully put away before bailing—and began her tip-toe exit, Stage Right. She held the lamp base over her left shoulder, ready to strike, as she silently headed for the stage.

Suddenly, a hand was on her back.

"Aaaaaaaah!" she yelled, whipping around and dropping the lamp.

"Relax, it's just me," Nate said, jumping back. His expression turned from surprised to embarrassed as he realized his presence had apparently terrorized her.

"Jesus. What are you doing here?" She bent down to catch her breath and pick up the lamp.

"I left my parents' spare gate remote in my classroom. I stayed over at their place earlier this week and forgot to take it with me. I'm going to dinner with them tonight, so I thought I'd swing by here first. Then I saw the side door was open and figured you must be in here. Mitch never uses that door."

Abigail exhaled and nodded as if this piece of information was the most obvious thing in the world.

"You sure you're okay?" he asked, rubbing her right arm. His touch sent a tingle up her spine.

"Yeah," she said feebly. "I just . . . I heard the door. No one knew I'd be here. My friend left early. I thought . . . I thought maybe it was Mitch. Like maybe he was spying on me or something."

Hearing these words out loud, Abigail realized how preposterous they sounded. For a moment she debated telling Nate about the letter, but thought better of it. Especially since she'd just thrown the poor, old, apparently lonely janitor under the bus.

No need to back over him.

"Mitch? Nah, he's not much of a spier," Nate offered, before quickly adding, "unless you touched his whiskey."

"What?" she yelped, remembering her solid backhand.

"Kidding. I know he comes off all gruff and hard as hell, but he's a big softie underneath." Nate began examining the signatures on the pillar, just as Abigail had a few moments earlier.

"How do you know he's a big softie?" she asked, wondering if Nate had seen a gentler side to Mitch.

"Oh, I don't really know," Nate stammered. "I figure all these harsh bastards have to have a soft underbelly. I mean, no one can be a miserable little shit all the time, right?"

Abigail immediately thought of Updike. She hoped what Nate said was true. It was, at least, for a few of literature's greatest villains: Mr. Darcy, Severus Snape, the Grinch.

Even Satan in Paradise Lost *had the ability to evoke sympathy from Milton's readers, and he's the damn devil.*

"I have to say, you guys definitely made a dent in here," Nate said, moving onto the stage.

"Thanks. It's coming along nicely. I have the trash left to do." She gulped as her eyes focused on the side door.

"Right. All three hundred and nineteen bags."

Abigail threw her head back in despair.

"I have to get going soon, but I could help you," Nate suggested. His eyes were soft and his smile looked sincere. At least she hoped it was.

Despite her current conundrum, Abigail was *dying* to get a little time with him. Maybe ask how his date went. She didn't want to be nosy; she'd settle for a few standard details. *Did you guys have dinner? Did you walk her home? How far can she even walk upright on those legs? Did you kiss her goodnight? Does she take her hair pieces out before you have sex? What does your chest feel like? Is it smooth and sculpted—can you practically taste that vanilla cologne if you lick . . .*

"Abigail, time's a'ticking. We gotta move if we're going to do this." She snapped out of her fantasy or nightmare—she couldn't decide which—to see Nate standing there, fully clothed, holding out a key in front of her. "I've got my car parked right outside. A few trips down the hill, and I figure this will be easy."

The two spent the better part of an hour loading and unloading and reloading. Abigail realized the trips would be more efficient if she stayed behind. This would've freed up room in the front seat, while allowing her to prepare the next load for pick up. But she didn't suggest as much. She was enjoying the snippets of conversation between loads.

Abigail learned Nate's family had been in Pennsylvania for five generations. That his father owned some sort of medical practice he was transitioning over to his oldest son, Nate's brother. That his grandfather, who seemed to be Nate's favorite, worked in a wine shop. Or a winery. Or a vineyard. Something to do with wine was what she'd gleaned from that forty-second snippet. Their exchange about rosé suddenly made sense, making her flush.

"You know, if you tried some good wine sometime, I think you'd find there's a lot more to like about it than some cheap college swill," were Nate's parting words as he dropped her at the base of Excelsior Primm. He'd apologized on the final ride down that he couldn't take her all the way to the train station, or to her home. The task had taken longer than expected, and he was now in danger of running late for dinner, especially when he factored in the now-necessary shower.

To Abigail, walking her normal commute was a small price to pay for finishing up the Little Theatre in a fraction of the time.

And the conversation was definitely an added bonus, she thought as she strolled down the sidewalk, the same shy smile that appeared an hour ago overtaking her face once more.

16

Criss-Cross Hooray

Abigail chewed on the side of her cheek, watching the ten faces on stage butcher fourteen lines of old Shakespeare. Rehearsals hadn't started out quite as she'd hoped. A seventh-grade boy who was cast as Paris had to drop out due to a mix up with his tennis club's schedule. A fifth-grade girl who signed up to be assistant director also backed out, citing her therapist's opinion that all this responsibility wasn't good for her anxiety disorder.

You and me both, sister.

Then there was the opening scene, the memorable Prologue that ushers in *Romeo and Juliet* and sets the tone for the rest of the show. Abigail had easily revised the lines to reflect the play's new direction, but no matter what she did, the scene fell apart.

"Run it one more time," she directed, squinting her eyes as she tried to assess who was speaking too fast and who was delayed. The kids began again, in unison:

"Two households, both alike in dignity,
In fair Verona, where we lay our scene . . ."

By the fourth line, her ears hurt. They were like the theatrical version of the *Bad News Bears*. Not helping matters was Tommy Otollo, a beanpole of a kid with a set of windpipes that was unrivaled. Abigail initially thought this would be a good thing, that Tommy's strong projection would lead the group, keeping all the other voices in line. Instead, he had become the baseball in the middle of a cake.

Abigail didn't have the heart to remove him from the Prologue, nor was she stupid enough to assign him the entire passage. Instead, she moved Tommy around the stage like a decorative lamp.

Maybe he would blend in better in the back.

Wrong.

Maybe we should feature him, front and center, since his is the loudest voice and Dieter isn't here anyway.

Wrong again.

Then she thought it might help if she took some of the attention off the ten kids. Perhaps they would sound better, more synchronized, if the audience had something else to look at. So she rearranged the scene.

The curtain now opened on the chorus as they stood in the courtyard of beautiful Verona. The stage would be dimmed, with scenes of the two families—and the lovers' frustrations with them—playing out on opposite ends. Romeo would practice his archery skills under the critical eye of Lord Montague as Friar Laurence stood nervously with an apple on his head. Juliet would gossip with the Nurse as a servant tied her corset ever tighter while Lady Capulet looked on.

Both scenes would deteriorate as the Chorus progressed: Romeo becomes resentful of his father's constant corrections to his stance, while Juliet is frustrated with her mom's endless insistence that the corset be tighter. The two were set to storm off in their respective stage directions as the Prologue wound down, providing plenty of visual stimulation to drown out the pre-pubescent voices. And Tommy. Oh, Tommy . . .

"Tommy? Tommy," Abigail yelled.

"Yes, ma'am?" Tommy, in all his awkwardness, had such an eager look on his face. He wore a goofy grin and gave his best deer-in-the-headlights impersonation anytime he was startled, which was all the time.

"Tommy, honey. Move to the right. All the way down. No, not the middle. All the way right. Keep going. Farther down. All the way . . . there. Thank you." He nodded incessantly once he realized he was in the correct spot. "Okay, kids. Let's run it again. One more time. Tommy, you lead. Everyone else, try to keep pace with Tommy."

They started over. Abigail realized this group had a distinct talent for taking a three-syllable word like "dignity" and turning it into a twelve-syllable abomination when said in unison. She moved to the very back of the theater to see if she could spot the problem from there.

"Fuck me," she uttered under her breath as she watched the performance.

Romeo and Juliet may escape this play unscathed, but we haven't eluded death yet. They're butchering this Prologue, and my job security.

"Ahem."

Abigail froze mid-thought. "Mitch," she said, widening her eyes and mouth as she turned around. "It's so nice to see you—I mean, for you to join us—I mean, of *course* you're welcome anytime."

Mitch stood there, staring down at her, expressionless.

I'm starting to sympathize with the Tommy Otollos of the world.

"It's shit," he eventually responded.

"It's . . . what?" she asked, shocked by this blunt assessment. Now it was her turn to stare blankly.

"Oh, it's stupid as all get out," he said, pointing to the kids on stage who had taken her distraction to mean they could goof off for a bit.

Abigail wanted to tell this man to go to hell, but she knew he was right. Though they had plenty of time before opening night, they also had many other scenes to master. She knew she wouldn't be as good of a director as she could be if the Prologue continued to plague her.

"What am I doing wrong, do you think?"

Mitch turned toward the stage, which currently featured nine children play-fighting each other while Tommy stood perfectly still in his newly assigned spot. He truly was an excellent lamp.

Mitch gave his lips a swipe with his tongue and clapped his hands before resting them on his narrow hips. He quickly pivoted back toward Abigail. "Well, for starters, you got too many voices."

"Okay."

"This is Shakespeare, not some damn holiday pageant where all the kids can get away with lookin' cute but stupid. We ain't rockin' around no Christmas tree."

"Right." She had no idea what he meant. Her blank expression ensured that.

"Oh, for Christ's sake, girly. I gotta spell it out for ya? Break it up." The kids on stage froze instantly, a response to his high-pitched, booming voice. Meanwhile, the lamp had grown eyes the size of saucers.

"It's—it's okay, kids. Take Five. Alex, you watch the cast. Make sure they're back here by three forty," Abigail yelled, trying to reassure them and herself.

"Yes, ma'am," she heard from backstage. This was followed by dozens of little footsteps and, eventually, the side exit door slamming. Loudly. This did nothing to qualm Mitch's irritation.

"Look, there's too many o'em and they ain't *gonna* get it right. They been at this forever and it's not comin' together." Abigail wondered how he knew this scene had been plaguing them. "So ya break it up. Curtain opens, a small group of two or three kids say the first two lines. Then another, then another and so on. Place 'em in groups all over the stage so the action keeps switchin'. 'Twill match yer visuals."

"Oh. Okay. I see," she said, meaning it this time.

Abigail turned toward the stage and began blocking the scene in her mind.

"An' use that lamppost."

"Huh?"

"That tall, freaky-lookin' kid. He got a loud voice. Give 'im the last two lines. Audience'll remember him."

"That makes sense." She giggled to herself as she turned back toward the stage, amused that they viewed Tommy in the same likeness, both in human and furniture form.

"An' yer little 'scenes' are fallin' flat, too."

"Yeah?"

"Hell, yeah, girly. Ain't you got eyes? Or are they always staring off somewhere? Anywhere but where they should be?" She didn't appreciate Mitch's condescending tone, but she wasn't about to look a drunken gift horse who could potentially save her career in the mouth.

"It ain't connectin'. *They* ain't connectin'," he said, pointing to the two sides of the stage where Romeo and Juliet would be placed. "Yer talkin' 'bout star-crossed lovers an' all this shit, but you ain't makin' no effort to show that's so."

Abigail scanned the stage for a moment. Suddenly, she gasped.

"I got it. They're star-crossed lovers, right? So we open, and the animosity between the teens and their parents is obvious, but what's *not obvious*—at least not yet—is how close yet far away the lovers are from each other."

Mitch stood there, listening, with his arms crossed. He reminded her of one of those sideline coaches who furiously chews tobacco and nods as a member of the coaching staff whispers the next play in his ear.

Two coaches. Like equals.

She tried not to let the prospect go to her head.

"So anyway, instead of having Romeo exit Stage Left and Juliet Stage Right, we'll have them *cross* and exit from opposite ends of the stage. They'll move in unison, Romeo behind the chorus, Juliet in front of it. Oh, wait. And when they exit, we'll have Juliet disappear first, then Romeo will turn around, almost like he feels—he *knows*—someone is there, but she'll be gone already."

Mitch nodded subtly, pursing his lips. It wasn't exactly ecstatic acclaim, but it wasn't bad for a man whose idea of courtesy was spitting just left of your shoe, not on it.

"Ooooh, they'll be total star-crossed lovers then," Abigail squealed, shaking her fists near her head. "It's going to be *so perfect*. Thank you, thank you, thank you." She threw her arms around him in gratitude. Mitch immediately stiffened, much like the foliage he'd devoted his life to.

The kids began to trickle back in. Abigail let go of the old man to discuss this new strategy with them. She examined their revised spacing once more from the bottom of the stage before issuing an enthusiastic "Take it from the top."

Abigail listened to each duet nail their lines as she slowly walked backward toward the front of the theater. She turned around once, flashing a proud smile at Mitch, only to discover he was gone.

17

Pissed Off in Periwinkle

With the Prologue in the bag, rehearsals were finally off to a running start. The good news kept rolling, as Abigail was even able to secure a production donation from the Kraemers. She was inspired to contact them after discovering their oldest daughter's inscription on one of the theater's pillars.

I'll never forget my EP days. See you all Over the Rainbow!!!

Abigail made sure to attach a photo of this throwback to her email. She was ecstatic to learn that Mrs. Kraemer's definition of a "small donation" was drastically different from her own.

Of course, my dear. Anything to support the arts. And the Primm. Art is so important to a child's upbringing. Especially nowadays. Count us in for twenty-five hundred dollars. I'll have my assistant contact the secretary for the transfer. See you on Opening Night.

Though Abigail quickly sent off an enthusiastic "thank you"—and internally praised this woman for saving her own bank account—she gulped when she reread that last line. *See you on Opening Night!*

Never in a million years did she think the Kraemers would actually show.

Apparently, Updike isn't the only one who wants to see a return on their investment.

Now the pressure was really on. If Updike's threat, the use of the Little Theatre, and the parents of twenty-seven kids didn't do it, the prospect of having to watch a disaster unfold in front of Manhattan's theatrical royalty was enough to make her flee the teaching profession for good.

Speaking of teaching, in addition to scaring the living shit out of her, the note also made Abigail a bit wistful. *Art is so important to a child's upbringing. Especially nowadays.*

Abigail knew the play was its own form of art. Of course it was. And if done right, it would be a beautiful piece these kids could be proud of. But art. Art-art. The letter brought back memories of *her* art. It was why she had gone to school, wanted to be an elementary teacher, and responded to Excelsior Primm's initial email in the first place.

Though she was excited for the dreams the stage would inspire for her club, she ached for her own art class—one that would likely never be within reach again if she couldn't first produce a success in an artistic field with which she had zero experience. She wondered if she'd chosen the wrong art form for herself. Or if the wrong art form was currently choosing her.

Fortunately, Abigail didn't have long to dwell on her doubts and potentially poor career choices. Soon after putting her additional hand-written thank-you card to the Kraemers in the mail, she arrived in a sleepy New York for Sophie's wedding weekend. Nate had graciously offered to man the two rehearsals she'd miss, while a sub would take over her classes. Abigail hated to do this so early in the school year, but she had made the commitment to Sophie nine months prior. True to form, Sophie was sure to produce one hell of a baby this weekend.

Abigail was still dragging her periwinkle bridesmaid dress through the train station when the group texts began. She had about fifteen seconds to throw her stuff in Sophie's aunt's condo before the day erupted into last-minute wedding errands.

A grueling ten hours later, Abigail and Mathilda managed to grab a reprieve. Though Abigail had come fully prepared with a new girl—Carla, a fifth-generation maple-syrup farmer—she was too tired to be herself, let alone anyone else tonight. Thankfully, Sophie's cousins were leading the second bachelorette party—the Queens edition. Well, the other "queens" edition, which promised to be even more debaucherous than the first. Since the drinking had technically started at lunch, the evening crazy-train left the station before anyone noticed the two weren't aboard.

This gave Abigail all night to work on the play's costume sketches from Brewhaha, a quirky little coffee shop she discovered on one of the many jaunts she and Quinn took into the city. She'd visited many times over the years but hadn't been back since that college internship failed to pan out. In fact, the more she thought of it, she couldn't recall visiting New York at all after that letdown.

A quick Google search revealed the place was still there, just two blocks shy of where she thought it was. Abigail turned the flimsy doorknob, causing the bell resting against the windowpane to come to life. The place was dark and musty, reminding her of an old forgotten library wing, but that's what she loved about it. And New York. They had personality. History.

She sidled up to the countertop, whipping out her notebook. A self-satisfied smile overtook her face as she basked in the notion that she'd get to spend the next few hours with her first love. Art-art. Her lips broadened with excitement as Abigail spread her designs in front of her.

There was a sketch of Lady Capulet's attire, which included an empire waist and deep purple hues with red accents. She'd also done some early work on the ceremony's layout. There would be a long red carpet, of course, emphasizing the importance of this event. The lovers would meet under a gold-trimmed awning that was sprouting new leaves and buds, symbols of a new beginning.

She rubbed her hands together before picking up her pencil. Abigail would be thinking about weddings all right, just not Sophie's.

Besides, this bride is a little less batshit than the one I'll be sharing a wall with tonight.

She was just about to fill in the details on Romeo's mask when her phone chirped. She assumed Sophie had discovered they were MIA, and figured she'd let Mathilda handle it. After the third chirp, she threw the phone into the hollows of her Madewell tote beneath her feet. Shaking off the irritation, Abigail began again, but the phone continued relentlessly. The vibration struck under her foot, causing her pencil to shift unceremoniously.

Abigail shoved a closed fist into her bag to retrieve it. The device seemed all too pleased to inform her she had seven messages.

MESSAGE 1

So . . . u banged that teacher yet? What's his name? Slate?

MESSAGE 2

Hope ur using protection. That other chick of his looks durrty ;)

MESSAGE 3

Let's grab a beer tonight. On the train now. Getting in early ahead of the rehearsal dinner.

MESSAGE 4

R u on a bridesmaid errand? Wouldn't that be SO Sophie to make u guys work round the clock? She probs didn't even get anything done b4 everyone arrived. Figured u'd do it all while she sits on her ass i bet.

MESSAGE 5

Remember that old Jewish man she used to bang? I fucking loved that guy. Do u think he still lives in the city? Wonder if we can track him down tonight.

MESSAGE 6

Staying at the Ace. Let's meet in the lobby at 9 then hit the Ginger Man. I think the last time we were there was like summer solstice 2015.

MESSAGE 7

Up in the room. Jesus, it's like hipster central here. Was it always like this? Fuck, I'm getting old. Call me.

Abigail was so irritated by the time she read the last text she couldn't even see straight.

Quinn had relentlessly suggested it would be a great idea if he got into town early. That way they'd have a night to just "hang" in the city, as he put it. Abigail told him over and over that she would be busy with wedding details. If he wanted to accompany her to Soph's rehearsal dinner the following night, that was fine, but her gentle assertions that his presence wasn't wanted or needed until that time fell on deaf ears.

She crumpled up the now-ruined sketch and slammed her hand down on her phone. Hard.

"Hey. There you are. Listen, I'm having a couple beers in my room, but I can still be ready by nine, I'm in room—"

"Quinn."

"Yeah. I mean . . . yeah? Do you remember how to get here? Just take the . . ."

"I told you not to come early, remember?" she snarled. "We had, like, a million conversations about it."

"You might've said I didn't *have* to come early, but it worked out. So I figured I'd surprise you."

"But I'm *busy* right now."

"With wedding stuff still? Shit, she has you guys by the balls. Put Mathilda on. She'll figure out a way to put that bridezilla in her place."

"No," Abigail said, taking a breath. "I'm at a coffee shop filling in some sketches for the play."

"Oh, you didn't say that. I'll come to you. Are you at Brew blah, blah or Serendipity 3? Don't tell me you're at a Starbucks. No true New Yorker would be caught dead—"

"*Quinn!*" The phone mercifully quieted down for a second.

"Quinn," Abigail said again, trying to take the edge out of her voice as she glanced around the room. She hated that she was causing a scene in the little coffee shop she adored. "I told you I'm working. I told you not to come early. I'll see you tomorrow at dinner, but I'm busy until then. Like. I. Said."

"Oh, c'mon, Ab," he retorted, his voice growing whiny in the most unattractive way. "I never see you anymore. You're always working. It's a kids' play. And it's a four-day weekend for you. Take some time off for fuck's sake. Besides, you sketch all day. I'm sure it'll be fine. The kids will never even notice if . . ."

"I don't know why you never listen," she whisper-screamed as her body seemed to levitate off the stool. "I fucking tell you something and you disregard it. 'Oh, it's Abigail. She's being oversensitive again. She's such a worrywart. It'll all be fine.' Why can't you understand this is important to me?"

It was once again quiet on the other end before Quinn meekly uttered, "Look, Ab . . ."

"No, you look." She was unable to stop herself. Abigail gathered her sketches and headed outside to prevent any further disturbance. "My life is my life and I get to decide what's important in it, got it? Stop dismissing my shit and start listening when I tell you something like 'don't come early.' If you can't, then I don't even know why I'm friends with you."

She listened for signs of life over the phone, but it was even quieter than before. Abigail knew she shouldn't have threatened the friendship, but she also knew she was at the end of her rope with Quinn not taking her seriously. She waited a few more seconds and then realized what she was hearing. Silence. It was the end of the line.

18

Wedding Weakened

Standing six feet from the gaudy bride two days later, Abigail scanned the crowd from her elevated place on the altar. She was happy her bouquet was there to occupy her hands, which constantly had the urge to leap up and attack the pale-blue bridesmaid dress with the unruly fringe. What made her less happy was the fact that she still hadn't heard from Quinn.

Last night's festivities came and went without a word from him. Abigail wasn't too concerned when he didn't show at the rehearsal, since he wasn't in the wedding. When she sat alone at the dinner, however, she felt a twinge of guilt, followed by panic. The idea was starting to sink in that she might have pushed someone she cared about so far out the door that he'd returned his key.

Doing another ocular lap around the church, Abigail had to look twice when her eyes landed on a clean-cut man sitting on the bride's side.

Quinn?

She stared at him, mouth agape. He sported the same serious expression he always did as Quinn focused his attention on what the priest was saying. What *had* changed was his Albert Einstein hairdo. It had been replaced by an updated look. The sides and back were clipper-cut short and blended into a longer layered top that was still a bit jagged but nicely styled. It dawned on her that the missing mop was why she hadn't been able to spot him earlier when she walked down the aisle, desperately searching for any signs of his scraggly trademark hair.

Halfway through Sophie's sister's reading of 1 Corinthians 13:4-8a ("Love is patient, love is kind . . ."), Abigail was caught red-handed, or rather red-faced. Quinn looked away from the happy couple to find her blatantly staring at him. She hadn't realized how obvious she'd made herself until she watched his eyes go wide with surprise. Her neck instantly grew blotchy, revealing a guilty plea.

In true Quinn fashion, he played it off. His face softened, and he issued a wry half-smile as he fixed his eyes upward as if to say, "Yeah, I got a new haircut. I'm a total sell-out. A tool. I know." He looked at her once more as he mouthed "Cool, huh?" and pointed to his head while shrugging.

Abigail had a lot of emotions running through her this weekend, and the sight of Quinn not only tidied up, but trying to convey that all was forgiven in the middle of a wedding, was too much. She offered a quick nod before turning her attention back to Soph and Bern. This was the smartest thing to do, she figured, considering her tears could easily be mistaken for wedding joy.

The friends made it all the way through the ceremony, dinner, and toasts before coming face to face.

"Oh, hello," Abigail stammered, looking up from her hands, which were amassed in a sea of foamy white chiffon dotted with glass crystals as she and Mathilda helped Sophie to the bathroom.

"Hey, stranger," Quinn offered, his words implying she wasn't completely off the hook.

"Hi, Quinn," Sophie said with all the energy she could muster, which was just above that of a sideways goldfish. "So nice of you to join us."

"You know what I would like to join?" Mathilda interjected. "The party soon. So how about you hurry up and pee so we can get to the task at hand. You know, actually celebrating your wedding?"

Abigail loved her for being an expert tension diffuser. Mathilda snatched a handful of fabric from Abigail's grip and continued to lead the bride toward the bathroom. From a distance, it looked like she was walking a very puffy and yappy white poodle.

"So," Abigail initiated, turning from the wackiness of those two back to the situation at hand.

"So . . ." Quinn replied, walking toward the designated smoking area and lighting a cigarette.

Abigail sighed, wishing she could disappear. Maybe throw on the low-cut black V-neck and buffalo check pants she'd brought for her Carla costume and emerge as someone new. Someone fun and carefree. Instead, she knew she was going to have to say what she'd been dreading. Though she hated confrontation, she hated the thought of losing a friend more.

"C'mon, let's go over there," she relented, pointing to an empty knoll. They began to walk around the grassy hillside. The daylight was fading fast, and a stiff breeze made Abigail's teeth chatter. Though she was freezing, Abigail was thankful Quinn kept his distance. Normally he would've tried to hook her arm in an overly dramatic show of chivalry. Or clasp her hand to pretend they were an old married couple. She stopped as they neared the edge, not wanting to divert their direction, nor lose their foundation entirely.

"So, look, Quinn," she began hesitantly.

"Ab . . . you know, I'm sorry if I fucked up your plans. I didn't mean to. I figured it had been a while since we'd hung and I thought New York, with all our history here, would be a good place to catch up. You know? Recharge?"

She winced, hating that something she did hurt him, even if it was deserved. Or felt that way at the time.

"I thought we'd have a few beers, talk about something other than work and be, you know, Quinn and Abigail again. At least that's what I wanted. But I guess that wasn't in your plan."

He threw his cigarette on the ground, which still had plenty of runway left, stomping it out with force.

"Of course, I want to spend time with you and you *are* a part of my life or plan or whatever." She paused, starting to gain some confidence. "But so is my job and so is this play and my students. This is my first *real* job where I haven't been labeled a complete failure yet. I guess it might mean that my own art and social life have to take a bit of a backseat, but I've got to try my best here. I can't have another failure like Sanctum, and I absolutely *cannot* fail at the very thing that made my dad the happiest. Not now that I'm already involved in it, anyway."

Shuddering at this thought, Abigail could feel the pressure building behind her eyes.

"We're still Quinn and Abigail," she continued. He flashed a bashful smile, revealing a hint of his nicotine-stained teeth. "But please understand that the days of college and going out every night and hanging twenty-four seven, spontaneously, just because it's . . . like . . . a Wednesday at eight thirty are over now. At least they are for me."

His smile disappeared.

"We have different goals," she clarified. "Your career is awesome. Really. Making documentaries is seriously amazing. But you work on your own schedule."

Abigail took a breath. Receiving no response from Quinn, whose hands visibly rooted around in his pockets, she had no choice but to keep going. "You're like family to me, Quinn. All of you are. Without the Kellys, I don't know where I'd be. But you've had me to yourselves for a really long time. I think *I* need to have me for a bit. To figure out what the fuck I'm doing. And what I want. If you really want to be a part of this next phase in my life I need you to be on board with that. I need you to let me be selfish here so I can be selfless elsewhere, okay?"

Though the mood was still awkward, her little speech went better than she imagined, given Quinn's penchant for outbursts. Of course, she also knew this was her he was dealing with. In the twelve years they'd been friends she had seen Quinn blow up at everyone and anyone, but never her.

Abigail could light his (new) hair on fire this very moment and he'd let it burn to the scalp before wearing the scars proudly.

"Quinn . . ." she gently prodded, trying to get him to transfer his stare from the scorched cigarette to her. "Quinn!"

"Okay." The awkwardness seemed to release as they fell into a meaningful hug. With his head still buried in her neck, Quinn whispered, "Why'd you have to go and get all mature and shit?"

"When I went and found twenty-seven kids," Abigail retorted, giggling softly as she pulled back.

"Whore." The two continued to chuckle as they linked arms like old times. "C'mon. I'll buy you a drink. They're free, right?"

"Yeah, I think so." She rolled her eyes in fake annoyance.

The two soon found themselves in a massive line for the open bar. Abigail took this opportunity to check her phone. The first text was from Mathilda, asking if everything had gone okay. The next was a video from Nate. It took a little time loading before an animated Alex popped on the screen. He was crouched on one knee, gazing up at a mop that appeared to be wearing glasses. Abigail could just make out Mitch in the corner of the frame, holding the fill-in Juliet high up on her "balcony."

"It is my lady; O, it is my love," Alex crooned through the phone.

The video was followed by another text.

IS HE A NATURAL, OR WHAT? IT'S AMAZING WHAT THESE KIDS CAN DO WHEN YOU PUSH THEM OUT OF THEIR COMFORT ZONES.

Maybe it was the bridal party drinks or the notion that love is supposedly in the air at weddings, but the moment produced an intoxicating mix of warmth and wistfulness for Abigail. Soon enough, however, she could hear Quinn's voice.

"Yeah, I'm okay," she responded as they ambled up to the counter.

"No," he laughed. "I said *rosé*. Do you want some rosé?"

"Oh, yeah, sure," she replied, her brain on autopilot as she processed the contents of Nate's message. Abigail locked her phone and—returning completely to the moment—quickly added "No!"

Quinn stopped abruptly, his hand holding a glass full of rosé remained mid-air.

"Sorry, I don't want rosé, thank you," she said to Quinn before turning to the bartender, who appeared to be running out of patience with her. "I'll have a merlot."

19

Sweat Equity

"We have no chemistry," Nate said, biting his lip and tapping his foot incessantly.

"None," Abigail replied. She rubbed her temple, trying to figure out where this all went wrong.

But it seemed so promising in the beginning . . .

"Shit . . . I mean, shoot. You didn't hear that, kids," Abigail yelled to the fifteen students looking on as Alex and Kennedy rehearsed the wedding scene.

"But I don't understand, I'm doing it like you told me," Alex whined as he looked at Nate, who was starting to become a fixture at these rehearsals.

"I know, my man," Nate said to the burly boy as Kennedy threw her head back, rolling her eyes in disgust. "But you're not comfortable grabbing Juliet's hands when she meets you at the altar. It's okay. It's not your fault."

In the back of her mind, this was a problem Abigail knew the production would face.

How do you cast a bunch of kids in a play about romance and marriage and death?

Abigail didn't think this was entirely a bad thing. She was somewhat comforted by the fact that a couple of teens weren't enthusiastic about marrying each other.

The only problem was, a couple other teens were.

What's the point of changing the play if the climax is disappointing?

"Alex, I know it's not easy, but you've got to relax. You're acting like you're afraid of Kennedy," Abigail told him. He brought his shoulders up to his ears.

"Alex is sweating and it's running down his shirt," Kennedy shrieked as a bead dripped from his head onto his baby-blue uniform collar, instantly turning the spot navy. "See?"

"Okay, kids," she said, trying not to sound deflated. "Let's do it again. Alex, try to shake it off. It's only a girl. Half your classmates are girls. And you don't even have to do anything. Not really, anyway. Just act happy and excited when you grab Juliet's hands. Smile and maybe—"

"Kid, you gotta feel it. And you ain't feelin' it. I could tell." Abigail didn't have to turn around to know that Old Father Whine had just walked in.

"Thank you. Thank you, Mitch," she uttered before turning her attention back to the stage. "I agree with what he's saying. You have to be excited about the whole—"

"Aw, it ain't got nuthin' to do wit bein' excited or actin'. He's scared of his own feelings." Abigail's eyes went wide. She was mortified for Alex, who was currently so red he was turning purple.

Great. And now we present to you "the wedding scene," backlit in a lovely shade of "mortified mauve."

"Let me ask you this, how long you been a cast?" Mitch inquired, leaning on his broomstick. The consensus was forever.

"And in all that time you guys ain't learnt to get comfortable wit one another?"

"It's fine, Mitch, it's just some jitters. They're at an awkward age, you know. Kids, let's try it again. Kennedy, walk down the aisle. Alex, grab her hand."

Kennedy managed to make it down the "aisle" with a hint of a smile on her face, an effort that was quickly tossed aside once Alex wiped his sweaty paw on his shirt before extending it to her.

"Eww," she squealed.

"Girly," Mitch yelled.

"Okay. All right. Look, guys. Let's all get comfortable." Abigail shook her arms out to her sides. "Kennedy, what's your worst fear in this scene?"

"That Alex is going to get his sweat all over me."

"Fair enough," Nate said, muffling a laugh.

"Alex, grab both of Kennedy's hands," Abigail commanded.

"Wh-what?" He flashed Kennedy a look of terror, like any minute now she might swallow him whole.

"Right now. Don't stop to think. Just . . . *do it*." Abigail's urgent order was enough to make poor Alex stop fidgeting and clumsily reach for his bride. Kennedy braced herself against the loppy kid's sheer forcefulness but then softened a bit.

"Interlock your fingers," Nate directed. The pair came together as awkwardly as one might expect for middle schoolers who were more familiar with the sensation of a cold screen against their fingers than another's soft skin. "See? What's the worst thing that can happen? Did you die? Did you wash away in a river of sweat? No. So, his hands are sweaty? Big deal. Mine are sweaty all the time. Especially around pretty girls."

Nate turned toward Abigail, who released a high-pitched giggle more suited to this prepubescent bunch than to their teacher. She wondered if anyone else could hear her heart pounding.

"Take it as a compliment," he continued. "One day you're going to be old and wrinkly and everyone's going to be dried up and you'll wish someone wanted to offer you a sweaty palm."

The kids snickered. This time it was Kennedy's turn to blush. She shot a playful smile at the floor before refocusing on Alex, who was still death-gripping her hands, his white knuckles visible to the audience.

"Completely comfortable yet?" Abigail asked, building on Nate's momentum.

"Yeah," they both said while standing stiff as boards.

"Then do it again. Kennedy, walk down the aisle and meet him. Alex, grab her hands. Both of you look at each other."

They did as they were told.

"Do it again," she directed.

"Again."

"And again."

The three adults watched as the pair eased into their interaction a little better each time. Without daring to move her head, Abigail shifted her gaze to see Mitch standing there, still propped up by his broom, with an amused look on his face. His smile was so broad the stage lights bounced off one of his gold fillings.

Abigail darted her eyes back toward the stage before Mitch saw her, but not before a long, closed-mouth grin overtook her own face.

"Again. One more time," she yelled. "Now . . . staring contest. Who's gonna win? Go!"

The cast broke out into jumps, claps, and giggles, while the two leads sported the same wide-lipped smirk Abigail had moments earlier.

"C'mon. Who's it gonna be? Someone's gotta get the other one to laugh."

The pair began to widen their eyes and snort as they tried to make the other break. Alex flopped his arms in an attempt to create a two-person wave, while Kennedy's feet tapped on the tops of his shoes. First left, then right. This only made Alex's wave more intense, which caused Kennedy's toe-tapping to turn into an all-out jig. The cast picked sides and cheered on their candidate until Alex started doing the Charleston and Kennedy burst out laughing.

"We have a winner," Mitch yelled, thrusting his broom in the air. The kids were too wound up to notice this outburst as they continued to cheer, but it was not lost on Nate and Abigail. They exchanged looks of astonishment before clapping and yelling just as loudly as the kids.

"Great, guys. Let's keep it going. Let's run the whole scene," Abigail instructed as they eased into the wedding ceremony. It was going so well until . . .

"Cut," Nate yelled, stacking one hand atop the other to form the "timeout" sign.

"Aw, fer Christ's sake," Mitch stomped his broom on the tempered hardboard stage.

"Sorry," Alex yelped. "I just . . . I didn't want . . . I mean, I never..."

"Alex, sidebar," Nate said as he moved to Stage Left. Alex ambled over, hunching a bit to bring his towering frame closer to Nate's ear. "So you don't actually have to *kiss* Kennedy, but you do have to get your face close enough to hers so the audience knows the intention of the scene."

Observing their conversation and Alex's furious head shake from a safe distance, Abigail called Kennedy over. After asking what her thoughts were on the whole "kissing" scene, Abigail also gathered that her teen bride wasn't sure how to handle such a close encounter, though she sensed a curiosity about her. Maybe even an eagerness.

"Ms. Gardner, sidebar." Nate waved her over as he patted Alex on the back and the kid bounded off. Abigail threw in an extra pat for good measure as she passed the boy.

"We need to nail this 'kiss'," Nate said, guiding her in close by the waist, his lips just inches from hers.

"Totally." She shook her head like an overeager child. Abigail forbid herself from moving any closer to him. She didn't want the temptation.

"They've got to get over this awkwardness if this play stands any chance at success. Do you see the way Kennedy regards Alex?"

"Yeah. My guess is she's both intrigued and disgusted by him."

"I get the same feeling from Alex." Nate paused for a second. "Well, maybe not disgusted. Frightened might be a better word. Damn. *Disgusted?* You think she's *disgusted* by him? Geez, that's a strong word." He looked physically hurt by this notion.

"Maybe not disgusted. Repulsed? Let's go with repelled." Nate's expression didn't dissipate as she tried to soften the blow. "What do you want? He's a teenage boy. Men can be gross. And clueless. And stupid."

His face continued to grimace.

"Trust me, she wouldn't be the first woman to be both oddly drawn to and simultaneously horrified by a man," she said, speaking from personal experience, of course.

"Whatever. This is the big moment in the whole play. We have to get it right."

She glanced over at the kids, wondering whether they were asking too much of them even if their lips never touched. Abigail expected to see a pack of innocent, cherubic-looking faces across that stage. Instead, she observed the twins taking a selfie, three boys clearly discussing how hot Honor looked with her hair pulled back (a look that was required for her Nurse headpiece), and her two leads whispering in each other's ears and giggling. Broad shoulders, small chest mounds, and blotchy skin were rampant.

They're inching closer to the students across the lawn everyday.

Part of her was proud she got to partake in this journey with them. And part of her was terrified.

They have so much left to learn.

She stood for a moment, admiring their still-goofy nature. Their silly curiosity would soon turn into a lifetime of torment involving sex, power, status, success, and ultimately—most importantly—happiness. Or a lack thereof. No matter how much Abigail willed them to stop growing and remain naively inquisitive about the world from a safe, childlike distance, she knew this wasn't an ending she could produce. Nor one she even wanted to, if she were really honest.

"Abigail? Thoughts? We need to get them through this scene, don't you think?" Nate said, encouraging her with his eyes.

She took one last glimpse at the kids in their natural state. It didn't take long for her eyes to land on Alex and Kennedy, who wore identical looks of terror as Mitch used his trusty broom to demonstrate how the kiss should go down. It looked like a woodpecker jabbing at a tree.

"Yes. Most definitely. We'll get them through it. Okay, kids," she yelled, trying to squash the visual trauma Mitch was bestowing upon their (hopefully) virgin eyes.

"You know how we broke through that last part where Juliet walks down the aisle? We're going to do that again for this scene where the priest declares you guys married and you . . . you know." Alex and Kennedy nervously fidgeted as the remainder of the cast looked on.

"Let's get into place," Abigail commanded, stepping in front of the two leads at the altar. "Now, Alex. Your turn this time. What's *your* biggest fear going into this scene?"

"That she won't like it. Or that she doesn't want my head near hers. Or maybe that I miss and end up headbutting her in the eye. Or what if I burp . . ."

"Okay," Nate interrupted. "Delivery. And performance. You're worried about delivery and performance. No big deal. Welcome to manhood. Let me tell you, Alex, every single one of us is worried about those two things. And not just during the first . . . *kiss* . . . but with every girl and every kiss after that. It's totally normal. It's even kinda cool you're so concerned about her and her feelings. Right, Kennedy?"

The girl flushed once again, but her grin betrayed any lingering disgust.

"So without further ado," Abigail announced, "let's go ahead and try—"

"Aw, what the hell, girly." Mitch stomped his foot in unison with his broom handle. "You think these two're a coupla zoo monkeys? Hell, they ain't. They're kids—and they're probably scared. Up on display like that."

"I'm not sure what you're getting at." Abigail tried to quash her frustration at these constant interruptions. "You want me to give them some privacy? Put them in the janitor's—in *your*—closet and tell them to have at it for five minutes? That's not gonna—"

"You ever done sometin' like this for the first time wit' a

whole crowd watchin' ya? 'Course ya hadn't. But you want 'em to. Well, I think that's worth somethin'."

"Okay. That's fair. Kids, you're being really vulnerable, and I'm happy to do the same. What do you want me to do? Sing? Dance? Both will be equally embarrassing for you. And for me. I'll even do it with Mitch's broom. Will that make you feel more comfortable?"

She was reaching for the broom in her best attempt at screwy-teacher-makes-an-ass-out-of-herself when she heard it.

"Kiss," the twins shouted as they sat cross-legged on the stage. They pounded the floor with their palms for good measure.

"Huh?" Abigail looked at the cast like they were aliens and not a pack of prep school students who clearly understood the value of social currency.

"Kiss," the tribe yelled.

"Kiss who? The broom? Fine."

"No. Kiss Mr. Carter," Reese said, pointing at Nate, who didn't seem half as mortified as Abigail did. No, these were definitely not naïve creatures.

"C'mon, girly," Mitch said, leaning against the theater wall and crossing his arms over his broom. "S'only fair. You want 'em two to make out? You do the same. Show 'em how it's done."

"Okay, first off, no one said *anything* about making out. And secondly . . ."

"And secondly, we'll show you how it's done. Kids, off the stage," Nate said.

"Nate, what are you doing?" Abigail muttered through closed teeth.

Nate waited for the cast to make their way down the steps before continuing. "We're going to run this wedding scene. Watch and learn something. Mitch, would you do us the honors?"

The kids quickly jockeyed for primo positions in the front row as Mitch ran over, letting his broom drop to the floor with a high-pitched thwack. He stood to the right of Nate, filling in as the officiant as Abigail slowly walked down the aisle. She stared straight ahead at Nate, willing him to telepathically convey what his plan was here before giving into her fate. If she were going to be a model for these kids, she might as well embrace her role as child bride.

What do I do? Do I go halfway in? Less than halfway? I need the kids to fully commit, but what if I lean too far and headbutt him in the eye?

Taking her last few steps until she reached her groom, Abigail could see now why the kids were always so hot. The heavy stage lights, the audience, and the pheromones were enough to make anyone sweat. Add in a dose of puberty and it was a wonder some didn't spontaneously combust center stage.

Running through the entirety of the scene, the stand-in Juliet replied, "I promise to love thee all the days of mine life . . . Romeo." Abigail tacked that onto the end of her proclamation to be sure there was no confusion.

The kids watched intently as Abigail overemphasized both the dialogue and her actions to show the children what to imitate. It wasn't until Mitch had declared them married and the two had removed their imaginary masks that the fidgets and squeals commenced.

"Thee may now kiss thy bride," the brusque actor said as Abigail hesitantly leaned in and Nate's lips found her where she stood. The contact caught her by surprise at first, but then she remembered all the eyes on her and she settled into their first kiss as husband and wife—and as fellow drama coaches with a room full of hormones standing by. It was the quickest three-

and-a-half seconds of Abigail's life, but the electricity from finally feeling Nate's textured lips and soft stubble would linger long after everyone else's attention had moved on. She suddenly felt hotter, though she was pretty sure this wasn't the stage lights.

The pair continued to hold hands, giggling at one another, just as the scene called for, though the laughs were genuine. She looked into Nate's eyes as they both shook their heads in disbelief. For the first time, Abigail noticed the small gold specks that danced around his irises.

The things you go through in the name of art.

"I've always wanted to play a priest, yippee," Mitch proclaimed, breaking into a little jig that was more suited to the jester than the clergyman. "C'mon, everyone. We just got yer teachers hitched."

He jumped off the stage and encouraged the kids to dance in celebration. Abigail had to hand it to him, he certainly brought out the celebratory atmosphere that a wedding called for. Mitch swung around from one person to the next as if this were a square dance, suddenly unhooking arms with Kennedy and locking hers into Alex's.

"Okay, you two. Ready?" Mitch called as he clapped his hands. "Go."

Just like that, the two leads smacked their faces together, their lips touching as the force reverberated through both of them. Abigail opened her mouth to say something, but Nate squeezed her hand and gave his head a quick shake. Alex's eyes widened as he took a sizable inhale and an even larger step back from Kennedy. Though his body moved, his hands remained firmly affixed to his bride's. It might have been a blink-and-you-miss-it moment, but she was relatively certain she just witnessed these kids' first kiss.

And what an awesome story to tell.

The excitement and joy left an indelible impression on her as well. Especially Mitch's excitement. Remaining in their own wedding-scene posture, Abigail turned back to Nate, who was still watching the scene play out in the audience. It took him a minute to catch her eyes.

"What?" he finally said as he turned to see her staring at him.

"Your hands are sweating."

20

Liquid Courage

A bigail lingered around school late that afternoon. Rehearsal had gone well, but she couldn't shake the feeling that there was still so much left unsaid. She'd laid in bed every night that week thinking about love, commitment, happy endings.

Are they ever truly real? Or are they figments of our imaginations? Or of someone else's?

She thought about writers—*real* writers, who were much more brilliant than she could ever be. Like the ones whose books lined her childhood study. A few remained loyally affixed to her current entertainment unit. Jane Austen, Zora Neale Hurston, Paulo Coehlo, Emily Bronte, F. Scott Fitzgerald, and of course, William Shakespeare. Abigail loved her father's *Complete Works*. Charles may have had an incomplete life, but those Shakespearean comedies and dramas? Those somehow remained intact, thanks to the hardcover rendition large enough to club a baby seal.

Still, that "work" didn't come without its fair share of tragedies.

She contemplated all this as she reapplied her lipstick in the private teachers' bathroom (she'd learned her lesson) and summoned some courage. She knew it was time to prevent things in real life from remaining incomplete. There were conversations that should have been taking place. Thoughts that were not spoken. Feelings left untouched. Questions that needed their answers, goddammit. Complete pairs. And she was going to start putting them together, one by one.

At least that's what she told herself as she tip-toed down the darkening outdoor foyer toward the Little Theatre.

She found him there, sitting quietly, contemplatively, on the theater's front bench. He scratched his waxy head as if something were bothering him. Her instinct told her to run up and embrace him, though she knew that would be the worst approach. Instead, she settled for a soft "Hi."

Startled, he turned to his left. "Whaddya want, girly? I'm all out of advice for today. Hell, for the rest of time."

The man who was so passionate and animated an hour ago now looked tired, glossy eyed. Mitch may have had a thick skin, but it was the texture of tissue paper, nonetheless.

"What I want to know is how you got to be so good at that."

"At what?" he shot back, contorting his face and displaying his hard-fought wrinkles.

"*That*. Back there. Those kids. You're very good with them, you know." She debated whether to sit next to him or keep standing. His general standoffish nature told her she was better off keeping her distance—a sentiment she couldn't get her heart to share in. "You're patient. Silly. Kind. And your advice is sound. They respect you. And *like* you."

"Aw, all that bullshit?" he guffawed, batting at the air. "You should know better. It's called actin'. Maybe if you inspired yer kids a little every once in a while, they'd be good at it, too."

Despite his stony words, Abigail could tell Mitch was uncomfortable. He leaned his weight on the palm farthest from her, talking in her general direction while making no attempt to meet her gaze. She'd hit a nerve. She couldn't give herself credit, though. Those *kids* had hit a nerve with him.

His face tried to wander away from hers, the way a dog, the most loyal of companions, does when he knows he didn't live up to expectations and must be confronted by this fact.

"Some of them are good at it, and *you* know it," she said, crossing her arms as she stared down at him. "And you weren't acting. I guess I'm surprised, is all. You taking an interest in our little play. To tell you the truth, I was terrified at first that you were going to try to wreck our rehearsals. Or tear through the theater angry or disruptive or . . ."

"Drunk?" He finally made eye contact.

There it was. The thought unspoken. It was the elusive adjective everyone ascribed to Mitch, but never dared to utter aloud, in his presence anyway.

Abigail was ashamed to admit it, but she wasn't up for the challenge of pairing the two likeliest of cohorts—Mitch and alcohol—together, either. It was a complete pairing all right, but one that left the whole of a man incomplete. The biggest problem with Mitch was the sum didn't equal his parts. She wanted to know why.

"You care about these kids. And you want to see them do a good job. I guess I didn't see you becoming one of our advocates, you know?"

"Aw, hell girly, we all got our demons." He shifted his tailbone on the straight-back metal bench. Abigail knew firsthand how uncomfortable that thing was, and she had substantially more padding.

"That didn't sound like a pack of demons talking to me," she challenged, though the breeze was beginning to smell of Dewar's.

He was the perfect picture of a melancholic country song. Sadness and sorrow. Longing and regret. Mitch and whiskey.

"Yeah, well, I got a family once, you know?"

"I know," Abigail said before thinking, suddenly worried he might suspect she'd read his letter. Mitch's eyes remained transfixed to the bushes just off to her right. He appeared to be lost in thought, perhaps about a life that was not of this time.

"Good bunch, too. Wife was a sturdy woman. Brave, steadfast. Good homemaker. Aww, what the fuck, good lovemaker." This mention made Abigail giggle. A sly smile entered his face as he looked up at her for a fleeting moment before bringing his gaze back down. He glanced around at the theater landing, his janitorial cart, and the environment that had slowly enveloped his reality for the past few decades until it became his new life.

"Daughter wasn't too bad herself, either," he continued, this time much more present than before. "But thought her mudder an' I were too strict. Too old world. Never let'er have any fun."

"So, what did she do?"

"She had'r fun and got pregnant at seventeen," he said, very matter of fact. "We were furious at first, but quickly got a plan in place. She'd continue on wit school, live here, we'd raise th' baby. All seemed good for a bit . . . 'til she realized her son o' a bitch boyfriend wudn't part of the picture."

Mitch paused for a moment, making a fist with one hand and placing his other palm over it, before continuing. "We made her—*I* made her choose. Live with us, go t'school, have a roof over yer head and family support . . . or get out on yer own. No help from us. Let yer bastard boyfriend take care of everyting and leave us out of it. Never tot it would happen, but she chose 'im. That was it. Never came 'round again. I started drinkin' more than a Scotsman typically would . . . which is sayin' a lot."

He laughed at himself, shaking his head, and she chuckled along with him. The comment wasn't without its tinge of sadness, though. Abigail could see the droop in the corner of his sun-damaged eyes.

"All that alcohol and anger made for a bad combo and a bad marriage, y'know? Wife finally left. Couldn't take livin' wit' me. I couldn't take livin' wit'out her. Last time I saw my wife was at'er funeral. Last time I saw my daughter, too. Only time I saw my granddaughter. No hellos or introductions or nuthin'. I stayed at the back o'the church, where misfits like sorry ex-husbands usu-ally do. Kept my distance. Tot I caught the little girl wavin' at me once, but then again who knows? Coulda been wavin' ta some-body walkin' in. Someone who was already in'er life. Her mudder caught her and turned'er right around. I got a few more glances at the back o'their heads. At my dead wife's ridiculously made-up face. And that was it. They were gone. But, long story short, I had a family once. Feelins once."

Abigail couldn't fill in the chapters between the life Mitch wrote about in the letter and his current existence at Excelsior Primm, but she knew it would be a gut-wrenching story when it was finally revealed. What surprised her even more was the vis-ceral reaction his story had on her. The man had it all and threw it away over pride.

Abigail knew she should feel sorry for the "victims" in this story, the wife and the daughter and the granddaughter, and she did—feel sorry, that is—but her utmost sympathy was with the offender. A shiny-headed man who'd found himself as alone in this world as she had. Whether by choice or circumstance, alone was alone. The single souls knew their own. It was a membership with no club. No solidarity for the solitary.

While she may not have known the middle chapters of

Mitch's story, she knew the ending wasn't certain. Or at least it didn't have to be.

"You could reach out to her, you know." Abigail's words were soft, as was her approach. She dug her nails into her fingertips, hoping a little physical pain might alleviate the emotional toll this man and his story were taking.

"Yeah, I could do a lotta things." Mitch placed his hands behind his neck, leaning forward and resting his elbows on his knees. It looked like a guillotine of sorts; a punishment Mitch seemed to think he deserved by the sounds of things.

"Just think about it," she encouraged. "The holidays are a great time for reuniting families, or if that's too much pressure, you can start fresh in the New Year."

The man didn't move. Abigail couldn't tell if he was burying anger or sadness under the two liver-spotted blades that now held his head.

She debated for a moment whether she should tell Mitch her own story. Maybe it would make him feel like love and loss weren't exclusive to him. Get him to understand that family dynamics are complicated, especially the parent-child relationship.

Charles himself transformed after his diagnosis from a somewhat demanding professor-father to a man consumed with silliness and laughter, to a small voice in a big body that required assistance to move. Grace had a similar journey, playing the hero when Charles was alive before her superpowers wore off and everyday tasks became her kryptonite. Abigail never loved them more or less. The nature of their relationship changed, sure, and it was only natural for resentments to build here and there. But that made them *human*. Fallible. Family.

She couldn't imagine a world where Jennifer would feel differently. Abigail glanced down at Mitch, the sight of a sorrowful statue, and decided now wasn't the time to launch into all that. The decision to omit her story didn't dissipate the tears that were welling in her eyes. But the knowledge that a pity party was the last thing this man needed—either for himself or for her—did the trick.

With a stiff jaw and clenched teeth serving as her walls, she managed to eke out, "We all deserve love, Mitch. We all deserve love."

For the first time, Abigail noticed his pathetically hunched-over frame. The result, no doubt, from decades spent in front of machines that only blew things away from him and never toward him. She gave him two parting pats on his bony shoulder before leaving quietly.

21

Romeo and Jesus Christ

"I cannot fucking believe you're making me do this."

"Shhh. Mathilda. We're in a church," Abigail whisper-yelled as they entered St. Benedict's theater. Feeling inspired and reinvigorated by her own cast's momentum, she'd decided to see what the other school productions looked like. *Our Town* wasn't set to premiere at Marshal Struthers for another few weeks, but luckily for her, the Catholic school's play was already in full swing.

Abigail wasn't so much looking to "steal" their ideas as she wanted to gain some context. See how their sets, costumes, acting, and overall productions compared to her own.

Besides, how could we steal from Jesus Christ Superstar *even if we tried?*

The thought of stealing from a Catholic school—even something as intangible as an idea—made her feel uneasy.

"I thought this was a theater," Mathilda said, sounding both confused and ignorant. While Mathilda's strict upbringing should have allowed her to school anyone on religion, she purposely shunned all mentions and practices associated with the topic. This was a habit that angered her parents to no end.

"It *is* a theater," Abigail said as she grabbed the heathen's arm and tried to lead her to their seats. "But I think it's also a church. Or at least it's where they hold their masses."

"What makes you say that?" she asked, still not receiving Abigail's many cues to stop asking questions before they made a scene. Abigail thrust her forefinger in the direction of a small but domineering crucifix that hung above the stage.

"Oh, sweet Jesus."

Abigail covered her face with embarrassment and forced them into the two closest seats she could find. She apologized profusely—for both the physical and auditory disturbances—as they made their way down the row.

Once seated, Mathilda piped down slightly. Abigail used the few minutes before curtain time to examine the playbill. The cover featured an illustration of Jesus on the cross. It was drawn from an up-angle, making the man and cross appear larger than life. Jesus's mouth was drawn with a very purposeful downturn. He looked sad. Disappointed. Betrayed.

Abigail admired the artist's use of color. The focal point contained various shades of browns, while the sky, peeking out from behind the image, contained bright whites, yellows, and blues. Though she found the image powerful, it also seemed very inside the box.

'Course, what image of Jesus on the cross isn't powerful?

"Christ on the cross. That's original," Mathilda said under her breath.

"Mathilda, seriously."

"What? You know the play's about Jesus. You can't think of anything better to put on the cover than that? It's so . . . one dimensional."

"I know. I see what you're saying." Abigail tucked the playbill into her purse as a xylophone-wielding nun let the theater know the production was about to begin.

"At least give Jesus some abs or something." Both girls burst out laughing. "What? He looks better with a little definition."

A full two hours later, the pair found themselves with Styrofoam cups in hand watching the stragglers emerge from the theater. Abigail focused on each guest's expression as she tried to ascertain whether they had enjoyed the play or not.

She thought it was a pretty good rendition, even if the lip-syncing was a little cheesy. One thing she didn't love was the all-white bedsheet tunics, which made it difficult to tell many of the characters apart. Abigail vowed to assign color themes to the Capulets, Montagues, and others to prevent this from happening to them.

Still, the depiction of Jesus' crucifixion did its job. Abigail left feeling sad. She felt sad for herself, sad for Jesus, and sad for the kids. Even with these emotions still fresh in the air, she couldn't shake the feeling there was something else they could've taken from this play. Obviously, it had a very powerful message. That much was certain. But she wondered if they hadn't maybe missed an opportunity for the kids to think critically. Come up with a different solution. Did Jesus *have* to die? Did his life *have* to end in tragedy? Was there no possibility of a happy ending?

Or perhaps, are we the happy ending?

"Did you enjoy the play?" The girls looked up from their coffees to see a nun approaching, her dark robe dragging across the floor.

"Yes, yes, we did," Abigail stammered.

The woman's eyes narrowed. "I'm glad you find the crucifixion of our Lord and Savior funny." The nun said this without a hint of emotion as her stare darted back and forth between the pair.

"Oh, no. Not at all," Abigail pleaded, absolutely mortified to be having this conversation.

"Of course, not," Mathilda batted her hand near the woman. "We enjoyed it. It's a very . . . traditional story."

"Are you the parents of a student here?" the woman asked. "Siblings, maybe?"

"No. I'm a fellow drama coach." Abigail was taken aback by her words. It was the first time she had outwardly identified herself in that role. Standing in front of this woman, her new title made her feel a bit like a fraud. This was her first chance to interact with a theater peer—a colleague—and she'd blown it by acting like one of her students.

Who are we kidding? Even they show more maturity than that.

"Oh, yes? Are you working on a play yourself?" the nun asked.

"We are." Abigail straightened up, giving her shoulders a quick roll before continuing. "I'm at Excelsior Primm. We're working on an alternative version of *Romeo and Juliet.*"

"Oh, how original." She scrunched up her long black sleeve to check her watch.

"It actually *is* original," Mathilda piped in. Abigail felt grateful for this support, though she was still a bit irritated that it was Mathilda's tomfoolery that got them into this mess in the first place.

"Are you doing a stage adaptation of one of the more modern-day versions? You know, that horrible movie with Leonardo DiCaprio and that . . . whatever that girl's name is."

"No, we're doing—"

"*Romeo & Juliet: Sealed with a Kiss?*"

"It's more alternative than—"

"*West Side Story?*"

"No."

"*The Tragedy of Romeo and Juliet?*"

"Quite the opposite—" Abigail tried to interject.

"*Romeo y Julieta?*"

"I . . . we tried to relate it to today's young audiences."

"*Gnomeo & Juliet?*"

"Okay. Lady, you're being ridiculous," Mathilda said, putting both hands in front of her like she could physically stop this tragic interrogation. "Why don't you stop listing *movies* and let her speak?"

"It's . . . it's *Romeo and Juliet*, but with an alternate ending. One the students came up with."

"Mmmm." The nun glanced around the reception area and openly yawned. Her mouth instantly swallowed her face, which was already stunted due to her mole-like eyes and habit.

"We thought the story was so sad," Abigail clarified.

"Well, yes, dear. It's a *tragedy*. These things happen, you know." As if to make her point, the woman's gaze moved to a huge crucifix to the left of the lobby doors.

"Yes, I'm aware." Abigail knew that better than most. She also knew she didn't love the idea of wallowing in these tragedies. Of letting their weight pile on top of you until you started to feel crushed by it, powerless to move. "I think that's exactly the point. They *do* happen. Like Jesus's story, people betray one another all the time. And teens take their lives all the time because they don't see an alternative. A way to end their suffering."

"What's your point?"

"My point is these stories don't have to end this way. Tragedies don't inherently have to be tragedies. So the students started to discuss what the characters could have done to prevent their demise and achieve a happy ending."

"Charming. I suppose if you've seen one version of *Romeo*

and Juliet, you've seen them all. Good luck with your little play."
With that, the woman walked off.

"Damn, those nuns can be mean," Mathilda said, still sporting
a look of indignation.

Abigail took a sip of coffee, trying to wash that asinine conversation down her throat with it.

"Excuse me." The girls turned to find a mid-fortyish man
with bad posture and a worn camel blazer standing behind them.

"Look, I'm very sorry if we were too loud," Abigail started,
wanting to cut this man off before they received another verbal
lashing. "I know this is a house of worship and we didn't by any
means intend to mock or . . ."

"Oh, don't worry about that. Did I hear you say Excelsior
Primm is doing an alternative version of *Romeo and Juliet*? That
ends . . . well?"

"Yes. The kids thought things could've been done to not only
prevent these tragedies, but to produce, you know, a happy ending?"

"So, you took one of the world's greatest tragedies and
slapped a Disney-style conclusion on it?" The man tapped on his
chin as if he were considering his ruling before issuing a final
verdict.

"Mmm, not quite. We approached it from the children's
point of view. Look, my cast, they're eleven to fourteen. Some are
the same ages as Romeo and Juliet. We took this as an opportunity
to explore a deep-seated issue like teen suicide. We wondered
what could have been done. How it could have ended differently
for them. These kids, they saw a way out for these two."

"Fascinating," the man said as he pulled out his phone and
tapped furiously before depositing the device back in his pocket.
"I love it."

"It's just . . . What?" Abigail was surprised by his comment.

"I love it. Or at least I love the idea of it," he added. He put his hand back in his coat pocket, emerging with a business card between his fingers. "I'll be in touch. God bless."

"Oh. Okay," was all Abigail could manage before yelling an awkward "Thanks," as he disappeared into a sea of boastful parents, congratulatory bouquets and children wearing bedsheets.

Abigail looked down at the card.

Kyle Kowalski
Arts & Entertainment
Eagle-Eyed Gazette

"My God," Abigail said as she turned to Mathilda, who was equally as surprised by these awkward encounters.

"Huh. At least your first review was a good one. I think?" Mathilda patted her dumbfounded friend on the back. "Apparently God really does work in mysterious ways."

22

The Queen of Tarts

Abigail debated whether to share her encounter with the journalist or keep it to herself. The problem was, she didn't know who to share it with.

Updike? Nate? The kids? What if they aren't ready for something like this? What if the guy hates our play? Would it crush them? Would it crush me?

Such were the thoughts that batted around her skull before she decided on her most obvious plan of action.

"Are you kidding me? How could this be bad? It'll be great," Mrs. Chang said as she mixed her morning tea and joined Abigail in their usual spot at the small circular table in the lounge. "The last time EP's drama department made the news was when Mrs. Vangundy fell off the stage and threw out her back at the Young Arts Theater Competition."

Abigail chortled before raising her hand to her mouth. "Sorry. That wasn't funny." She furrowed her brow and straightened her lips.

"Oh, yes, it was," Mrs. Chang argued. "She wound up in the arts section with a picture of her spread eagle."

The two women convulsed once more. When the fun was over the older teacher grabbed Abigail's hand and cleared her throat, adding "Updike will be proud."

Abigail didn't quite know what to say. She was used to fielding these statements in relation to her dead parents, but she couldn't honestly remember the last time she had the opportunity to make a real-life human proud.

"We all will be," Mrs. Chang continued, shaking their entwined hands. "You know what you're doing. You're finding your way. I think it will be spectacular—and all the better, since the media will be there."

The lounge door swung open as Nate walked in. He paused for a second, taking in the sight of the two women sitting across from each other, hand in hand, gratified expressions on their faces. Mrs. Chang imparted one last squeeze before rolling her eyes in fake annoyance as she exited the lounge.

"Morning. What was that about?" Old City Coffee in hand, Nate walked behind Abigail to check his cubby.

Hoping to shake whatever lingering excitement or sentimentality was in the air—after all, there was nothing to be proud of yet—Abigail stood and headed to the copy machine. The only paper she had in her possession was last week's test on chapters five through seven of The Yearling, but Nate didn't need to know that.

"Oh, nothing. Just a little teacher-to-teacher mentoring."

"You need mentoring?" he teased.

She glanced over her shoulder to throw him a side eye. Sure enough, that impeccable smile was on display.

"No," she retorted, focusing extra hard on her copies. "Well, maybe a little. But not from you."

"Oh, so we're more peers than mentor-mentee, then?"

The playful environment was quickly morphing into flirtation.

Abigail tried to deny this was the case. That the space simply became warmer with two bodies near one another, but she knew that wasn't it. One of the lounge's main window frames had bent last week after a careless football player chucked a pigskin in that direction. Luckily, he'd missed the glass, but the nasty indentation prevented the window from closing all the way. This was not a welcome addition in early November, as the room was freezing.

Definitely feels a little warmer.

"I was simply asking Mrs. Chang for some advice," she said, closely examining her printouts, which would go straight into the trash once Nate was gone.

"Hmm, sounds . . . tantalizing."

Yup, the room was hot. And so was Abigail.

That word choice was no accident.

"Maybe you could share the news with me." He walked over to the printer and leaned in close—a little closer than your average peer would typically get. "Friday night. Over a little wine."

Abigail was locked in his hazel eyes which, depending on the light, transitioned from hickory to olive, though that hint of gold always remained.

"But what about Bethany?" she asked. She didn't want to ask, mind you, but she forced herself to.

"Oh, God. Bethany?" Nate squeezed the skin between his eyes, as if the mere mention of her name could trigger a migraine. "She's my dad's partner's daughter. He's the orthodontist in my dad's dental practice."

The perfect teeth suddenly made perfect sense.

"Bethany just moved back to Philly after graduating from college. Our dads thought it would be nice if I showed her around, which I did. I guess she took a liking to me—probably because I'm one of the few people she knows out here who didn't

go to her high school. Three dates, and two drinks later, she's
screaming at me on a street corner, accusing me of 'banging the
blonde with the bad ponytail.' So we can safely say Bethany's in
my rearview mirror."

Abigail wasn't sure whether to be relieved or mortified at
this revelation. In either case, things seemed . . . messy.

"But won't your dad be mad?"

"Nah," he said, batting the air. "In the grand scheme of
things, this is such small potatoes. He can't afford to spend time
worrying about bullshit like that."

Abigail wasn't sure what to make of this situation. Dating as
an adult with live parents was foreign territory to her. She tried
picturing her dad setting her up with a colleague's son. Boasting
about the suitor's top-notch education, emphasizing his father's
contributions to the literary world, dropping hints about how
wonderful this sort of "meeting of the minds" would be for the
two families. The thought sent a chill down her spine. Suddenly
she empathized with Juliet.

Abigail looked at Nate once more. Biting her lip, she instantly
became self-conscious of her own teeth, which were admittedly
on the larger side for her face.

"Come on, she's . . . she's . . . she's *Bethany*." Nate bent backwards, throwing his eyes and hands to the sky. He straightened
back up before continuing. "But she was right about one thing.
I'm sure I looked like I enjoyed talking to you that night, because
I did."

She prayed he couldn't hear her swallow the large lump in
her throat. Or notice her lip twitching as she tried to keep her
composure. Suddenly she wasn't so sure if it *was* a good idea to
date a coworker. Especially one this cute.

But still . . .

"I won't push it," Nate continued, "but I'll be at Sipz, the wine tasting room on Sixth and Market, this Friday around five if you find yourself in the neighborhood."

Nate ended his proposition by tenderly rubbing her elbow. Abigail was grateful to be wearing long sleeves at this juncture. She would've died of embarrassment if Nate had any clue that underneath the silky gray sleeve of her bow-neck blouse was an arm full of goosebumps and pit stains growing larger by the second.

Abigail's voice was so meek she couldn't tell if any sound came out while her lips mouthed "okay." Nate flashed her one more famous grin as he turned and headed out the door, which was open just long enough to let a stiff breeze blow through. Abigail shuddered and turned toward the tweaked window, which issued the final confirmation that this moment had, indeed, ended. She thanked the long-sleeved gods once more before heading off to first period.

"He just threw the invite out there and left? I can't tell if that's hot or douchey," Mathilda said over the phone as Abigail paced frantically behind the Little Theatre before rehearsals began. She'd been trying to reach Mathilda all day, not wanting to forget any minute detail of her encounter before she could pass it on.

Abigail had gone into panic mode as soon as she replayed the scene in her head from the safety of her classroom. She started to think about what she'd wear before thoughts ballooned into an all-out ethical dilemma on the trials and tribulations of dating a fellow teacher. Especially as a new teacher. Especially as a new *female* teacher.

There was no denying that her heart . . . and other parts . . .

wanted to explore this connection. But what she wanted, more than anything, was something she already had.

This job. This play. This school. These kids.

Mathilda had failed to see the problem and told her as much. The problem she did see was that an insecure, mousy alien had somehow taken over her friend's body and was now whisper-shrieking at her through the phone.

"Who are you?" Mathilda scolded. "Eliza Doolittle? Jesus Christ, Abigail, he isn't Professor Higgins, and this isn't one of your shitty Hepburn love stories. Get a hold of yourself."

"I know. I know that," Abigail retorted in her hushed panic. She quickly looked over her shoulder, confirming she was still alone before continuing. "But it's . . . he kind of just stopped seeing someone. And we *work* together. He's close with some of the students in my play. So much can go wrong."

"So much can go wrong for them, or for *you*?" Mathilda countered as she cross-examined this foreign creature.

In all the years the girls had known each other, Abigail had never gotten worked up about a boy. It wasn't that she didn't like dating. She enjoyed the company, the sex (mostly), and the ability to prove she could affix herself to something. That she wasn't a perpetual party of one. But her heart was never really offered up. She tended to maintain a strong ambivalence, even a slight dislike, for the guys she dated.

One after another, they all came and went. Except for a few bad apples, they were an upstanding bunch: patient, kind, and (mostly) loyal. All the things one would assume Abigail would want. Yet they would never do. She found one peculiar reason after another as to why Trent's hobby for disassembling things, Dylan's desire to work on Wall Street, and Robert's love of Pomeranians would ultimately be the relationship's undoing.

Her friends told her these explanations were ludicrous at best. A handful of years back, she'd even confided in Mathilda that Trent had confronted her about her ambivalence. A Vertical Horizon song was playing over the sound system at a local Temple bar. Abigail was so caught up in the music that it took her a moment to realize he was trying to get her attention.

"A song about a good guy who tries to do everything right but it's still not working for the girl," Trent had yelled over the 1999 classic, bringing his head closer to hers. "Kinda sounds like you and me, huh?"

That night, for the first time, Abigail had no response to a boyfriend's statement. Trent had been right. Not just about himself, but about all the relationships she had ever willingly entered and then felt involuntarily trapped in.

Though Abigail never wavered in her beliefs regarding love and happy endings, those were things reserved for other people. Not her.

"This has absolutely nothing to do with me, Mathilda," Abigail argued as her pacing intensified. "It's just . . . it could get messy. Complicated, okay?"

"All relationships are messy, Ab. And everyone is complicated. It kind of goes with the territory, you know?" In the background, Abigail could hear Mathilda's standard lab noises: paper shuffling, keyboard tapping, the occasional "No, not that blood sample, the other one."

"Yes, but not *all* relationships involve twenty-seven other kids. Unless you're, like, Mormon or something. Anyway, we're getting away from the point."

"Which is?"

"That this isn't even a relationship." Abigail smacked her thigh with her hand. "I mean, there's a working relationship, yes. But my *point* is that, I . . . things should stay professional. Okay? That's my point. And I'm asking you for some simple advice. On what to wear. To meet a colleague. Over wine. To discuss . . . work."

Abigail knew she sounded foolish. She felt foolish. And she knew Mathilda wasn't buying it. Not for one second. But sometimes when you commit to a stance, you have to see it through.

"You can't simply turn and run after you've already developed your argument," her father used to say when he'd help her with her essays and felt the conclusions lacked luster, decisiveness.

"So, anyway, that's what I was calling about. And now, unfortunately, I must go because we took so much time arguing over a non sequitur that I need to start rehearsals. So . . . thank you for your advice. Talk later."

"Don't mention it," Mathilda said.

Abigail closed her eyes, chastising herself for such a dumb fucking conversation. Thankfully, the one reprieve she had going for her was that Nate was back with the soccer team this week, helping Coach Kay secure their spot in the semi-finals. She inhaled through her nose, ready to put her personal life to the side and head into the theater like the fearless leader she was, or at least tried to be. Exhaling, she opened her eyes to go inside.

"I don't know what the hell is wrong with ya, girly. Wit' all of ya."

Abigail flinched. She turned to see Mitch leaning against the side door, shaking his head, a look of disgust on his face.

"Can't no one have a normal conversation anymore? Huh? Has that gotten to be too much for ya?"

"I was simply asking for a little personal advice." Embarrassed, she began to sweat. She tried to inconspicuously wipe her brow while pretending to block the sun from her eyes.

"Oh? A little personal advice?" Mitch stood upright, placing both feet flat on the floor, arms crossed, like a barrier she would have to go through before continuing on her idiotic way. "S'that what it's about? Have ya got a head on ya?"

This last question puzzled Abigail. Of course, she had a head on her. She knew this for a fact because it was starting to pound. "Well, do ya? Ya sure got a huge lump a meter or so above yer arse. Y'ever think maybe ya should use it?"

Abigail self-consciously pulled up her staple check pants as she smoothed down her front.

"Seems to me you should do a lot less askin' and a lot more actin'."

"You're right," she relented. "That was unprofessional of me. I'll go in there right now and get rehearsals started."

With her head down, she tried to move past the custodian and into the Little Theatre, but the barrier didn't budge.

"Aw, fer fuck's sake, girly, you that dense? I ain't meanin' those kids. I told them to shut the hell up and run the banishment scene. Needs work. You don't feel the longin' and the heartbreak. I told 'em to practice 'til we do."

"Oh. Okay." Now she was completely lost. Was this about her or the students? Or Mitch? Or Nate? Abigail had no idea how to respond to this man. She never had, and frankly, she was losing the will to try.

"I'm talkin' about *you*. Less askin', more actin'. You got instincts, don't ya? Hell, yer a smart girl. Or at least, yer s'posed to be. Since when do ya have to ask yer way through life? You don't need a life coach or a goddamn conference call to figure out what *yer* feelin'. You tink dat udder girly knows what *yer* feelin'? Fuck me."

"I . . . I suppose you're right," she said, slightly amazed that the drunken ramblings of this man may, in fact, be correct.

"I don't get ya. The whole lotta ya. So worried about what everyone else is doin' and thinkin' and what everyone else is doin' and thinkin' bout what yer doin' and thinkin'. See if ya can bog yourself down a little more in hysterics, why don't ya?"

Abigail let out an exasperated laugh as she examined this point. In retrospect, she did feel kind of overdramatic at the big production over something as simple as wine with a cute co-worker. She also felt like an imposter. Yes, she was acting. She was acting like the leader she thought these kids needed without actually embracing the role.

No wonder they're having trouble connecting with certain scenes.

"And while yer at it, get a life," he continued, clearly on a roll. "Fer fuck's sake, you got a date wit a lad who ain't half bad. Put on your Sunday best and that tart makeup y'all smatter on yer faces and sit across from 'im. Smile and nod when he talks and laugh at his jokes. Just blows me mind that it's dis hard for you people."

Mitch lit a clove cigarette, which was strictly prohibited on school grounds, but that didn't matter to him. No one was going to tell the OG custodian—who'd been there longer than the "Primm" in Excelsior Primm—that he couldn't smoke. "Keep it simple, stupid," he added as he exhaled his first puff.

Together, she and Mitch did a bang-up job explaining to the kids how they needed to empathize with the main characters' plight—to try and understand what it would feel like to have the one person you love in all the world so close to you proximity-wise, but so completely unattainable.

"What if ya had somethin' ya loved more than anythin' and it was taken away from ya in an instant, never to return?" Mitch snapped his fingers as he posed this question to the kids, who were gathered around in a huddle.

Abigail knew what this felt like. Twice over. She knew Mitch did, too. Three times over. As she stood there in the audience and watched him address the students on stage, she knew he wasn't simply explaining method acting. He was talking from experience. These, it seemed, were roles they were both born to play. She considered this for a moment before swiftly moving on, refocusing her attention on the cast. The old Abigail would've gotten caught up in her own issues. The new Abigail was perfecting her performance as a confident, focused leader.

The rehearsal went so well it put them a day ahead of schedule. Abigail was sitting with her feet dangling off the edge of the stage, tapping notes and itinerary changes in her notepad app before leaving for the day when Mitch approached once more.

"So, you know what you gotta do from now on?"

"I do. I'm going to work hard to make sure the kids empathize with their characters. And I'm going to voice my concerns and critiques earlier. Oh, and I'm going to put my personal problems aside until I'm off school property. They need a consistent coach and I intend to be one, so I . . ."

"Lord, I talk, yet she hears nutin'." Mitch held his arms out as he addressed the theater's ceiling. "Goddamn, girly, you got tha biggest sack a'haggis between those two lobes of yers. I'm talkin' about *you* and yer datin' life. You feel somethin' for that pretty boy? Go fer it then. Don't overthink it. Keep it simple. Stupid."

Abigail suddenly felt very stupid. And very small. She'd been schooled all afternoon by a lonely old man who seemed to have it all figured out a lot better than she did, despite his current relationship status(es).

She instantly thought about the letter and Jennifer. She wanted so badly to bring it up. To tell him that he was right earlier.

That we are all a pack of imperfect humans trying our best not to royally screw things up for ourselves—or others—and that he was one of them. *Jennifer* was one of them. That there was still time. It wasn't too late. He wasn't too old.

An entire family could be waiting on the other side of stubbornness. A new beginning. The second act.

Instead, she simply smiled and said "Okay."

23

A Rosé by Any Other Name

"**I**'m sorry I'm late." Abigail barreled into Sipz, finding Nate at the tasting counter. She'd been playing the game of "how late should one arrive for an unofficial non-date?" earlier as she slowly walked from the train station to the wine bar. She'd stopped to apply a fresh coat of lipstick when the tube fell from her fingers and into the gutter. Not wanting to arrive with one maroon-colored lip quadrant, Abigail had flung herself into the nearest CVS. She was now moister and later than she'd intended, but her lips were "Frivolously Fancy" perfection.

"Hey, you made it," he said, giving her a side hug before turning back to the pourer at the counter. "It actually gave me a chance to chat with Dan here. He owns the place. He and my grandfather go way back."

"Hi." She waved at the older man, who sported black-rimmed glasses and patchy white facial hair. He nodded back in return. "This is a great little spot." She scanned the crowd, which seemed to consist of young professionals and academic-looking types. Most of the men wore no-iron collared shirts and shiny belts, while the women stood holding wine glasses in thick, practical heels. She pictured Dan being one of them back in his day.

"Yeah, it's cool," Nate said, accepting two glasses with a little ruby-red liquid sloshing around in their bowls. He kept one for himself and handed the other to Abigail.

"Here, try this. It's called a tempranillo." There were those pearly whites. Abigail felt her heart flutter. His eyes—his *smile*—were so bewitching.

No wonder Bethany sank her claws in and didn't want to let go.

"You come here a lot?" Abigail swirled the contents before dipping her nose into the glass's airspace, as Nate instructed. The bulb instantly fogged over with her warm breath.

"Sometimes," he said, doing the same. "I love these urban tasting rooms."

"Yeah? Why's that?" She took a sip. The wine burned and caught in her throat, though she did her best to hide it.

"See, the beauty of this place is you can try out a bunch of different labels and varieties for little money and a solid buzz. It's like *The Bachelor* of wines. Just keep sampling until you settle on one you like. Or, in your case, like *The Bachelorette*, I suppose, since we're trying to match you up today."

"I didn't realize you were into bad reality TV." Abigail eyed him suspiciously.

"Eh. We all have our weaknesses, right?" *God, he's charming.* "So, how'd you like that first wine?"

"Too strong."

"I think you mean too complex, too multifaceted. Gotcha. We'll take it down a notch." He turned back toward Dan, pointing to another selection on the laminated wine menu.

Nate slid a ramekin with oyster crackers closer to them, holding the bowl up for Abigail and popping a few in his mouth. She fixated on his face as he chewed, watching his rosy lips and square jaw move up and down. She remembered the angles of that jaw well. Abigail had wanted to reach out and grab it as they practiced the wedding scene.

"You all good with rehearsals next week?" he said, giving his lips a final lick. "I love helping, but Coach Kay could really use the extra eyes with finals coming up."

"Oh, yeah, we're fine," she said, waving him off.

Dan pushed her second tasting, a red, transparent elixir, in front of her. "Pinot noir," he said, taking a couple steps back.

Abigail nodded her head before turning to Nate. "Speaking of school, I can't believe how far Alex has come. He's really blossomed over the past few weeks."

God, why do you do this? You finally get this guy off school property and all you can talk about is "kids and play," "kids and play."

"So, what'd you think of this one?"

Humming into the wine glass, Abigail raised her eyebrows as she took another sip.

It was fruitier than the last selection and didn't burn quite so badly on the way down. But it was a long way from good, in her opinion, and a long way from the rosé she was used to. Of course, she would drink this all night if it meant she could stay here, staring at him in his denim shirt that showed a hint of his shaved chest, as he talked about her new favorite subject: their kids.

"This wine's okay, but it has kind of a fertilizer smell and aftertaste." She handed him the glass with half remaining. Nate threw it back like a shot before turning once more to Dan. He double tapped his next selection on the shiny menu, which earned a head tilt from Dan.

"Yeah?" the older man said with a half-smirk.

"Yeah," Nate confirmed.

Dan disappeared in the back, leaving the two alone at the tasting counter.

Taking this as her cue to get off the topic of school, Abigail said, "So tell me about this grandfather of yours."

Nate went on to describe summers spent with him in Central Pennsylvania.

"I thought the farm work was so cool," he said, with an air of nostalgia. "I loved chasing his border collie, Lily, up and down the hills. My favorite, though, was finding new ways to repurpose the wine bottles."

"That sounds nice," Abigail added, trying to picture childhood summers filled with more than just books that were read outside on a nice day. Though her dad had loosened up significantly after his terminal diagnosis, it was too late to enjoy the fun aspects of summer. Water balloon fights, hanging onto a rollercoaster, riding bikes. Those activities involved muscles and motor skills, something Charles had lost in his left arm by the time his zest for life finally kicked in.

"A hummingbird feeder."

Nate's fist tapped the counter, causing the oyster crackers to tremble.

"I'm sorry?" she said, shaking her head to remove any lingering fantasy that was playing out in her own mind.

Nate turned closer toward her, resting his elbow on the counter and his head in his hand. She could tell he used very little product with how easily his fingers combed through the honey-colored strands.

"It was my favorite wine-bottle project. My mom loved the feeder. I gave it to her one Sunday when she and the rest of the family came up to the vineyard. Sundays were family days. Looking back, though, that was like a three-hour trip just to have dinner with Gramps and I in the summer."

Abigail nodded and smiled politely.

"Anyway," Nate said, clearing his throat and standing up straight. "Enough about my boring childhood stories. Tell me about yourself. What's your story?"

It was the question Abigail loathed.

Where should I start? Do I mention my dad's retirement from teaching at forty-eight? Trading in the Mazda RX for a handicap-accessible Astro Van? Having to get out of my seat at every red light to prop his head back up because it would flop down whenever the van stopped? I could continue on after that. Regale him with tales of a mom who kept it together just long enough for Dad to die, but not long enough to take care of her minor, fatherless child. I could mention how she showed her love through packages of zany items, including forty pairs of socks, that showed up on my door as I got older. Or perhaps go into detail about the last time I saw her before the diabetic episode that took her life. When I screamed at her about the rat problem she'd let spiral out of control. That would take care of years eleven through twenty, anyway . . .

She stopped scratching at the wooden bar to find Nate staring at her expectantly. Her fingers instinctually went to her neckline, which was undoubtedly pink and splotchy by then.

"Well, there isn't much to tell, really. I'm just—my story's boring. Like you said, no one wants to hear about other people's pasts."

Abigail nodded before fixing her eyes on her water cup. She focused on the sole black speck at the bottom, unsure how to proceed. As good as she was at analyzing and telling other people's stories, her own autobiography always left her unsure about what to reveal.

"Here, try this one," Nate said, swooping a blush-colored liquid under her nose. She looked up to see a newly uncorked blushing bottle that was lightly perspiring positioned between her and Dan, who sported an unsure smile.

"Did you just hand me a rosé?" Abigail said with astonishment. She'd been so caught up in her self-consciousness that she hadn't seen Dan re-emerge.

"Hey, the first rule of *The Bachelor* is that every girl needs a rose now and then, right?" Nate finished his joke with a rib poke, sending the same butterflies through Abigail's system as it had the first time he'd done this during Alex's audition. The pair took their new drinks over to a high-backed table in the corner. Though the lighting was lower over there, it lent a soft glow to the whole scene.

"Cheers," she said, holding her glass out. "To good times and good wine."

They clinked their stemware as Abigail took her first palatable sip of the night, savoring its familiar strawberry and rhubarb flavors.

"Don't worry," she added, her mouth still in the glass. "I won't tell Quinn you caved on the rosé."

"What's with that guy, anyway?"

"Oh, he's harmless." Abigail waved her hand dismissively.

She told him about their high school years, making sure to mention she never felt any chemistry whatsoever. "Since then, he's been like a brother to me. He and the whole Kelly clan have been great."

"That's awesome," Nate said, admiring the painted canvases along the wall. From the looks of them, Abigail imagined these were from wine-and-paint parties. The jagged swirls and angular circles gave away the newbies, who had neither the confidence nor the skills to capture these shapes in one swift stroke. "My mom always said, 'the more people who love you like family, the better.'"

Nate took another sip, then furrowed his brow. "Although . . . that phrase, 'like a brother?' That can be a mortal wound if you don't picture yourself as a branch on someone's family tree, if you know what I mean."

She did know what he meant. She knew Quinn knew what it meant as well. There just wasn't any other way to put it—to a potential date, to those who made assumptions, to the person being compared to family. Quinn was a BFF, of course, but that seemed like such a patronizing way to describe what they had. Their bond went beyond friendship. It ran to the bone. She'd do anything for that idiot, but deep down she knew the one thing he'd want more than anything was the one thing she couldn't give.

Her phone buzzed in her purse against the high-back chair. A likely text from Quinn, who sent anywhere from four to seven uninitiated messages a day.

"So," she said, picking up her wine glass and putting her nose in it. She narrowed her eyes as she spoke. "You have a lot of experience in the 'friend zone,' or, I guess in this case, I should say in the 'family zone'?"

She kicked Nate playfully under the table, the tips of her Lulus tan suede ankle boots unintentionally making direct contact with his tibia.

Nate grimaced, sucking air in from the side of his mouth.

"Yeah, that can be tough. I've received that talk and I've given that talk. You can ask Bethany about that one. I'm pretty sure she's trying to slide into my DMs through a catfishing profile. She is *not* one to be ignored."

Abigail giggled and rolled her eyes. She could picture Bethany's spindly fingers furiously rattling off a message tied to a profile pic from some obscure online model.

"But the best thing to do in those situations is to be honest. After all, it's hard to get mad at honesty."

"Right." Her eyes darted around the room.

Meanwhile, Nate's eyes grew larger at this seeming realization.

"It's none of my business, but you *have* told him this, right?"

"I . . . I would—I *will*," she clarified, tilting her head. "The subject hasn't come up, and he clearly knows how I feel."

Thoughts of dead parents, talk of other men, tuning out in the middle of his own family story. Ugh, we're officially out of date territory and into . . . I don't know, Dr. Phil territory?

"Well, fortunately for you, you're no shrinking violet." Nate tapped the side of his black Chuck Taylor against her calf.

"What's that mean?" Abigail said with a laugh, gesturing wildly and knocking her knuckle against a painting of a pumpkin with a disproportionately large curlicue stem.

"I seem to recall crossing paths with a pretty fierce hurricane that whipped away in a blue fury—or flurry—sorry, it's the wine—some time ago."

"That was Trixie," Abigail argued, feeling all the embarrassment that had been forgotten a while back. "One of my many alter egos. It's a long story, just know she's way braver than I am." She shook her head in disbelief as she recalled that night—or at least as much of it as she could—and how rude she was to Nate.

Trixie could have such an attitude . . .

"Oh, c'mon. I don't believe that. I think you're selling yourself short."

Abigail brought her right shoulder to her ear. A heavy silence lingered as tipsy conversation swirled all around. "You know," he finally said, "you remind me of a line from one of my favorite books growing up."

"What's that?" she replied skeptically. "*Little Shop of Horrors?*"

Nate sighed and looked into her eyes. He had an expression that was both calm and serious.

"'You are braver than you believe, stronger than you seem, and smarter than you think.'"

"Pooh," she shouted. Abigail used to read these books to Ev when she and Quinn arrived back at his house after high school. She thoroughly enjoyed these encounters, particularly as the books were new to her as well. The boy and his bear had been banned in the Gardner house due to its "immature, idiotic language," according to Charles. "That's A.A. Milne . . . and Pooh," Abigail confidently declared.

"Actually, it's Christopher Robin, but I'll give you partial credit."

"You know what I mean," Abigail said, lobbing a balled-up cocktail napkin at him. "I love that quote. How'd you know?"

"How could I have known?" Standing up, Nate reached for the bottle and her glass. "Apparently the truth was staring you in the face this whole time and you didn't even know it." He set her newly poured wine down and the two locked eyes once more. Abigail could feel the energy building in her body. Her fingers tingled as she willed him to stay where he was, to linger a little longer.

"How do you like the rosé?" he asked, breaking eye contact and returning to his seat.

A few minutes later, they walked to the train station at a fast clip on account of the impending storm. The wind added another complication, quashing Abigail's hopes of a romantic, leisurely stroll and perhaps their first kiss (their first real kiss, anyway).

She wondered what Nate was thinking but had no way of knowing, aside from asking him to fill out a quick survey, which didn't seem appropriate. Abigail was hoping an electrifying, end-of-the-first-date-can't-wait-for-the-second kiss would turn things around, but the weather and his almost unmanageable pace dashed those hopes.

The atmosphere inside the train station wasn't much better. It was damp and dank, with passengers eager to get home ahead of the storm. People shoved past each other, muttering obscenities into phones and shaking the first signs of rain off their coats and onto whatever was in their paths. The humidity started to kick in as passengers disembarked, while others ran toward the cars.

A train pulled into the station as Abigail said, "I guess this is me." She wasn't guessing, though. It was her train. She simply had nothing else to say and no further reason to stall.

"Okay. Have a good night," Nate said as he held her elbow, helping her into the car. His effort was a bit too enthusiastic for this crowd, as they both received pushback once he'd managed to get her inside. Barely inside, that is. It would be one of those train rides where you pray your nose doesn't come into contact with the film on the sliding doors' windows. "We'll have to try wine tasting again sometime."

"Uh huh," Abigail chirped, trying to sound upbeat. She doubted he'd even heard her as Nate had already turned halfway around. Clenching her jaw, she steadied her stance for a train ride from hell.

"Oh, just one more thing."

"Wha—" And there it was. His lips were on hers. It wasn't an all-out, one-for-the-storybooks kiss, but a real-world kiss. It was abrupt and pointed, full of intention but clumsy on delivery. They were surrounded by the sights, sounds, and God-awful smells of the station, which she imagined were a mix of wet paper and rodent repellent. Nevertheless, they were sharing a moment. One that would never happen again: the first kiss. It was imperfect and she dug it.

"Hey, back the *fuck* off," she yelled, sending Nate flying backwards a solid three steps onto the train platform.

"Sorry," she blurted out, throwing her hand out to him as if she'd sent him plunging off a cliff. "Not you, I mean *you*."

Nate looked past her to an older-looking man with crazy Doc Brown hair, who stood behind her with a satisfied expression on his face. Abigail threw her finger out, stopping just short of driving it right between his eyes, and instructed the man to find somewhere else to stand.

"I thought you weren't very brave," Nate yelled as he took another few steps to clear the platform.

"I'm not. That was Trixie talking. And maybe the rosé," she said as the doors closed.

Abigail tapped her fingers on the grimy plexiglass window, wishing she'd opted for a rain-soaked moment over the rat-filled station. She wasn't picturing a scene straight out of *The Notebook* or *Breakfast at Tiffany's* or anything . . . Okay, she was. Fortunately, she pulled out of her fantasy long enough to see Nate, still standing there as passengers whizzed around him, blowing her one last kiss.

I guess perfect moments are rarely . . . perfect.

24

Gone Viral

ack at school, rehearsals continued to run at the same steady pace Abigail had grown accustomed to with this group. This tended to consist of one request for the girls to be quiet, a mini meltdown from a cast member who felt he or she was being outshined, a line feeding for a scene that was mastered weeks ago, and a wild-card situation Abigail could neither predict, nor prevent.

This week's drama was courtesy of a polyester allergy they discovered Birdie had. Abigail had found matching violet and crimson chokers at her new favorite secondhand store, and had brought them in for the twins to try on as part of their Lady Capulet and Montague costumes. This caused Birdie to develop itchy red patches along her neckline. While Abigail was thankful no further symptoms ensued, the kids administered their own diagnosis. It was an STD. From John Henry.

"She probably got it while they were behind the stage," Kennedy said as Birdie popped her uniform collar in a failed attempt to hide the redness from the others.

I guess the marks do kind of look like hickeys.

"Kids, please," Abigail yelled. Begged. Pleaded.

How do they even know what an STD is? And what do they think those two were doing behind the stage? What were they doing behind the stage?!

As indignant as she was about this accusation (and its validity), she was even more amazed to learn Birdie didn't know she had a polyester allergy. Apparently, school uniforms had come a long way since Abigail was a student. Today's cool kids sported digs made from cotton and hemp.

"You mean, you've never worn polyester? Like in your *life*?" Abigail asked. Though she was astonished by this notion, her questions came off more skeptical and accusatory than she'd meant.

"Oh, my God. Ew. You think our mom puts us in polyester?" Reese said, stepping in front of her sister.

"Yeah. She's like a health freak," Birdie said, yanking on her neck. "And don't try to finger our nanny, either. Our mom would totally fire her if she bought something from an unapproved brand."

This conversation, possibly the most ridiculous one Abigail had ever had in her life, was delivered without a trace of humor.

These weekly disturbances were entertaining at best and energy draining at worst, but Abigail wasn't about to complain. As a group of prep school kids performing Shakespeareish after their requisite class time had ended, they were welcome to serve as the fashion police.

The one thing Abigail did want to complain about was Mitch. He'd withdrawn recently, becoming a virtually silent shadow who sat in the back of the theater for only a few minutes at a time. She wondered if maybe her own reactions to his outbursts, which no longer made the weekly schedule, had caused him to retreat. She sure hoped not.

In the meantime, Abigail did what she could. She waved to him when she saw the stage lights reflecting off his bald spot. He waved back. At least she thought he did. You never could be sure with those blinding lights. Or with temperamental custodians.

She couldn't complain about Quinn, either. In fact, she had to hand it to him. He'd handled the whole "big date" like a true friend. And she kind of needed one, considering that Mathilda had been putting in long hours on the Boomer Bandit. Abigail was happy that her friend was hard at work on her own passion—taking other people down—but she was practically bursting at the seams to talk to someone about Friday night.

She'd managed to get Sophie on the phone for a few minutes, though that conversation mostly consisted of new townhome-decorating ideas and lots of yelling at Bernie. That's why Abigail was so pleased to see Quinn's name pop up on her phone that morning, asking how her date was, although she was pretty sure he didn't honestly want to know.

Abigail showed her appreciation by sparing him all the traumatizing details. In fact, she hadn't provided any details, since she hadn't returned his text. Directing the kids to run through the fight sequence again, Abigail whipped out her phone as she stood on the steps leading down the left-hand side of the stage. She'd taken to focusing on this act, as she felt Alex and Kennedy were getting a little too excited to practice the wedding scene.

It went well, thanks for asking.

She reviewed her response, wondering if it was impersonal and a bit too polite. She sighed, hating cyberspace and the notion that you couldn't take anything back once you put it out there. This caused her to overanalyze even the most simplistic prose.

He's no Quinn, though, didn't even try to get to second base. The nerve of some people.

Instantly, the three dots appeared on her screen. Quinn shot back the bashful smile emoji, the universal symbol for "this conversation is over, but we're ending on a good note." Abigail knew it well. She used it often. She sent one last angel emoji back, confirming their all-good status.

"Excuse me," a voice said from behind. Abigail quickly clutched her phone to her chest. Frankly, she was getting tired of people interrupting her train of thought and surprising her from behind. She tried to quash that irritation as she turned around to find . . .

"The reporter?"

"Yes," the man said. "Formally, Kyle Kowalski."

He removed his bifocals, producing a small cloth that he used to wipe them and then his head, in that order. He placed the cloth back in his tan crossbody bag and pulled out a small notebook with a pen tucked into its spiral. This visit suddenly felt official.

"I'm here for a statement. I was thinking you could walk me through this . . . 'play' of yours."

Abigail swallowed hard, trying to maintain her composure. She pleaded with the sweat beads forming on her brow line to go back in. "Uh huh," she squeaked.

"So, you think you've got a better ending to *Romeo and Juliet* than Shakespeare, huh?"

"A different ending. I never said *better* . . . exactly." She fiddled with her first-initial necklace before making herself stop.

"That's pretty clever. And brave of you. Messing with a classic and all."

"I guess so." Abigail had never missed Mathilda more. This

was her first experience with a journalist. These open-ended statements and leading questions made her feel more like she'd just robbed a senior center than produced a school play.

"Nervous about how it may go?"

"Umm, no. I mean, nothing outside the usual, I hope." She certainly wasn't going to tell this man that her future teaching career and lifelong art-class aspirations depended on it. She also hated the way she sounded, like one of her sixth graders trying to act casual around their crush, while shitting their pants on the inside. Come to think of it, this wasn't entirely different than the way she'd been acting around Nate recently.

"Care if I chat with the cast a bit?" This notion did cause Abigail to care. A whole lot.

The kids? He wants to talk to the kids. Why?

Though ambivalence tended to reign supreme among this cast, unpredictability did as well. You never knew what was going to come out of their mouths. Especially after a day like this, with talk of STDs and who did what behind the whatever. Abigail knew her own recent behavior hadn't been the best either, as she stared down at her phone.

She quickly uttered an excuse about needing permission slips, not wanting to reveal the new ending, and no photographing minors. A few more mundane questions seemed to pacify this guy, who finally made his way out of the Little Theatre and off school property. She hoped.

Once Kowalski was out of sight, Abigail knew she had to take back control of this group, which had broken out into a pretend sword fight the second she'd become preoccupied. The Thanksgiving holiday was a week away, and she'd be damned if the break—not to mention their general slacking-offishness—killed this whole production.

"Kids, gather round," she yelled as she hopped up the steps.

"Who was that guy?" John Henry asked as a few other "yeahs" chimed in.

"Maybe it's her boyfriend," Reese suggested.

"No," the young boy insisted. "Mr. Carter is her boyfriend. Where is he anyway? Did you guys break up?"

"Okay, kids, knock it off," Abigail said, visibly annoyed that all they ever wanted to talk about was sex, dating, and the like.

"And where's Mitch?" Birdie asked.

Pointing toward the back of the theater, Abigail turned to see the bald-headed reflection had disappeared. She hoped—nay, *prayed*—he hadn't been there to witness that abominable exchange between her and the paperboy.

If he did, he probably left in disgust. And who could blame him?

"Now kids, c'mon," she said, getting back to the task at hand. "You're focused on the wrong things. Who is and isn't dating whom and who is and isn't here is not important." She took a small pause for dramatic effect.

"I'm here. *You're* here." She made eye contact with each child. "Now, Thanksgiving break is right around the corner. You know what happens two weeks after that?"

"The play?" Alex answered.

"Yes, the play. Do you want to throw all this hard work and extra hours away because you're not focused?"

No one answered, as it was a rhetorical question, but Abigail still felt better for having posed it.

"I know the holidays are all about family and eating and decorations—and I want you to enjoy it—but this year you have homework. Run your favorite scenes with your family. Call it 'Theater Thursday' instead of Thanksgiving. Or something like that."

The idea of an assignment over the holiday wouldn't play

well with this bunch, but she hoped they had the passion in them anyway. She wanted them to want this play to succeed as much as she did. Except she wasn't sure they had as much—if anything at all—to prove. Abigail, on the other hand, had everything riding on this.

So she gave it one last shot.

"Three weeks, kids. We're three weeks from curtain time. You wrote this yourselves, this is *your* play. Make it the best you can. It's not about letting me down; don't let yourselves down."

Thanksgiving was nice for Abigail. Different, but nice. It was the first year in forever that she failed to make the trek up to Boston for her aunt's shindig. This also meant she wouldn't be spending the rest of the holiday weekend in Martha's Vineyard with the Kellys.

"Oh, but you *always* come to the cottage, dear," Mrs. Kelly had whined after she was told Quinn had gotten nowhere with his pleas. "It simply won't be the same without you."

Abigail knew the feeling. She was anxious about not spending a traditional family holiday with some family, even if it wasn't her own. But she still didn't feel completely comfortable with the Quinn situation, and this was Ev's first holiday since returning to school after their "episode," as Mrs. Kelly referred to rehab. Abigail felt the brood maybe needed a chance to reconnect, while she perhaps should pull back a bit.

Instead, she heated up a manager's special turkey breast for her and Brutus. She watched the parade on TV, looked out the window, and drew to her heart's content. She didn't even change out of Thursday's clothes until late Sunday morning, when she joined Mathilda at Poppy Grove.

"You seriously took Brutus out in your pajama pants? At four in the afternoon?" Mathilda asked indignantly as they glued little glass crystals to the masks for the kids' wedding scene. Abigail had assembled a whole table full of seniors to help with the masks, promising the cast would come by for an encore performance after their big debut.

"Yes. Why is that so hard to believe? And besides, they're tight. Closer to, like, yoga pants. Everyone wears yoga pants on holiday weekends. It would be weird if you didn't."

"Tell me again why you're changing the play?" asked Beatrice, an old woman with a pinched face but a very steady hand, as she glued crystal after crystal at lightning speed.

"Because we thought it would be nice." Abigail was tired of this question. She'd given a passionate response when a few people had inquired early on, but she sensed they never quite grasped the idea. Or maybe they did and didn't agree with it. Either way, it shook her confidence every time she was asked.

"It provides a creative outlet for the kids, helps with problem-solving, gives them something to be proud of," she continued in her best car-salesperson voice. A senior knocking out two and a half masks an hour wasn't one she should brush off. "And think about it. How many of the world's great novels—movies, works of art, even—are centered on death, tragedy, sadness? What if they didn't have to be?"

Beatrice looked up, breaking her stride. She pursed her lips, squishing her face even further in the process, making it look like she'd just eaten a Lemonhead. "But the world is sad sometimes, sugar," the old woman said, thoughtfully. "That's real life. Look at me. My husband died twenty years ago. I've been here for eight. My kids and grandkids rarely come to visit."

Abigail thought for a moment. This was the logical argument, yes. She knew that. And tragedy, true tragedy that involves acci-dents and misfortune, cannot be avoided. She of all people knew that, too. But there was more sadness in the world than that. There was self-destruction. Depression, addiction, acts of violence and malice that can step in at any moment and stop someone's life on a dime. Everest and Mitch knew this. Grace, to a large extent, was also part of that category. Abigail, a byproduct. She couldn't help but think that Beatrice's loneliness and lack of visitors fell somewhere in there as well. Romeo and Juliet's true ending certainly did.

"But people can change things sometimes, you know?" Abigail finally said. "They can learn from past mistakes—theirs and others—and maybe make different choices for the future."

Beatrice continued gluing silently, though Abigail could tell she was listening. Her hands had noticeably slowed. "And just think, if you could've gone back and made your husband get that prostate of his checked when he first started complaining, you would have, right?"

"I suppose, yes." The old woman nodded as a crystal lodged under her long fingernail.

"And if you did go back and got it checked and he recovered, what kind of narrative would you have written about your future? How would you have wanted your love story to play out?"

"Well, I guess I would've written a real happy one. With a nice ending," she said with a smile. Just for a moment, Abigail could see Beatrice was there, in whatever plot she had created, living out the ending in her head. "But by the mere fact that love stories have endings, honey, doesn't that mean happiness has to end? Someone has to go first, after all."

"You're right," Abigail relented. "To have life you have to have death. To have light, you have to experience the darkness. But I bet it would be a hell of a story. And I bet you'd live it all over again if you could. And I'd bet you a glazed donut over there that people would be happier, feel more fulfilled and have a bit of a brighter day after having read your story."

"I bet you're right," Beatrice said, flashing a mouthful of dentures. "But I want the glazed donut anyway. You can have the cruller. I don't work for free, you know."

25

Chasing Ghosts

bigail was happy to see that the performance overall
showed improvement after the Thanksgiving break.
She could easily tell who had practiced and who had not, which
was both encouraging and disappointing. She was also disheartened to see Dieter wasn't at rehearsal their first day back. Abigail
made a mental note to talk to Updike about it.

Then there was Alex. She shook her head in amusement
watching him chat up the girls. It was awesome to see the young
man he was becoming. He even seemed to have gained a few
more inches and a couple mustache hairs, in addition to an
understudy. John Henry had been following him around like a
shadow all rehearsal—asking about his holiday, if he liked his
new Apple Watch, what he was doing for Christmas. Alex appeared to enjoy the attention, especially from a kid who was
already fairly popular.

She glanced across the stage to see that the twins were still as
giggly and gossipy as ever. In fact, they were staring at her. Birdie
hid something behind her back while Reese whispered in her
ear.

Squinting her eyes, Abigail gestured for them to come over.

"Here," Birdie said, thrusting a red-and-white-striped box at her. "It's an early Christmas present."

"From our mom," Reese added. "We helped pick it out." They could hardly contain their laughter.

Abigail opened the box, unwrapped the tissue paper and held up the most hideous sweater she'd ever seen. It was red, with a giant Christmas tree in the background that was framed by a fireplace and a cat wearing a Santa hat.

"Umm, thank you?" Abigail wasn't sure what to make of this gift or whether she should stop holding it up, for fear the other kids might make fun of it. "Did she make this herself?"

"Oh, my God, no," Reese said.

"She doesn't even get it," Birdie chimed in.

"Do you want to enlighten me then? Are you inviting me to an ugly sweater party?"

The duo howled once more. "No!" they yelled in unison.

"It's polyester," Birdie said as the other fell over onto her sister's shoulder. "Our mom got it on sale on Black Friday. Apparently, there's a Kohl's on the way to King of Prussia."

Abigail's face quickly matched the color of the sweater as she died of embarrassment. Tales of the allergy and the twins' idiotic teacher must've made the rounds at the Thanksgiving table. Once she got past this initial mortification, though, Abigail had to admit it was a pretty clever and funny gift.

"Better be careful, or I'm going to attack you with this sweater," she yelled as she held it in front of her, walking stiffly toward the girls like Frankenstein. "I don't even remember which one of you has the allergy. I can't tell you apart after the holiday."

The cast laughed and chased each other for a bit before getting into position for the transition between the Prologue and the first scene, in which the audience is introduced to a bustling Verona.

By the end of rehearsal, they hadn't gotten as much done as she would've liked, but Abigail was glad to feel such positive, high energy after the long weekend. Abigail looked up as she was dismissing the kids, hoping to catch a glimpse of Mitch's bald head in the back, to no avail.

She headed backstage, picking up crumbled notes and an abandoned EP sweatshirt as she waited patiently to see if he would emerge from his office. After a few minutes, she gave the door a feeble knock and went inside. The windowless space seemed even muskier than usual, with the smell of moldy leaves and old wood filling the air. Mitch wasn't there, but his janitorial cart was. Abigail quickly checked his private stash hidden under the garbage bag supply to see if it had been touched recently. Though the whiskey bottle that nearly ended her teaching career had long been drunk, this one didn't look like anyone had partaken recently.

The other item that was still there was the letter. It leaned out of the middle desk drawer, just as it had when Abigail originally found it more than a month ago. She thought about this past holiday and what it might've been like for Mitch. Unwilling to picture him sitting alone at a card table, eating a TV turkey dinner with one stubby candle burning, Abigail chose to remain positive.

Maybe he talked to Jennifer on the phone or in person and it went really well—so well that he's sworn off alcohol. Maybe he's made himself scarce here because he's making himself available somewhere else.

God, she hoped this was the case.

"I'm really beginning to think we're going to pull this off," Abigail said as she and Nate made the hour-and-a-half drive to visit his grandfather outside of Kutztown that weekend.

"Of course you're going to 'pull this off,'" Nate said, taking his hands off the wheel of his maroon 2009 Nissan Xterra to make air quotes. "It's going to be great."

"Thanks. I may keep this job yet." She pulled at a hangnail, stopping right before the point where it might bleed. Abigail needed something to do with her hands, which were jonesing to reach up and play with Nate's hair. Maybe place that errant lock behind his ear. But that was way too forward for her. Instead, she stuck to the one thing she was confident in: her words.

"Say, have you seen Mitch lately? He's been pretty MIA. You didn't steal him away for the soccer team, did you?"

"I didn't, though he could definitely show those kids how to shove their foot up someone's ass," Nate snickered. He grew serious before continuing. "Why is that even on your radar? I mean, with all you've got riding on this play and all."

"It's not," she shot back. She hadn't expected him to question her own inquisitiveness. Abigail turned to look at Nate, but his eyes remained focused on the road as they passed farms and signs for wineries along the Berks County Wine Trail.

Apparently, his grandfather takes this winemaking thing seriously.

This was the same thought she pondered when Nate had mentioned his grandfather's proximity to this trail a half hour earlier. She was constantly amazed to see how his face lit up when he discussed this area or his grandfather, or any of his family, for that matter.

Abigail got a vicarious taste of Nate's family life over the holiday weekend, which he spent at his parents' second home in the Poconos. Those four days seemed to be consumed by festivities and lively conversations, with the whole family—his mom, his dad, his brother's family, and his sister and her fiancé—all under one roof.

The pair got to chat a bit on Friday until Nate needed to get ready for the annual family photo, which was taken up at Koziar's Christmas Village. They also FaceTimed for a whole four and a half minutes that Sunday before two little high-pitched voices squealed, "Uncle Nate! Uncle Nate! There's a coyote outside. Come look!" and burst into his room to drag him to a window on the other side of the house.

It warmed Abigail's heart to know families like this actually existed—that it wasn't just a Hallmark Movie Channel myth, though she wouldn't have been surprised if his mom turned out to be Candace Cameron Bure.

The compact SUV turned onto a two-lane road. It felt like you could see for miles since all the grapes and other crops had already been harvested. Though the land was brown and barren now, Abigail could picture what it would look like in late spring, when everything would be in full bloom and the landscape lit up bright green.

God, I hope I get to see this place in six months.

The plea caught her somewhat off guard, and not just because she didn't pray. She rarely looked too far into the future, preferring to settle for the present instead. It felt safer that way. Less disappointment, more predictability. Six months was a long time from now.

So much can happen. And what if I'm out of a job by then? Would we even survive? Would I?

With these scenarios swimming in her head, Abigail hadn't noticed they'd turned onto a dirt road that led up a small hill until she was staring at yet another estate. She sat up tall. There was an open shed with peeling gray paint up ahead and a ranch-style house with a screen door even farther up the hill.

"This is it," Nate said, parking across from the shed in a little dirt turnout. His face lit up immediately, causing Abigail's heart to drop.

A stout older man with a white button-down shirt tucked into his Levi's quickly emerged from the house, wiping his hands on a rag before pulling on a suede jacket.

"Come on," Nate said, reaching for her hand to help her up the dirt road.

Gathering her composure, Abigail widened her eyes and brandished her biggest "It's *so* nice to meet you" expression as the broad-chested man barreled down the hill.

Truth be told it *was* nice to meet him. Gerald—or Jerry, as he liked to be called—was quite the charmer. He had a larger-than-life presence, smiley eyes, and a big, barreling laugh, almost like Santa. His happy-go-lucky attitude was infectious. And not just to her. Nate was practically beaming as they sat in Jerry's living room sipping fresh-pressed cider.

Nate howled as Jerry told them about one of his recent poker nights, which she'd heard much about. "And then Bill says 'Lewis, you got three of a kind. What the hell ya foldin' for?' And Lewis stared at him blankly—real stupid-like—for a minute, before looking once more at his cards, at the community cards and then at Pete's cards before he finally said 'aw, shit' and whacked his cards right off the table."

Abigail found Jerry's nature refreshing. He was a wonderful host, showing the pair all around the estate, stopping to tell stories wherever and whenever he was inspired by one. He was gentlemanly, too. Jerry ran back up the hill to grab Abigail one of his heavier jackets when he noticed she was struggling with the wind chill, despite her protestations that she was fine.

Even though the house on the hill was a solid walk from where they stood, Abigail could hear Jerry's voice perfectly as he picked up the phone before returning to the pair.

"Oh, yes. Hi. How are ya? You'll never guess who I've got here."

Nate took that time to point out various sentimental land-marks along the dirt hill. One was two large tree stumps near the turnout where they parked, "where we used to take our lunchtime break," he said. "We'd bring these pails and identical thermoses down with us. I thought hot chocolate was the same thing as coffee until I was twelve."

"Don't laugh," he said as he wrapped his arms around her from behind. Suddenly, she wasn't so cold anymore.

Leaning against Nate with her ankles crossed, Abigail closed her eyes. She let the sun, which was just peeking through the clouds, hit her face as she inhaled the scene around her. The warmth enveloping her was intoxicating. She could picture kids running around this estate, just as Nate had. The dusty overalls, muddy boots, and sticky mouths from raiding the strawberry trellises. Running up and down the hill with a border collie. Warming up by the fire. Saying, "Hi, Dad!" or "I love you, Mom!" as a parent came to pick them up or drop them off. Injecting new life into this estate, this family and those titles, which had become dirty words to her. They were monikers Abigail rarely uttered, as she had no use for them. Their pronunciation felt foreign in her mouth.

This might be my favorite happy ending.

"Hey, quit it, ya love birds," Jerry yelled as he rejoined the pair. "All that sugar'll seep into the soil and the wine'll get too sweet. We don't make any of that ice wine 'round here. You gotta go down the road for that."

Abigail was starting to feel like a real connoisseur by the time they'd arrived back at the house. Jerry had a way of explaining things, even complicated things like fermentation, clarification, and filtration, in such a straightforward yet entertaining manner. If Jerry were involved, she couldn't imagine anyone walking away unenthusiastic about a subject matter. Especially one that involved tasting a new edition or, as Abigail learned, a new vintage wine.

"We had Nouveau Weekend a few weeks ago, so drink up," Jerry said, referring to the annual two-weekend event where winemakers debut their new batches. This sentiment was repeated once more as Jerry packed up a case of chardonnay for them to take home after lunch.

"Now, you gotta promise to bring this one back to see me, ya hear?" he added, closing the trunk after Nate plunked down the case.

"I will, old man," Nate said. He poked Jerry in the belly. The "old man" instantly swatted his hand away before grabbing his wrist and pulling Nate in for a big bear hug.

"I love ya, kid. Remember that." Jerry pointed at Nate and winked. "And you, little darlin', boy, aren't you a peach."

Abigail smiled bashfully as Jerry pulled her in. She stiffened at first but eventually gave in to Jerry's warm hug. How could anyone not?

Holding Abigail's elbows and stepping back to an arm's-length distance, he added, "You two take care of each other."

The phrase suddenly made her wonder about Nate's grand-mother, presumably Jerry's wife or partner. The way he said this, with a glimmer in his eye, made her think it wasn't just age that brought this advice. It was loss. Experience. Love.

I'm going to ask about that love story one day. If I ever get the chance.

Nate and Abigail were soon engulfed in a cloud of dust driving down the hill. Soaking in the last few hours, Abigail was simul-taneously weightless and weighed down. She could see herself here—like, really *see herself* here, in this place, on this estate, with this man. But could he see himself with her? Not to men-tion her demons, baggage, and sulky bull terrier. She might've been on her own, but all these items made her a package deal.

Abigail failed to notice the cute little barn-dotted farms this time as they whizzed past. She also failed to notice when Nate turned up another dirt road, a different one than before. It led up a much steeper hill—so steep that when she finally faced forward, Abigail could no longer see the terrain purportedly in front of them.

Nate swung the car to the right and yanked the parking brake up.

"C'mon. I'm taking you to my favorite spot," he said, issuing a now-familiar wink as he exited the car. She heard the trunk open, a little clanking, and footsteps heading toward a picnic table that sat under a lone, barren maple tree.

Abigail smiled softly to herself, realizing this daydream wasn't over yet. She found him sitting on the table, his feet resting on the bench. The view overlooked Grimville, where wineries buttressed RV parks.

"Thought we could use a little alone time," Nate said, positioning the bottle of wine between his legs and digging a corkscrew out of his pocket. "Jerry can leave you craving that." He shoved the sharp end directly through the foil as the cork came out with a steady, satisfying pop. Nate took a swig before passing it to Abigail.

"Oh, he's wonderful," she said, batting at the air. Not wanting to decline his offer or disrupt the mood, she took a small sip from the bottle. Truth be told, all this high energy had been exhausting for someone who was used to quiet, still settings. Ones that were perfect for reading or creating.

"Is . . . everything okay?" Nate cocked his head toward her.

Abigail straightened up, jerking her head in a way that sent her hair over her shoulders.

"Of course, I'm great," she said, flashing a toothy smile as evidence of this.

"Mm'kay." Nate tapped on the bottle, producing a distinct

ping that broke through the silence surrounding them. "You seemed a little quiet back there. I hope Jerry didn't say anything that offended you."

She felt a lump grow in her throat. Jerry didn't—couldn't—say anything that offended her.

"It's just . . . I don't exactly share the same background as you," she said, swirling a twig between her fingers. "With the whole happy, healthy . . . normal family and all."

She went on to tell Nate about her childhood. How it was simple and quiet until her dad's diagnosis when she was eleven, when the family descended into chaos and appointments and hushed conversations about the future that only took place after Abigail went to bed, though she always cracked her bedroom door to listen in.

She mentioned how utterly lost she felt when she started high school, just months after her dad died, and how Quinn and his family were godsends. People she'd cherish, though she'd never be a Kelly. Always an interloper. The child Mrs. Kelly metaphorically took in out of the cold when it became clear Grace couldn't handle the tasks that came with raising a teenage daughter on her own.

"I'm ashamed to say that when she died—I was devastated, of course—but after that initial mourning period passed, I felt free." Abigail exhaled. She was truly beginning to feel light and free. She had a job she knew would make her dad proud, an after-school project that tapped into her creativity, financial security for the first time ever, and a man that she adored, who came with an equally adorable family. Who didn't seem to be running for the hills (well, another hill, anyway), as she spilled her guts about a life that couldn't have been more different than his. One he probably couldn't imagine, even if he tried.

No, he wasn't running. He wasn't moving at all. After a few seconds, Nate squeezed her left hand, his fingers entwined with hers. He turned to face her completely, with tears in his own eyes.

"What a load to carry. I'm sorry you had to deal with so much," he said, placing his other hand on top of their fist.

"Nate, I . . ."

He grabbed her face with both hands and pulled her into him. Their lips explored one another for just a second until they opened up. The kiss sent shivers down her body. Abigail could still taste the buttery wine in his mouth and feel the adrenaline from their conversation, as she struggled to grab air where she could.

The two fell over sideways onto the picnic table as Nate kicked the wine bottle between his feet off the bench. It tipped onto its side, making a glugging noise as the contents emptied.

Nate laid Abigail flat on the picnic table, lowering himself on top of her. His lips made their way down her clavicle, catching her necklace in his teeth. He looked at her for a second.

"You're so magical," Nate uttered as he further unzipped her puffer jacket. Abigail ran her hands through his hair, closing her eyes and arching her back. She had no idea what he was going to do next, but *God* she wished that zipper would hurry up.

A low gurgling sound cut into her euphoric state. She waited for a moment, not wanting to be hasty—and not knowing exactly what he was into. Opening her eyes, Abigail confirmed that Nate had indeed stopped. His left hand was still clutching her zipper, and his right knee remained up against her thigh, allowing a slight amount of pressure on her pelvis without placing his entire weight on her. But his head had turned. He was fixated on something near the end of the picnic table.

Another series of rapid gurgles commenced. Abigail sprung onto her elbows, whipping her head around to see where Nate's eyes were pointed. Sure enough, there was a gigantic wild turkey standing there. Its head bobbed slightly as it called out, giving its feathers a good shake once it was done.

Banging on the table, Nate yelled "Hey! Move along!" but the turkey seemed unfazed. Abigail rolled onto her side and tried clapping at it, which elicited a vacant gaze. It was then that she heard the low gobbles of other birds as the rest of the fowl came up the backside of the hill to join its friend.

"Nate . . ." She tentatively grabbed onto his jacket as the turkeys started to surround the table in a sick role reversal.

"We gotta get out of here," he said, his head collapsing onto her chest as they laughed at the hilarity of this situation.

26

Playing Around

Abigail sat in the lounge and took in the burnt-coffee air. She smiled as she exhaled. There was nowhere she'd rather be than sitting here, on her campus, waiting to discuss one of the many novels her dad had already dissected for her before overseeing her own version of a happily ever after.

Speaking of the play, Abigail was glad to see Mitch had reclaimed his normal role as critic, though his suggestions were harsher than ever. He didn't have a lot of patience with the kids, adopting a tone that sounded strained or even hoarse by the time rehearsal ended. The children took most of his criticisms with a grain of salt or an eye roll, which infuriated him more. Abigail, on the other hand, was trying to tell herself it was irrational to be afraid of a seventy-two-year-old brandishing a snow blower.

While she was hoping beyond hope that he and Jennifer had (re)connected, that didn't seem to be the case. Or if they had, Abigail gathered it didn't go very well. She added the father-daughter pair to the list of "VIP" seats from the old PC in the teacher's lounge and printed off an extra invitation to send to Egg Harbor. Abigail retrieved the invite from the printer and walked over to the counter to grab an envelope and pen.

"Hey. There you are," Nate said with a sweet smile as he walked into the lounge. Though he'd set foot in this room a million times before, today was different. There was no apprehension or nervousness or even odd sexual tension. This time, Nate strolled straight over to her. He quickly looked right and left before giving her a short, sweet kiss on the lips.

"Here I am," she said, resting her hand on his chest. "Don't tell anybody, but I was snorting glue sticks in the PC corner." It was her attempt at witty banter.

"Oh, maybe you can sniff on this instead." He handed her a purple iris that clearly came from the school grounds. This would be another knock against her in Mitch's eyes, she was sure.

Abigail wanted to throw her arms around Nate's neck and drink in his woodsy cologne. She never seemed to tire of that. But they were on school property and they had yet to declare their relationship in writing to Updike, as the Excelsior Primm teacher's guidebook demanded. Besides, even if they had, she knew it wasn't a good idea to display affection around school.

We'll have to save that for later, she thought, a devious grin overtaking her face.

Seeing as how they still had nine more hours to go before they were off school property, Abigail turned her attention to a more pressing matter.

"You know, Dieter's attendance has been pretty horrible since we got back from break." She scrunched her brow, awaiting Nate's take on the subject. Though this was also his first year teaching full-time at EP, his experience as a sub and sometimes assistant coach meant he'd developed an enviable familiarity with the school and its subjects.

"We haven't even been back for two weeks, Ab." Nate walked over to the cabinet, emerging with a Dilbert mug that said "Mondays . . . Am I rite?" next to a shrugging Dogbert. He filled it with some tap water, retrieved the iris from Abigail, and plopped it in the mug.

"No, no—I know." She leaned against the counter as she nervously fiddled with her hair. "His schedule sounds so erratic."

"I know. It's not his fault. It's that goddamn drug-addict brother and trash mother."

"Nate."

"It's true," he continued. "The crap going on in that family—it's a communicable disease they all have. Are you worried about his parts in the play? If so, I can talk to Updike."

Though Abigail appreciated the offer, she wanted to see the woman herself—a sentiment she never thought she'd have. Despite a few solid weeks with no negative attention—no attention at all, for that matter—Abigail still felt the need to prove herself to this woman. Yes, some face time was exactly what this situation called for.

How can she turn away a teacher concerned about the well-being of one of her students?

This was the thought she pondered as she walked that cold, white marble hallway that felt like the Green Mile. For once, the headmistress was in a fairly upbeat mood when Abigail entered. Unfortunately, there was little she could do for Dieter, the sturdy woman explained.

"Mrs. Ebbisham makes the proper phone calls when he'll be absent, and he never misses more than two days in a row without a written note," Updike acknowledged while sifting through the pile of papers on her desk.

"But don't those absences add up at a certain point?" Abigail asked, confused.

"Of course they do, but that's none of your concern. Leave

that to the board and myself." Updike raised her head before continuing, a knowing smile creeping up her face. "You didn't make the mistake of giving him a starring role in your little play, did you? If so, I think it's time to recast. If you even have enough participants to do that."

Abigail wanted to explain that it wasn't Dieter's role she was worried about; it was his home situation. But Updike had made her wishes clear.

"On that note, I wanted to mention how well the play is shaping up," Abigail said, trying to inject a little positivity into this conversation. She saw little point in ending an Updike session on a down note if it could be helped.

"I'll alert the media." Updike's eyes wandered back down to the memo in front of her.

What even were those papers? Who has an entire desk full of papers anymore?

Lifting a thickly stapled stack from her desk, Updike noticed the newspaper underneath it.

"Oh, look at this. I guess *Our Town* premiered," she said, retrieving yesterday's paper. The movement caused a waterfall effect as the documents resting on top of it resettled on her desk. "For the first time this year, anyway. And what's with St. Benedict? They did *Jesus Christ Superstar*? Really? It's not even Easter."

"Right?" Abigail took this as her cue to sit down and possibly even commiserate. "I mean, we have an entire upcoming holiday season based around Christian figures and they choose to overlook that in favor of Andrew Lloyd Webber?"

The two shared a moment of superiority as they doled out harsh criticisms to their top competitors. By the time they were done, Updike had even yelled "We're gonna kick those Catholics' butts come festival season."

Walking to the train station, Abigail was beginning to feel a little more optimistic about her role at Excelsior Primm, but more than a tad disheartened by Dieter's current position. She was happy she'd not only managed to make Updike cackle, but also got the chance to show off the playbill's cover. It featured the winning artwork from a design contest she'd held on campus. While the winner had received their own copy of *The Complete Works of Shakespeare*, as far as Abigail was concerned it was her own victory: she was incorporating some of her passion for art into her current gig.

Saying she couldn't utilize her art training at EP wasn't entirely true. There were the backdrops of Verona Abigail had designed from her window seat in the evenings with Brutus by her side. Not to mention the intricate masquerade wedding ball masks she'd created from Brewhaha during Sophie's whirlwind New York wedding.

The kids had been thrilled with their face pieces when she'd debuted them after the Thanksgiving break. She was happy with them herself, considering the majority of sequins were glued on by the Centenarian Club, Abigail's playful nickname for her assisted-living allies. Thoughts of the masks reminded her to confirm the kids' post-production matinee at Poppy Grove, along with Saturday night's date with Mathilda. She completed both tasks on the train ride home.

Abigail breathed a sigh of relief once these plans were locked away. She was content to remain in the normal rhythm of life, staving off the impending holiday chaos as long as possible. Unfortunately, her upcoming busy schedule came with a side of guilt. She knew the older lady in 3B would judge her for the additional time away from her other responsibilities.

"I've noticed your dog's home alone a lot," the neighbor

had said a week earlier when they ran into each other in the building's entryway. "I can tell because he whines at the door for exactly three minutes after you leave before he resigns himself to his fate, then starts whining again around four. That's when I think he has to piss."

Abigail was ashamed it took this urinary intervention to get her to see how often she was gone. Not just from home, but from her friends' lives as well. Brutus had become a latchkey kid, while her friends' names had been replaced by play sponsors, Nate, and the school on her iPhone's recent call log.

Back home, Abigail shot a quick text to Quinn as Brutus yanked her down the building's front stoop—a clear sign her absence was felt, at least in the bowels of the beast. They strolled a whole two blocks—practically a full marathon for Brutus—before he threw himself under a park bench. Abigail took a seat. She was happy to catch a few calm moments outside, though her brain was too distracted to focus on her current surroundings.

The barren trees and patchy brown grass reminded her of Mitch and his cagey nature. She hoped the VIP invite might cheer him up a bit—that someone thought enough of him to save him a front-row seat at something, anything. Though Mitch's invite was hand delivered to his unoccupied office, Jennifer's was tucked away upstairs. Abigail had gotten this close to mailing it earlier that day, but decided to sleep on it instead. Soon, her thoughts crept to another dysfunctional family, the Ebbishams. Dieter was the sweetest little boy—so eager to please and full of promise—but had no outlet or advocate to speak of. Abigail sighed, knowing she couldn't make everything better for everyone, but wanting to try anyway.

27

Exposéd

ieter had shown up to school the following day but hadn't made it back since. That was six days ago. Abigail had stared all week at the copy of *Oliver Twist* she'd brought in for him, which was patiently occupying the right corner of her desk. She thought the story of an orphan who beats the odds might inspire him. At the very least, she figured it couldn't hurt for Dieter to know someone was thinking about him. Paying him a little special attention.

Despite Updike's wishes, Abigail had left no fewer than five messages for Mrs. Ebbisham. A few of her calls were sent directly to voicemail, which let Abigail know this was an active number and the woman was purposely avoiding her.

It felt like someone else was avoiding her as well.

Apparently, I'm quite the pariah nowadays.

Abigail took comfort in hearing the snow blower each morning, though the lawn work finished a little earlier than usual nowadays. The motorized sound and gasoline smell always made their way into the teachers' lounge, assisted by the early December breeze and that bent window frame that had also been ignored. Aside from starting earlier, Mitch also seemed to save his evening duties until everyone was off campus, as he was no longer present during the after-school hours that occupied rehearsal time.

Putting her newfound creeper skills to good use, Abigail made her way to his back office during her off period, just before lunch. Sure enough, the VIP invitation she'd left for him sat on his rolltop desk, unopened. The long white envelope also laid there, peeking out of its drawer like a tongue that continued to mock her.

She tapped the drawer open a bit further, revealing a grainy black-and-white printout of what appeared to be a school picture. The girl looked to be about seven or eight. She had long, lighter hair, which was pulled back by a huge bow. Her smile was so wide it extended to her eyes, revealing a mouth of missing teeth. There was something about the girl's eye creases that was familiar.

Though she couldn't confirm it, Abigail assumed this had to be his granddaughter's school photo. Whether this was a recent pic or years old was anybody's guess. The image's poor quality was almost certainly from the oldest printer in the faculty lounge—the one hooked to the PC.

The vision of Mitch sitting in that dark lounge after sundown, searching for any signs of his family on the internet and printing what little evidence he could find, was too much for Abigail. She placed the print-out back in the drawer and slipped the letter into her messenger bag before her brain could issue any sort of protest.

Abigail swiftly made her way out of the theater and into the lounge. Retrieving the second invite from her bag, she scribbled a quick note to Jennifer.

I know, personally, that your dad would love to see you.
—Abigail :)

Abigail knew the happy face would seem childish, but she was hoping it would add an air of lightness and optimism for Jennifer. She tucked the note and VIP invite in with the letter, smacked a stamp on that wretched white envelope, and tossed it in the mail slot. Breathing a sigh of relief, Abigail stood back and smiled at herself. Mitch and Jennifer Beaton were now (un)official members of Happily Ever After Productions.

Abigail was on a roll—one she didn't want to quit. She strode proudly down the hallway to find Updike sitting at her desk. The woman's eyes were glued to an open file folder, per usual, while a half-peeled Cuties sat on a saucer next to her left elbow. Abigail took a deep breath before beginning. "I hate to sound like a broken record . . ."

She braced herself for the onslaught of sarcasm and spite.

"Don't worry about it," the headmistress said, picking at the rind as she continued to scan the document in front of her. "Dieter has been formally removed from the school."

"He—he has?" Her eyes darted around the room, searching for some sort of solution or sense, but finding only fake foliage. "I can't believe she'd do that. What irresponsible parenting. And before the holidays and semester's end. Oh, I can't . . ."

"*Miss* Gardner," Updike said, surprising Abigail in a manner only she could. "Dieter was removed *by* the school."

It turned out Excelsior Primm's Board didn't take kindly to the boy's extended absences, either. The issue had been compounded by the bad taste Dieter's brother had left in their mouths a mere four years earlier. Mrs. Chang had taken the liberty of filling Abigail in on Deacon during one of the young teacher's groan fests as she debated whether to intervene—against Updike's advice—or not. Apparently the elder Ebbisham had been expelled after a trashcan fire in the boys' bathroom was linked to a lit joint, which Mitch had linked to him. Abigail learned Updike had stood up for Dieter back then, saying the boy should not be punished for his brother's indiscretions.

Feeling scorned by Mrs. Ebbisham's constant inability to "get the lives of her and her family together—especially that older one," Updike revealed she was not going to bat for round two. Once she was notified that Dieter's accrued absences needed to be addressed by the Board, she let them have their wish this time around.

"Besides, Mrs. Ebbisham is delinquent on her last tuition payment," she added, biting into the Cuties like an apple and sucking some of the juice off her bare nail. "No doubt the result of a thorough cleaning out by that little narcotic-fueled kleptomaniac. I shudder to think what will become of him when he finally leaves home for good. He'll terrorize the whole city."

"But . . . what will become of Dieter?" Abigail wasn't sure she wanted to know the answer.

"Despite being the cold-hearted person I may seem, Ms. Gardner, I do have a soul. I followed up after the Board meeting, and Dieter will be homeschooled through the rest of the year. This will give Mrs. Ebbisham a little time to get her act together and enroll him in one of Philadelphia's many public-school programs. Or not."

He's kicked out of school and being punished for the sins of his mom and brother? He'll be homeschooled because it's easier on her. *But* home *is his problem. It sounds like his own personal hell. And maybe she'll get it together and put him in a new school next year. "Or not!" What?!*

Anger poured through her body as Abigail dug her fingernails into her palms.

This is so fucked up. What kind of mom just lets her kid get re-

moved from school—from middle school? *And you. What kind of headmistress lets a parent drag a child down with them, with no intervention from the school?* You! *Yeah, you. I'm talking to you.*

But this inner turmoil would remain just that. Updike had already buried her head back in her paperwork, and Abigail hadn't uttered a word.

"Will this create a problem for your program?" Updike finally pandered after a few seconds.

Abigail was indignant that this—*this*—was the "problem" she was choosing to focus on.

She thumbed at her necklace, praying for some superpower that would allow her to stand up to this woman while simultaneously saving that little boy. Instead, she resumed her submissive role.

"I guess . . . sort of. We can insert an understudy slip in the program, I suppose, since they're already printed." Abigail didn't mention that she'd hedged her bets, strategically placing Dieter in easily replaceable roles. She didn't want to give Updike that satisfaction.

"They're beautiful, if you haven't seen the finished product," she continued. "I know you saw the cover art. That was Chrisanne's submission, she's an eighth grader. Dieter actually came in third. He was in class the day the contest began. And the day submissions were due. It was a pretty close race between the top three. He wasn't *always* absent."

Abigail's small nod was rebuked by a strategically placed coffee mug that Updike raised to her lips. Below it read the headline "Play . . . Right? Theater Programs Heat Up in Area Schools" with the subhead "But Just How Hot is *Too* Hot?"

It was an op-ed piece in the Arts Section of the *Eagle-Eyed Gazette* detailing how competitive drama programs had become in recent years, particularly among the private school sect. There was talk of Hollywood-like set donations, kids recruited specifically for drama programs, time allotted in school for rehearsals, and even an allegation that one school poisoned another group's lunch at a local competition.

"That all sounds terrible, but I don't understand what that has to do with us?" Abigail replied after the headmistress read a few tidbits aloud. "We weren't even at the competition where Murray Avenue supposedly came down with salmonella. And if you ask me, it was maybe not the smartest idea to bring sushi to an outdoor drama competition in the first place."

Updike continued in an over-exaggerated voice.

"I met Abigail Gardner, sixth-grade literature teacher and drama chair pro-tem at Excelsior Primm, as she and a cohort were taking in the local rendition of *Jesus Christ Superstar*." She came to a dead stop and glared at Abigail for what felt like a full minute.

"At first, I thought she was spying, which she very well might have been, but Ms. Gardner's attempts to take her kids to the top involve altering complete classics. Reinventing the wheel, so to speak, to make the play more 'entertaining' for today's audiences. The middle schoolers even practice a kiss at every rehearsal, which is often met by hoots and hollers from the peanut gallery."

The rest of the conversation was a blur. There was flailing. Of the hand and newspaper varieties. There were quotes allegedly attributed to her that were read aloud. Abigail personally thought the quotes were quite mundane, though she couldn't recall saying those *exact* words during her exchange with Fuckhead Kowalski.

"I don't understand. No one even interviewed me. I've been misquoted," she tried to interject whenever Updike came up for air.

Try as she might, Abigail couldn't evade the personal hell raining down upon her. It didn't matter if the quotes were harmless. "You absolutely cannot agree to an interview without going through the Board. And myself. Don't you know that? Don't you know *anything*?"

Abigail backed out of the room shell-shocked, tripping on a potted plant that was placed too close to the doorway.

"How utterly wrong I was about you. You're *nothing* like your father."

The words hit her harder than any school bus ever could. She opened her mouth to protest—an audible croak quickly escaping before she realized she hadn't formed any argument. Updike was right. She'd learned nothing from all those years.

"If you ever pull something like this again, I'll yank you out of that classroom myself and make sure you never set foot in another school. I've got to call the Board right now to give them notice. Close the door," was her final command before banishing the girl to the hallway.

"But . . ."

"*The door!*"

28

Everything Ends

*A*bigail stood there facing Updike's closed mahogany door in silence, hoping the feeling would soon return to her face. She quickly realized, however, that she did not want to be standing there when Updike phoned the Board. Though the headmistress had generally implied her job was safe—for now— she knew the Board could override her if this turned out to be a massive PR nightmare.

Look what they did with Dieter.

She used the remaining few minutes of lunch to call Mathilda, the only person Abigail knew who had any experience with the media. She caught the young detective as she was heading into a briefing on another petty theft. They spent most of the time talking about that case: a seventy-six-year-old man who had forgotten to lock his back door after he returned from gardening. Fortunately, he was unharmed, aside from his wounded pride, due to his absent-minded action and the loss of four hundred dollars.

"Try not to sweat it too much, Ab," were Mathilda's only encouraging words regarding her friend's own loss of pride. Abigail appreciated the sentiment, though it was little consolation. She'd finally found a job she loved—one that allowed her to use the knowledge her dad instilled while maintaining her creative edge—and she'd screwed it all up without even knowing it.

Abigail realized Mathilda had her own problems, though, and her own dream job to get back to. She was thankful she'd answered at all, especially with how MIA Abigail had been lately due to the play.

"I love that I'm a 'cohort,' though. Feels kinda good to be on the other end of these things. Like in a bad way," Mathilda said as they wrapped up.

"I'll keep that in mind when I'm back on the job market, thanks."

Abigail took a page out of the family handbook and finished out her last two classes with a stiff upper lip. She hadn't heard anything more from Updike by the time rehearsal started, which was fine with her.

No news is good news.

Entering the Little Theatre, she plastered on a fake smile in an attempt to lighten her disposition. The kids made this mercifully easy as they bounded around the stage, thrilled to don their costumes for the first fitting. It was also the first rehearsal without Dieter—first "official" rehearsal without him, anyway. Witnessing the look of enthusiasm on Tommy's face as he was promoted from the second row to Chorus Kid #1 was a bonus as well.

"I'm going to say the heck out of those lines," he bellowed.

Abigail basked in this lighthearted moment, eager to remove the weight of today, if only for a few seconds. She was happy Tommy was happy. She was also happy that he didn't cuss.

See, it's not all bad. They may make out, but at least they're not potty mouths.

"You'll see," Tommy said as he ran to block his new center-stage position. "I have what it takes to lead the band."

"Chorus," she corrected.

"Chorus. Right. *Totally*. I got it, Ms. Gardner." He flashed her a double thumbs up and a dopey smile full of large, crooked teeth. Abigail silently thanked his parents for waiting on braces. She didn't want to imagine the light show he could produce with a spotlight and a little hardware.

The kids did relatively well with their fittings, which occupied the first forty-five minutes of rehearsal. There was only one meltdown from Reese, who wasn't happy that her sister's corset was closer to her favorite shade of pink than the crimson it was supposed to be. If this was the only incident she had to contend with, Abigail was pleased to accept this small victory after the day she had.

As a reward for their good behavior, she let them keep their costumes on as they rehearsed the new ending.

"Thou hast been assembled here for a wedding of grand proportions," Marshall said as Friar Laurence. "What we doth witness between these two souls is love of thy truest form—a love that shall flourish with eternal affection, from this day forward."

"Whilst my respect for you is strong, dear Mother and Father," Kennedy began, turning from Romeo to address her parents, "my love for my new husband appears ever stronger. Faces can remain hidden for a fortnight or two, but my adoration for this man is unbridled. Neither I, nor my love, can hide our true affections any longer. Therefore, I am doth compelled to tell you the truth, and reveal that I am now a Montague."

Kennedy expertly unmasked Alex on her first attempt, revealing her husband's true identity to hysterical gasps, and leaving Lord Capulet to support his lady in her surprised, weakened state.

"I'll have your head," William yelled, raising his fist to the sky in outrage.

"Stop. Cease this rehearsal immediately."

Abigail shuddered at the command resonating from the back of the theater. Though the voice wasn't screaming at the top of its lungs, Abigail was well aware who it was without turning around. It was Updike, plain and simple.

No masking that one.

Closing her eyes and taking one last calming breath, Abigail turned to find Updike padding down the aisle toward her. The headmistress' makeup seemed a bit more disheveled than usual, with her blue eyeshadow and coral blush migrating outside their normal lines.

Abigail didn't know exactly what had transpired with the Board, but she knew it was bad.

She eyed the side door for a second, determining she could likely outrun this linebacker of a woman if she tried. Instead, she planted her feet firmly on the floor, broadening her shoulders. Her hands turned into fists as she let the resentment of the past few hours—the past few *months*—culminate there. This encounter may not have involved swords or fountains, but she felt every bit as much conviction as Romeo had when he slayed Tybalt, a monster twice his size.

If I'm going down, I'm not going down without a fight.

Preparing to battle for the house that Gardner built, Abigail challenged, "Headmistress Updike-Montgomery, I'm sure this can wait until after rehear—"

"I'm afraid it cannot." Updike's gravelly voice was even more serious than Abigail had anticipated, which she didn't know was possible. "I'm sorry to inform you that Mr. Beaton—Mitch, as you may know him—passed away earlier today. My office received a call about half an hour ago. I'll give an official word tomorrow during the announcements, but I know your little club had a special bond with him, and since you're still on school property, I thought I would let you know now."

Sniffles and a few whimpers erupted behind her. Just as when Updike had entered the theater, Abigail was hesitant to turn around and face what awaited. In fact, she refused to move anything at all. It was only then that she noticed Updike's bloodshot eyes and puffy nose, symptoms of a larger state Abigail had been blinded to in her internal rage.

"I want—I want to let you know he loved you all in his unique way," the headmistress added, swallowing hard and clenching her fist around a tissue. The sniffling behind Abigail continued to build, filling the silence between Updike's words. "He wasn't the easiest person to get to know, but I'm sure you kids had an effect on him."

Abigail knew, at this point, that she had to turn around. To face a firing squad much worse than any prep school Board.

She would never be able to recall the exact words she got out in the seconds that followed. It was nothing profound. That, she was sure of. There was no beautiful soliloquy that was going to save the day. No rewriting this ending. Death, in real life at least, could not be undone. It was a luxury she had perhaps taken for granted in letting the children alter history.

Updike told the group they would need to vacate the theater so the school could secure Mitch's office and obtain his personal effects for his family.

Jennifer.

"No one has been back there, correct, playing in Mitch's office?" The headmistress's eyes connected with each child on stage.

"No."

"No."

"No, ma'am."

"No. No, no, no."

The last four denials came from Abigail, though they had nothing to do with the sanctity of Mitch's office (which she'd broken anyway). She sealed her lips, trying to keep her jaw immobile, but it quivered regardless. She was afraid to breathe, fearing it would all fall apart. She was afraid to look at any specific student for the same reason. Though her own eyes were blurred by tears not yet released, she could hear wailing, Stage Right. Abigail didn't need her full vision to know that the tall figure who had recently appeared so manly was crying like the child he was. She wanted to run to Alex, to all of them. But she felt she had little to offer. Her "it's going to be okay" sentiments seemed incomprehensibly inadequate.

The room appeared to be getting smaller and hotter. It felt like the stage spotlight was pointed directly on her, though in reality it was pointed at the children. Abigail had to get out. She might not be able to embrace every cast member like a parent would—not that she remembered what that was like—but she could at least save them from watching their coach crumble.

"Ms. Gardner, I'm going to need to see you outside for a few moments," Updike said, issuing Abigail a rare reprieve.

Walking down that long theater aisle was a blur. She knew she'd uttered another useless phrase to the kids, something about "It'll be all right—I promise" or "Hold tight." Frankly, she didn't know where to go from there. Abigail was quickly learning that the pain you face yourself was somehow easier to grapple with than the pain bestowed on others. She wished she could act as a shock absorber, have the news bounce her backward, while granting the kids a pass from the experience of grief.

No such luck in the real world.

Though she hadn't done anything to spare the kids from hurt, waves of sadness, frustration, and longing crashed against her fragile demeanor anyway. Abigail's forehead and nose made contact with the cold, red brick as soon as the theater door shut. Updike remained silent as she shook, her body pressed against the wall like she was receiving some warped form of corporal punishment. Shaking soon turned to heaving, which brought guttural sobs. Updike offered an equally cold pat on the shoulder, seizing upon a momentary break in the hysteria.

"What happened?" Abigail finally uttered. She took one look at the bench to her left, recalling her meaningful conversation with Mitch, and broke out into double-breath spasms once more. She was doing her best to quash her hysteria just as a pair of footsteps accelerated down the hall, threatening to undermine her efforts.

"Ab? Ab! You okay?" Nate's eyes were wide and his mouth was long, yet tight.

She once again found herself speechless and sightless. When he got to her, Nate placed both hands on her shoulders.

"I'm so sorry you had to find out this way," he said, putting his head near hers.

"Find out what in what way?" She pulled back, looking him in the face.

"About Mitch and his illness. It was never my intention . . . I never wanted to keep it from you. He is . . . he was very private, you know?"

She shook her head violently. No, she most certainly didn't know.

Abigail lifted her arms, forcing them down as his elbows immediately gave way. She placed her hands back in front of her, keeping the world at a safe distance, as the sobs once again took her sight and sound.

"Mr. Carter, why don't you go assist Madaline with the children? I know they could use you right now."

"Yeah, of course." He threw one last pained look at Abigail before rushing into the Little Theatre to save the day.

"Kidney disease," Updike revealed once they were alone.

"Huh?"

"It developed into end-stage renal disease."

Abigail's eyes darted all over the floor.

Kidney disease? How could he have renal failure? I would've sensed if he were that sick. I have tons of experience with this. How could I have been the last to know?

"He didn't want to spend his days hooked up to a dialysis machine, so he got on a kidney transplant list," the headmistress continued as the pair stood awkwardly near the bench, though neither opted to sit. "One became available, and he went in to sign the paperwork before Spring Break of last year. While he was there, the doctor stepped out of his office for a moment, and Mitch got a look at the donor waiting list. Up next after him was a thirty-seven-year-old man. After that, a fifteen-year-old boy. He took himself off the list and spent the summer trying some alternative therapies in the Czech Republic."

"Czech Republic?" Abigail mouthed, trying to absorb this story.

"He was feeling better for a bit. Unfortunately, his condition worsened over the past month. He continued to work if he physically could, though he got very, very sick right before the Thanksgiving break. Mrs. Chang stopped by to give him some of her family's leftovers. She said he looked frail."

Abigail had such a hard time picturing this feisty grandfather in such a way. He was older, yes—and he wasn't a large man. A little on the tall side, but thin by all accounts. Still, "frail" and "sickly" weren't words she would ever use to describe Mitch.

"He seemed okay at the last few rehearsals," Abigail added, wiping her eyes to reveal a huge black streak across the fleshy part of her hand. "A little grumpier than normal, I guess, but he was so reserved right before break that I kind of welcomed the change."

"Ms. Gardner, Mitch wasn't around in the last few weeks before break. He made a valiant attempt to resume his normal workload earlier this month, but that only lasted a few days. His condition just got the better of him and he was too weak."

Abigail's head throbbed at this revelation. There were just too many facts being turned upside down. Sure, Mitch had taken a smaller role right before break, opting to stay in the back and observe the play from afar, but you couldn't say he wasn't around. There were at least a handful of times she could point to that said otherwise.

"If he wasn't there, then who . . ." She let her question trail off, realizing precisely how the *Gazette* had secured such a de-tailed account of their rehearsals.

That shiny-headed mother fucker.

"Anyway, he didn't want many people to know. Listed Mrs. Chang as his emergency contact. I'm not sure you're aware, but Mitch didn't have much family."

"He did," Abigail immediately shot back, earning eye contact from Updike in record time. "He did have a family. He had a daughter." She could barely bring herself to think about Jennifer, let alone utter her name.

"He told you about that, did he?" Updike mused, relenting

with a sigh that told both of them they were on the same page.

Abigail didn't say how she knew. She simply took the head-mistress' offer to let Nate and Madaline handle the rest of the day, which would involve a lot of soft talking, arms around shoulders, and waiting for parents to arrive.

Abigail stared vacantly ahead on her numbingly silent train ride. The stillness continued as she entered her apartment, the door opening smoothly for the first time in months as Brutus merely lifted his head at her presence.

She thought she'd be relieved to be home. To have no one look at her as she chose whatever form of grief she preferred. But she found no solace there. Only bare walls and used books. These leather-bound works had been a source of comfort. The built-in wall unit was one of the apartment's selling points. Once filled, she thought this modest library would allow her to transport a little piece of her home near Bryn Mawr to her new adult digs.

Now, their presence felt judgmental, retributive, suffocating. Like the books had betrayed her. That by forcing such a large part of her past into her present, she may have somehow altered her future.

She suddenly hated that entertainment unit.

"You stupid shelves!" she yelled, projecting her anger onto the inanimate wooden planks that held her father's treasures. "Why did you have to exist in the first place?! And you . . . you dusty, old, lifeless books. Why do I have to look at you every day? Why are *you* what I have left? Why do you matter so much?"

With all her strength, Abigail shoved the books clean off the shelf. Brutus quickly fled through the walk-in closet to the far end of the bedroom. He was not used to seeing this sort of rage from Abigail, who had thrown her upper half onto the abused shelf as she sobbed, this time silently.

After a few minutes she gathered herself and turned around, leaning on the very same shelf for support. She surveyed the damage. It wasn't too bad. Yes, all the great authors she had grown up watching her dad admire were scattered all over her floor, along with a chipped vase from a side table that was collateral damage.

And then she saw it. *Paradise Lost*. Its spine had snapped.

29

The End of the Innocence

Abigail stared out the window at the twisted beetle-bung trees as her big toe kept the rocking chair in motion. Holding her pencil loosely, she sketched the trees' odd angles, framing the frozen pond and icy banks that sat just outside the windows of the Kellys' cottage in Martha's Vineyard.

The last few days had been peaceful. She'd rented a car, taken Brutus and fled—something she was apparently very good at. She hadn't picked up her phone or checked an email. The pile of books still laid exactly where they'd fallen.

Brutus sat by her side, her right hand patting his head in a non-committal fashion. She looked out past the trees and held her breath, trying not to cry.

She was sick of crying. Sick of the pounding headache and fatigue it gave her. Abigail could feel her heartbeat as she temporarily cut off her oxygen, hoping it would inhibit the bottomless inventory of tears.

I can't believe he's gone and he didn't fight and he didn't even tell us—me—he was leaving. I can't believe this is happening to another family. Another girl without her dad. Another man with an incomplete life.

She exhaled deeply as Brutus did the same. The house was once again peaceful, devoid of all movement and signs of life.

Suddenly, Brutus' head shot up. Taking a few sniffs of the air, he bolted from the room.

"What's the matter, Brutus? You see a ghost?" she asked in a hoarse voice that revealed it had been far too long since she'd last spoken.

"No, but I have."

Abigail flipped around in the chair, rocking it almost hard enough to tip her right out.

"Quinn, what are you doing here?" she asked when the slightly less paranormal creature finally walked down the hallway with a dancing bull terrier at his feet. Abigail could tell Brutus was grateful to finally have some new life in the closed-up space.

"You didn't answer," he said, holding up his phone. He removed his coat, hanging it on a hook above his third-grade soccer picture. "I was worried."

"Your mom gave me away, huh?" Abigail wasn't sure whether she was annoyed, comforted, or plain relieved that Quinn was not, in fact, a ghost.

I've been staring into the abyss for far too long.

Quinn tapped on his phone screen and held the device up once more.

"Hello, darling," a throaty female voice sang out. "I heard what happened with Abigail. Ugh, such an unfortunate situation that she, of all people, doesn't need. Listen, I was thinking, I wouldn't be surprised if she wanted to get away for a bit. You know how she likes those long drives. Remember when Grace died and you two ended up traveling all the way to New Orleans? Anyway, I'm all for a little break, but this time, she doesn't have you. And I-ninety-five is icy. I'm not sure how much she drives anymore, so this all has me a bit worried, you know. Call me."

Abigail rolled her eyes and leaned her forehead against the chair.

"Aw, don't be too hard on old Mrs. Kelly," Quinn said as he slowly approached the rocking chair that was still tilted backward, its slats making Abigail look like she was incarcerated from the neck down. "Although once I called her back she was behind my plan a hundred percent to come up here and check on you. I believe her exact words were 'go see our girl.'"

Abigail wanted to find phrases like this endearing. And she appreciated Mrs. Kelly's efforts to make her part of the family, even going so far as to call her and Ev "my girls" up until recently, in an act of assimilation. But she was Mrs. Kelly's girl because she was no longer someone else's.

"It was nice of her to let me use the cottage," Abigail said as she examined her snot-soaked sweater cuff.

"C'mon, you know she always loved you. We always loved you," he said, turning to make eye contact with her as he sat at the grand piano in the middle of the living room. It was huge and sleek and black, a complete contrast from the rest of the room's rustic décor. But that behemoth somehow tied the room together, maybe because only a family like the Kellys could pull it off.

Quinn fiddled with the keys, improvising a melody before settling into some of the classics he grew up playing.

They talked about their wonderful summers up there, idealizing the fond memories and laughing at the not-so-perfect ones. Of beds that went unslept in. Of scary stories about axe murderers told to Ev. Of made-up, sudden-onset green bean allergies in an attempt to get Mrs. Kelly to cook instant mashed potatoes instead.

"Remember that time I tried to jump Mr. McAlister's chain-linked fence to pick his raspberries and ended up hanging from my finger, thanks to the barbed wire on top?"

"I had to run all the way back to get your mom," Abigail said, turning in the direction of the fence. "I've never seen anyone run that fast in an evening gown. I thought your dad was going to *kill* you."

"You and me both," Quinn said, spinning around on the piano bench to face her. "Or the time we were all supposed to go to dinner, and my mom made us promise we wouldn't dirty our outfits at the beach, so we said we'd only get our feet wet? Then a big wake from some asshole speedboater came crashing in, soaking us up to our waists."

"Didn't that wake knock Ev down altogether?" Abigail continued to giggle, wiping her eyes.

"Yeah. It pulled them like three feet in. I think we ended up blaming the whole thing on them. Saying they'd gone in the water and we were the upstanding citizens who went in to save them from that 'killer wake' by that 'irresponsible boater who was probably drinking alcohol—and he didn't even look twenty-one,'" Quinn added, pressing his hands to his cheeks.

"Oh, God, you're right. We *did* blame Everest for that. And that wave. And that boater. Essentially, everyone but us."

They savored the lighthearted, fun moment. The things nostalgia is made of.

"Hey," Quinn said, breaking the newfound silence that allotted just enough time for thoughts to return to their previously disturbed state. "Are you okay?" He grabbed the rocking chair by its front legs, forcing it to go still.

"Yeah," she muttered, slowly unraveling her contorted body parts under a blanket that had morphed into a disappearing cloak of sorts.

"I needed to get away for a bit." She straightened up and fell into a more natural posture within the chair. "Needed . . . some space, you know? To think."

She told Quinn that Updike had offered to arrange a sub for Friday. And that Nate could take over that night's rehearsal since "he's already here every day, anyway," Updike had added in a somewhat suggestive fashion when she conveyed this idea to Abigail that fateful Thursday.

"The children need a stable presence in their lives right now," Abigail said to Quinn, who had gotten up to look out the window, catching the last few minutes of light before dusk faded to black.

"And you don't think that was *you*?" he said, turning away from the window to face her.

The swiftness of the inquiry surprised her.

"I—I don't think I'm the best person for that job, no. Not right now." The shame of that sentence weighed heavily on her. She *wanted* to be that stable presence. To stand tall against whatever adversity would come her way. But she couldn't seem to get there. She just never quite made it happen.

"Jesus, Ab, fuck." Quinn brushed past her, knocking the piano bench and causing her chair to rock once more. "You don't think that's what you were providing all along? That those kids didn't see you as a source of strength?"

She softly shook her head, not wanting to stir up memories of fleeing Excelsior Sanctum for the safety net of a younger audience, only to wind up fleeing once more.

"Why? Just because you had—you had some *bad shit* happen to you? Because you took a tragedy—no, *two* tragedies—and instead of creating a third, you *made* something of yourself? Because you said 'fuck this, I'm going to get up every day and I'm going to see beauty in the world and I'm going to create beauty in the world through my art and I'm going to *be* the beauty in this world.' Huh? Because that's what you did, Ab. You said 'Fuck. This.' And you created it anyway. And you marched on and never wanted anyone to feel sorry for you. You took that shit, and made a beautiful person out of it. A person Charles and Grace would be proud of."

There it was. That old, familiar sentiment.

"That's a nice thought and all, but directing a middle-school play for rich kids hardly qualifies as adding beauty to the world." She hated that she was crying again. Her crusty sleeve did its best to keep up with her eyes and nose, but this one was a runny cry. She fought the urge to blow her nose in the afghan blanket. "A play and a group of students I ran away from, I might add. My façade came crashing down pretty quickly."

She brought her knees back up to her chin, reassuming her ball posture.

"Yeah, well, you add beauty to my life." Quinn flashed her a frustrated look as he moved back toward the piano. "You're pretty fucking amazing if you ask me. But what do I know? I'm just some washed-up, one-hit wonderfuck."

"Quinn . . ."

He sat down, banging on the keys once more before eventually transforming his strokes into light tapping. Quinn looked across the room at his parents' old record player before breaking into the opening chords of "Piano Man."

"Damn, those two loved to think they were hippies," he said with a chuckle, shaking his head and ending the tune just before Billy's harmonica would have commenced. He walked over to his parents' record collection, thumbing through the albums. "How 'bout we put on the real thing? They are the only hippies I know whose entire record collection consists of rock 'n' roll. Look at this. Springsteen, Dire Straits, the Eagles, Fleetwood Mac, Petty."

"I think I saw your mom play a Simon & Garfunkel album once, does that count?"

"Is this what you're referring to?" Quinn asked as he held up a black-and-white record sleeve. A picture of Art Garfunkel in a tuxedo was plastered across its cover.

"I sincerely hope not, but what do I know?" Abigail's cheeks were beginning to hurt from all this activity.

"See if you know what *this* is." Quinn slyly pulled a record from its sleeve, careful not to reveal its cover as he set it on the turntable.

Cheesy eighties rock filled the air as a male singer suggested that all she wants to do is dance. "Ooh, I know this one," she exclaimed. He reached for her hand and pulled her out of the chair.

"The Eagles—no—Don *Henley*. This is . . . *Building the Perfect Beast*," she proclaimed.

"No. You're close, though." Quinn took off his shoes and began sliding around the floor in his socks. He spun on his heels, shooting finger guns before waving her over.

"No, I'm sure it is." Abigail swayed warily at first, eventually relaxing into a steady beat.

"Don't you know *The Very Best of Don Henley* when you hear it?" Quinn ran his hand through his smooth hair, breaking into the famous *Pulp Fiction* dance.

The pair continued to bop around in the middle of the room— the same room where they used to perform over-the-top ballet duets while Mrs. Kelly sang. Where they acted as the world's worst back-up dancers when poor Everest would practice their lyrical routines.

The tunes soon gave way to a more stoic melody. Abigail

and Quinn stopped their child-like bouncing, unsure of how to proceed now that the pace had changed and "The End of the Innocence" was upon them. Quinn held out his hand, a move he'd done a hundred times before, mostly with Abigail but with other girls, too, throughout an adolescence marked with debutante balls, cotillions, and as many parties as the Kellys could squeeze into a holiday weekend.

The pair came together in unison, as they always had. They swayed to the tune, Quinn's hand on Abigail's waist as hers rested on his shoulder. It was an old, familiar fit.

"Nate called," Quinn whispered as if they were in a room full of other waltzing twelve-year-olds. Abigail lifted her head, furrowing her brow as she tried to make sense of that. "Apparently you listed the Kellys as your emergency contacts."

Though she had long forgotten that, his words instantly reminded her of how much she had in common with Mitch. Two unmoored souls trying to find love and support where they could, whether that be a long-time co-worker or adolescent best friend.

"That's a total invasion of privacy, you know," Quinn continued. "Him going through your file like that. He could get fired."

"I know, but you won't tell anyone." She put her head on his shoulder.

"Why's that?" They turned and turned, locked in their Quinn and Abigail synchronicity, his mouth inches from her ear.

"Because you care about me," she said softly but confidently. "And I care about him."

"Oh, *that* old line."

Quinn bent down, nudging her head until their foreheads touched.

"Why wasn't it us?" he whispered. Her eyes fluttered open in surprise, though she kept them fixed on the ground. The pair swayed through the duration of the song. Abigail let out a nervous chuckle, which Quinn returned in kind.

"Because of this," she eventually answered, letting go of his hand and gesturing around the room.

"This house?"

"This *home*."

Quinn stared at her in confusion, "The Last Worthless Evening" fading into the background.

"These memories. Those memories," Abigail continued, pointing to the dance floor, then to the piano and finally to the framed photos that sat on top of it.

"So, we have too much history?"

Abigail fervently shook her head. "We could never have *enough* history. I love you—all four of you—because we can never have enough history or memories or laughter."

Quinn stared silently at the ground. He appeared to be thinking hard.

"You were my emergency contact, for God's sake, Quinn. You're my soft spot. You and Ev and Roger and Marie. You are my family."

They danced a little longer, in small, sloppy circles. Quinn chuckled lightly and shook his head, though his stance remained warm, loving.

"Just promise me this," he said, tightening his hands behind her neck. "The role of dance partner, campfire companion, synchronized swimmer, big brother—those are the roles I cherish. Those will always be mine, right?"

"Who else's would they ever be?"

30

Skeleton Keys

A few days after her encore performance as a teacher who flees when things get rough, Abigail found herself back on campus. After all, the show must go on, as it always does. This one had a helping hand from Nate, who took the reins and ran with them, saving the day as only he could.

Forgiveness hadn't come immediately as she dialed him late Sunday night.

"You have to understand how private of a person he was, Ab," Nate had uttered in a low, slow voice after their circular arguments got them nowhere. "Mitch was very prideful. Never wanted to show any weakness. I love you, but it wasn't my place. Don't think it didn't tear me up inside, though."

The words had cut through her like a laser beam, leaving her warm and illuminated. That life—the one with the muddy boots and border collie and children—came flooding back to her. She'd killed off that scene on her drive to Martha's Vineyard, chastising herself for even considering it could be a possibility.

"I—I love you, too," she finally said after a few tense beats when she swore she could hear Nate's heart through the phone.

And she certainly understood Mitch's stance. After all, Charles's own diagnosis abruptly brought about the end of his teaching career. He simply couldn't bear everyone's pity, or the looks that would come as they observed his slow demise.

Back at school, Abigail was surprised to see how intact the production was. Not that she thought her absence, or, unfortunately, even Mitch's, would cause the whole school to crumble. Still, it felt odd to learn that everything was just as she left it.

Abigail gave a short nod to death and grief before beginning rehearsal that afternoon.

"Challenge Romeo and run the fight scene again, John Henry, this time with more gusto," she directed in a voice ironically free of any emotion.

Though she tried her best, Abigail's heart and mind felt a million miles away. In brief, unfilled moments, her thoughts turned to anything but the play. She thought of Mitch and his last months on Earth. Of Jennifer and her daughter. Of Charles and Grace. Of little Abigail Gardner.

Change, death, the impermanence of it all. Why is it that nothing gold can ever stay?

She toyed with this age-old question again and again, simultaneously loving and hating her father for introducing her to the great philosophers of the world. They carried the deepest thoughts and, it seemed, the heaviest hearts, which they passed onto their readers the way a childless aunt might will you an antique clock. It's complicated, it's pretty, it's valuable, but it may not be worth the trouble it requires to determine how best to utilize it. Or in what manner it should be displayed.

Abigail also thought of Quinn and that night at the cottage, where a slight death seemed to occur. Or perhaps a mourning. For times past, words unsaid, innocent, impenetrable adolescences that were locked in memories and photographs, but were never to be relived in this flawed adult world.

Abigail and Quinn had curled up on the couch under a wool blanket that night, listening to old records and staring out the windows until the sun began to rise. She remembered him whispering something to her before she fell asleep. When she awoke later that morning under a dark sky that hid a fully risen sun, he was gone. His presence and smoky Patagonia fleece sweater had been replaced by a down pillow.

She wished she could say time at the Kellys' cottage had healed all, but it hadn't. There was one noticeable change in her, though. Abigail vowed to display more confidence as she juggled the hats of director, screenwriter, seamstress, set designer, and fill-in parent.

The only task she did not enjoy was stagehand. She avoided the back right corner of the theater like the plague, staying as far away from Mitch's old office as possible. Not that she had any choice. A chair had been placed up against the door, requiring the children to give that area a wide berth as they maneuvered backstage.

That was fine by her.

No need to unlock the past and free any lingering demons.

Though John Henry played the scene the way she'd requested, her mind remained fixated on all the unfinished business and skeletons that surly old man undoubtedly kept locked behind those four walls.

The final dress rehearsal was a long one. The kids were tired. The room was a mixture of excitement and nervous anticipation that had begun earlier that day when some of the play's older participants were allowed to sell tickets during recess and lunch. A few especially responsible kids, including Alex and John Henry, even went classroom to classroom, enticing students with a two-dollar savings if they bought tickets ahead of time. At eight dollars a pop, the kids hauled in two hundred and sixty-four dollars in advance ticket sales.

"Must be all the parents," she theorized to Nate, counting the loot after the last student had been picked up that evening.

"Right, because parents think ahead like that and send their kids to school with extra cash to save that whopping two dollars on a child's play ticket," he quipped, flipping a wad of ones in front of her nose. "Especially these parents, the tight belts that they are. It's probably all the dads who want to get a look at their kid's hot drama coach. Especially her backside."

"Nate." She leaned in his direction, smacking her shoulder into his.

Abigail stayed late that night, but encouraged Nate to go home. Though he objected at first, she was finally able to convince him that some alone time in the Little Theatre would be good for her.

"I want to wrap my brain around last-minute staging adjustments," she said, gathering the cash box and accompanying spreadsheet for Nate to take with him. "And I want to check the lighting. And make sure all the backdrops move in and out swiftly. And account for all the props. You know how those kids like to sneak off with them. Remember when Honor conveniently 'forgot' she'd taken Juliet's bridal bouquet home?"

"Okay," he said, hesitantly accepting the day's haul. "But you could get out of here a lot quicker with a little help." He held her tightly.

"Nate, I just . . . "

"I know," he relented. "I'll give you some time." Nate pulled back a little, kissing her on the forehead. She melted into him, so thankful for his understanding and support. "After all, a true 'artiste' needs time to produce her masterpiece."

"*Our* masterpiece," Abigail retorted, feeling like a shithead for the resentment that flashed through her sometimes, though she was referring to the entire cast's efforts.

After one more long, butterflies-inducing kiss goodbye, Abigail busied herself with the reserved seating assignments. She hung around for an extra half hour, not wanting to leave just yet and looking for any excuse to stay. She batted the curtains and swept pretend dust that supposedly coated the stage. She also removed any signs of debris from backstage that might cause a child to trip in the dark, like an errant feather or a poorly placed piece of tape. These efforts—sincere as they were—were all in vain. Abigail knew the cleaning staff would be in before the start of tomorrow's school day to get all this in order, but still.

I don't know who the new head custodian is, but I certainly know they won't give a damn about our play.

It was then that she saw it. The light bouncing off the gold-painted doorknob caught her attention before she had the sense to look the other direction. As much as she wanted to avoid the man, his stubborn presence didn't seem to want to avoid her.

She approached the room slowly, as if an actual skeleton might pop out and terrorize her. With a shaky hand, she nudged the chair aside and tried the door. The knob turned a few centimeters to the right before refusing to go any further. The locked door was a relief, in part, as it meant she wasn't invading Mitch's privacy all over again. But it was also another loss. For whatever he kept behind that iron curtain would surely be whisked away, if it hadn't been already.

Secrets, promises, regrets left behind. All would be discarded, unresolved. He'd have to take those with him to his grave.

It was a devastatingly sad thought Abigail had as she stood there, staring at a cheap piece of metal that carried so much weight.

31

Take a Bow

S tanding in the adjoining classroom that would serve as the play's reception area, Abigail noticed her hands shaking. Opening Night was finally here, and if a little brass doorknob felt heavy, the pressure of this night was positively chest crushing. There were facts she couldn't deny that added more anxiety to an already tense situation.

Fact: you have no experience with theater; they only picked you because you were the low woman on the totem pole.

Fact: you don't know how to keep your mouth shut around reporters.

Fact: Updike hates you and is waiting for you to fail.

Fact: you had a total freak out and skipped town; responsibilities and adulting be damned. AGAIN.

Fact: Updike still hates you.

Heading backstage, the area mercifully ran like a well-oiled machine ahead of curtain time. Abigail peeked out into the audience, proud that they'd managed to pack in a strong crowd, despite a few empty seats in the VIP section. There were still fifteen minutes until curtain time, but Abigail knew at least two of those spaces would remain empty all night. She hadn't had the heart to replace Mitch's and Jennifer's names with two others. She figured it was a fitting tribute to leave the seats empty, though she willed her eyes to stop looking at them.

Scanning the rest of the audience, Abigail also found it odd to see so many adults on campus. Sure, she'd done back-to-school nights and parent-teacher conferences, but it was quite different to see such a large group of wealthy, middle-aged humans trying to build each other up with feigned excitement. There was something else altogether foreign about this group. They were *parents*. Single, still married, and remarried. A few with nannies in tow. They'd all put their social schedules, binge-watching sessions, and cocktail hours on hold to watch their little darlings act their hearts out.

Yes, all the parents were here. Except hers. It was a stupid thought, she knew, but Mitch wasn't the only presence missed that night.

Get it together. You're a teacher, not a student. You don't need a parent in the audience. And you certainly don't need anyone saying you've done a good job.

She was the adult now. It was time to act like it. That would be the role she would play tonight for her kids. Abigail made a quick run to the teacher's bathroom to blot her face, puff up her already flat curls, and reapply lipstick. Standing in front of the mirror, she forced herself to look squarely at her entire reflection, instead of focusing on whatever new flaw she'd discovered.

It wasn't her best look. It wasn't her best light. But it would have to do, as time kind of continues on, whether you'd like it to or not.

Soon enough, Nate and Abigail joined the cast in one final pep talk, held in a tight circle in the adjoining classroom. Once again, it was Nate who did most of the talking. He spoke of courage and creativity. How far they'd come and how wonderful each and every one of them was. He eventually quieted down. All heads turned to Abigail, eagerly waiting for her to speak.

With twenty-seven sets of little eyes on her, she mustered a simple "I know you'll all be wonderful. Just . . . be your wonderful selves. Have fun and be happy. The rest will fall into place." She quickly uttered an excuse about checking on the box office so she could break away from this group huddle with some dignity still intact.

"How's it looking in there?" Mathilda asked as Abigail made her way to the front of the theater. Abigail knew Mathilda's nights away from the precinct were precious, which was why she was thrilled when her BFF volunteered to oversee the ticket sales with a few of the older club members. The kids were equally thrilled, as they thought it was "cool to work with a cop."

"Good. Almost ready for showtime."

Abigail looked around at the guests coming in. Though her eyes settled on that dreaded bench, her spirits lifted as she saw an elderly couple sitting on it hand in hand, the tips of their shoes hanging a few inches off the floor. They never uttered a word, but took in all the excitement through convex lenses that made their eyes appear twice their size. The man had a large bouquet in his lap, while the woman held onto the string tied to a balloon that said "You Did It!"

A real-life happy ending. Sitting right here in front of me.

Not wanting to get too sidetracked, Abigail turned back toward Mathilda. "Thank you again for helping tonight," she said, conscious to stand far back from her friend, who was flying around the ticket sales table, dodging her helpers as she made change and handed out playbills.

In addition to Mathilda, Abigail also had help from Quinn,

who graciously offered to film and edit the play from the back of the Little Theatre.

"Hey, if you can make some money hawking copies, why not?" he'd said a few days ago when Abigail voiced her regret at not being able to see the full production from her backstage vantage point.

After welcoming a few more late VIPs, Abigail soon received the text from Nate she'd been both dreading and expecting.

5 min. til curtain up—3 min til Sasha gives xylophone warning. Head backstage. XX

"Here goes nothing," she said to Mathilda as the pair hustled to complete the final ticket sales and secure the cash box.

"Oh, please. You'll be fine. How bad can it be? Jesus was sporting one of those crocheted clip-on beards for . . . Christ's sake."

"I'll probably need one of those if this goes horribly wrong and I have to go into hiding," Abigail said as she placed her hands on the theater's double doors.

"Not to worry. I already ordered us two on Amazon. You know, so we can spy on our next production a little more discreetly?" Abigail loved Mathilda for her disarming attitude. It was what made her a great detective, and a great friend. The girl knew exactly what to say and how to put you at ease.

Walking back into the theater, Abigail immediately caught sight of the red banner she'd proudly displayed above the stage's classic red curtain. She'd surprised the cast with it earlier that night, unfurling the long sheet that touted their posse's nickname in sparkly gold letters. The kids were encouraged to add their signatures to it as a nod to the pillars of productions past.

Mrs. Chang and Updike entered the theater and were soon upon Abigail, their eyes wandering up to meet hers.

"Happily Ever After Productions. HEAP, for short. What an adorable name," Mrs. Chang said, giving Abigail's shoulders a playful squeeze before she politely excused herself.

"I'm sure it's a 'heap' of something," Updike muttered as the pair made their way to the VIP seats.

The next eighty minutes were a whirlwind for Abigail and her cast.

While the club's name might not have impressed Excelsior Primm's feared leader, the actual play seemed to be a different story. Abigail caught a few glimpses of Updike's face from backstage, and she was proud to see the children kept her full attention. Nothing had ever been able to do that, in Abigail's experience, not even the papers on her desk.

Updike wasn't the only one who appeared to enjoy the show. From what Abigail could see, the audience looked genuinely amused at this alternative take on the world's best-known tragic love story.

Alex and Kennedy nailed their parts, scoring some "oohs" and "aahs" from the audience when they air kissed during the wedding scene (Abigail made sure there was no contact after Kowalski's scathing op-ed).

Even the gaffes were met with love and adoration—and there were a few. John Henry's blade flew off his sword handle during the fight scene, and a last-minute, unexpected shoe change by Marshall meant he was now tripping over his floor-length friar robe.

Abigail's heart sank the first time this happened when he was running off the stage after co-conspiring with Juliet on her masquerade wedding. The little boy's shoe snagged his garment and his face came *this close* to making contact with the stage. His recovery, however, and the crowd's lighthearted chuckle assured her that this merely made the play more endearing. By the third time Marshall stumbled—despite her best attempts to tie up the garment—even Abigail allowed herself a laugh.

Naturally, there were also a few stutters, lengthy pauses, and word substitutions here or there, but nothing that detracted from their plot or centralized message: that love could, in fact, be enough. That if it's strong in conviction and commitment, it can conquer all. Even in ancient-seeming Verona.

The final curtain was met by a round of applause and hollers. The review was clear. The kids had killed it. There was an electricity backstage that confirmed they had done a wonderful job, whether they were told so by anyone else or not.

By the time the cast came out for their bow, the crowd was on its feet. The accolades started at an ear-piercing level thanks to Tommy's rather large family, who happily cheered their hearts out for Chorus Kid #1, also known as Stage Hand 3.

Abigail willed her nerves to vanish as Alex and Kennedy met center stage for their final recognition. Given how warmly the play had been received, she had no reason to fear stepping onto that stage herself. But her palms clenched, and her forehead glistened anyway.

Bringing the tips of her fingers to her lips, Abigail shot off an air kiss to Nate, who was positioned Backstage, Left. They had done it. All of them had. They had taken the greatest tragedy in literature and re-written it with a happily ever after.

If only life worked that way.

She banished this thought long enough to see that Alex and Kennedy had their arms stretched out in her direction, their eyes willing her to step out of the darkness and into the spotlight.

Abigail walked slowly, thoughtfully, with an air of humility. She issued an equally humble smile and wave as Nate passed a bouquet of pink lilies and white roses down the chorus line until they settled upon Alex, who personally delivered them to her. She did her best to accept them in an overly gracious manner, touching her chest and giving Alex and Kennedy a long group hug.

She reached down to receive the bouquet, only Alex didn't budge. Instead, he plucked a single white rose out of the arrangement, laying it at the foot of the stage. From the corner of her eye, Abigail saw Nate passing a second item—a microphone— down the line. Her heart pounded as her body broke out in a thin layer of perspiration.

Alex took the microphone. He fumbled with it a bit, started to speak, then realized he hadn't turned it on. Abigail was proud to see how well he kept his composure as he flipped the device's switch and started again.

"We dedicate our opening night performance to our good friend and, uh, the guy who kept our school clean and pretty, Mitch Beaton," Alex said enthusiastically.

Abigail's hand involuntarily flew to her mouth. She wanted to bolt from this stage and this theater. To outrun this pain and keep ahead of discomfort for as long as she possibly could. She'd train like a world-class athlete just to have a shot at it. Her limbs began to tingle as her mouth went dry. Her body was ready for flight, but her heart . . . well, her heart couldn't take it anymore.

She was an excellent escape artist, it was true, but the recovery period—filled with shame and embarrassment and emotions that settled heavily upon her frame—was too much. Instead, she solemnly backed away from center stage, giving Alex the full floor. He pulled a piece of notebook paper from his maroon velvet pants.

"Mitch was kind of a hard guy. He didn't like sissies," he said to the audience's laughter.

Abigail wondered if most of the parents even remembered who Mitch was, but between the phone calls Nate and Updike made and the "In Memoriam" poster board with his black-and-white photo on the side of the theater, she gathered many did.

"He wanted all of us to do the best we could, and he knew that we had to be strong to do that. But he wasn't a mean guy. In fact, I think he pushed us because he loved us. He might not've been our teacher or an official club member, but he was as much a part of this play as anyone. He showed up to rehearsals, gave us his honest opinion, said 'nice work, youngin' when we improved and 'Aw, that's crummy. That's the best you got?' when we didn't."

Alex waited for the crowd to die down before continuing.

"Our play was better because he watched us, and our trees and bushes always looked beautiful. We didn't know it at the time, but Mitch was real sick. He died before he got to see our play, but I think he would've liked it. He probably wouldn't have said he loved it, he wasn't very emotional, but I think we would've gotten a 'nice work, youngins' tonight. We wish we could hand him this flower ourselves, but he would've hated that anyways. He probably would've thought we got it from school property, huh, Ms. Gardner?"

More laughter followed as Abigail did her best to blink back tears. She had forgotten up to this point that she was still in the spotlight and not admiring the young man from backstage.

"So, instead, we want to say that we performed in his honor, and if he is watching it from . . . somewhere . . . we hope he liked it. Thank you."

The crowd burst into another round of applause. Though Alex's entourage only consisted of his two parents and a younger sister, he had the entire crowd clapping like he was one of their own. Like they somehow had a hand in producing this magnificent young man who not long ago looked like an awkward, whiny child.

The kids might have written another's happy ending, but they didn't get theirs.

To Abigail, tonight's success still bore a sadness, ensuring that Shakespeare's work once again ended the way it was intended.

All at once, the cast pulled a giant wad of gold confetti from their pockets, throwing it up in the air and declaring, "To Mitch!" Their mood was celebratory. They were excited to do this for him.

Maybe he had a front-row view somewhere. Somehow.

While she was feeling sorry for herself and for them, the kids were celebrating the accomplishment of a major task, which Mitch was a part of. That it came to fruition, both thanks to his help, and despite his ultimate absence. Abigail moved obligatorily to the microphone and wrapped her arm affectionately around Alex's shoulder.

Looking down at the boy, she said, "Thank you—so much—Alex, for that amazing speech." Abigail straightened up and looked out into a sea of parents who had quieted down to hear from their kids' leader. She was sure they could hear her short, pointed breaths through the microphone. "Mitch would be so proud. You captured his essence perfectly and you're right. He will be very missed."

Abigail swallowed hard. She knew she didn't have much left in her—not after this night and not after this week.

"And thank *you all* for coming. For giving us and your kids your support. It means more to us than you'll ever know. Now please, join us in the adjoining classroom for punch and cookies."

Flicking off the microphone, Abigail went to hand it back to

Alex, but something stopped her. She couldn't leave this night feeling defeated. Deflated. She was tired of the disappointments. Of always feeling things could have gone better if only x, y and z. Maybe she couldn't bear the weight of the world, but she could achieve what she set out to do. She could make this a happy ending.

Turning on the mic and bringing it back to her mouth, she added, "I just want to say what a joy this whole experience has been."

The crowd quieted down once more as a few parents sat back in their seats.

"Your kids, they're amazing individuals, especially this one." Abigail put her hand on Alex. "Things—like tonight's performance or even a life cut short—don't necessarily turn out the way you want them to. And these high expectations we create for ourselves, they really just set us up for failure. But when you live in the moment, embrace the chaos and bask in the bliss, the ride is a heck of a lot more fun. People like Mitch, who maybe know their days are numbered, have embodied this *joie de vivre*, this zest for life, for ages. It's about time the rest of us took a page out of their book and did the same. Because although this experience was trying and sometimes even maddening, I wouldn't trade it for the world."

She paused to look at her cast. The group was staring back at her, most with slight smiles on their faces.

"Your children are growing up," Abigail continued. "Trust me, these are not the little kids who came into this theater four months ago. Our time with them—our time with anyone—is limited. But as Mitch showed us, we can get mad about it, squander it, or we can throw ourselves headfirst into whatever experiences may still await us. These kids did that tonight and through the course of this production. I've learned so much from them, and I hope you have as well. Good night."

The crowd applauded. Abigail noticed a few moms even had tears in their eyes. She hoped her words meant something. They did to her, at least. This death and dying stuff was beyond awful, but she'd also never seen anything as beautiful as someone letting go of all their day-to-day nonsense and ego and airs and just *living*.

The tragedy is that it takes a terminal illness to teach us this.

Abigail's upper body collapsed onto her thighs the second the curtains closed. She felt like she could finally breathe for the first time all night. That the load put on her back four months ago—and the aspirations of twenty-seven kids, plus one lonely janitor—had finally been removed.

A few kids ran up to her for hugs before quickly bounding off in search of cookies, punch, and their own bouquets from their parents. Abigail remained on stage as everyone filtered out. The theater soon fell silent, letting her know it was safe to reopen the curtains.

She walked onto the now-empty stage, which felt substantially larger than it did minutes earlier. Her eyes went straight to the only other object occupying the space, the white rose. She debated whether to remove it or leave it there. It was true, not everyone got their happy ending. A kidney, the ability to marry the one you love, a "good job" from your harshest critic, the praise of a parent. Happiness comes in many forms for many people. Tonight, it came in the form of a packed house and a cast that felt they had done something. Other wishes would remain just that.

"You did it," said Quinn, filming her as he moved on stage.

"Quinn, put that thing away." She batted at his camera and turned her head in teasing defiance.

"You know how long I've been waiting to hear you say that?" Before their talk at Martha's Vineyard, a joke like that would've elicited nervous laughter from an uncomfortable Abigail. Truth be told, Quinn probably never would've said it at all. But now that the air was clear, they were both grateful to be able to make light of the situation. "Seriously though, Ab, you did great. It's gonna make an awesome video, too."

"I'm sure it will. And thank you—so much—for your support," she said, giving him a big hug, the kind reserved for only your closest friends. "I mean it. And not just for today or the past few months. For the last twelve years. I was serious when I said you guys are my family. I would be nothing without you."

"Can you look into the camera and say that one more time?"

"Thank you," she said, grabbing the lens and doing an extreme *Wayne's World* close-up.

"You're welcome, though I don't think I'm the only one you have to thank."

"Oh, my gosh," Abigail said, remembering the larger world waiting outside those theater doors. "You're right. Mathilda. She's probably freaking out with all those kids."

"Yeah . . . her and some others." Quinn put the camera down by his side and made his way up the theater aisle. "I'll see you by the dessert table."

"Save me a cookie," she yelled, kneeling to collect some of the memorial confetti. Another pair of arms was suddenly around her.

"Have I ever told you my girlfriend is absolutely amazing?" Nate kissed her neck before helping her up. Abigail chuckled, wrapping her arms around his neck. "Really. She is. I'm going to have to introduce you to her sometime. Just don't talk to her about wine. She's a real dummy on that subject."

Abigail threw her small fistful of gold dust at him as they stole a few quick on-stage kisses. Before long, a lone groupie burst through the door.

"There he is," Marshall proclaimed, successfully running

down the aisle now that his costume was off. "That's Mr. Carter, Dad. He's the one who told me I'm . . . I got . . . what did you say I have again, Mr. Carter?"

"I said you were multi-talented," Nate said, grinning. He jumped off the stage to greet this pair.

"See, Dad? I *told* you." Marshall turned to his father as if he'd just proven the world was most certainly round to a truther.

"I never said you weren't, Marshall." The father sported a look of embarrassment that he tried to clearly display to both teachers. "I never said you were—or *weren't*—anything. You couldn't think of the word Mr. Carter had used."

The threesome chuckled as Nate threw his arms around the pair. He escorted them up the aisle and out of the theater, promising that they didn't want to miss Mrs. Chang's Snicker-doodles.

"I'll be right behind you," Abigail shouted as she regained her moment of solitude.

32

The Rest Is Still Unwritten

Alone once more, Abigail's attention returned to the top of the stage. While she loved the idea of the rose remaining there for days, eventually drying up but looking beautiful nonetheless, she knew its more likely fate was that the new head custodian—one who had no history or attachment to this school, this theater, these kids—would instantly sweep it into the garbage once they cleared out for the night.

That was a thought she couldn't bear. Abigail reached for the rose as another hand suddenly appeared from the audience.

"Oh, good. Someone else had the same idea," a female voice said from the darkened pit below. Abigail couldn't see her face, but she knew instantly who she was. She bolted down the stage's side steps, afraid if she didn't reach this apparition fast enough, the being might disappear. With the stage lights out of her eyes, Abigail took in the human form. She had curly blonde hair, a jean jacket and a face that betrayed a life much harder than her likely age. It wasn't an unfamiliar look to Abigail.

"Miss . . . Beaton?"

"Yes," the woman said delicately, though her face failed to

soften. "Thank you for the nice words. I think he would have liked that."

A million thoughts ran through Abigail's head. She had no idea where to begin.

Do I offer my condolences? Ask how she liked the play? No, that's stupid. What about the tribute? Was that nice enough? Oh, my God, the letter. Shit. Should I apologize for meddling in a matter so obviously personal? WHAT IN THE WORLD DO I SAY?!

The woman offered a polite, if slightly forced smile. "Look, my father and I . . . we had some rough times," she finally began.

"Oh, but he loved you," Abigail proclaimed, shaking her fists in front of her as she made use of that nervous energy. This surprise outburst caused Jennifer to take a physical step back. "I mean, he absolutely loved you. Adored you, really. You and, oh, forgive me, I can't remember her name."

"Cadence. Her name's Cadence," Jennifer said in a low tone. She allowed a sigh to escape, which seemed to express both her frustration and her attempt to be patient with this overeager teacher.

Apparently, patience and Mitch Beaton went hand in hand. Jennifer's mom needed to be patient when he came home at two a.m., too drunk to make it up the stairs and into bed. The butcher had to be patient when Mitch accused him of padding the meat scale and overcharging him, always managing to get a crack in about the business owner's foreign status in the process. And Jennifer. Well, Jennifer was tired of being patient. She explained all this to Abigail in one short, pointed rant that left her breathless by the time she finished.

"But he wasn't all bad," Abigail argued. "I mean, he had his bright spots."

Inhaling deeply, Jennifer said, "I know my dad loved me.

And I'm sure you and this club filled a void in his life from his first family. Well, my mother and I and, later, my daughter. I refer to us as his first family, for some reason. Not like we're royal or noble in *any* sense of the word." She laughed at the seemingly outlandish notion. "I guess I figured he had others on the side. Or other women at least. Put the hurt we caused him and the hurt he caused us behind him. Locked it in a box somewhere and threw away the key."

Abigail wanted to say something—*anything*—that would make Jennifer feel they weren't his first family, but his only family. His true loves. She knew how patronizing this would sound to the man's daughter, however. She'd heard it a million times from people who knew her own parents to varying degrees.

Your mother would've loved to see you walk across that stage, Abigail, her grandmother had written in a graduation card a few years back when Abigail obtained her teaching certificate. Abigail did not attend that graduation ceremony, despite the Kellys' insistence that they would be her cheering squad. *She would've given anything to be there for it. You're by far her proudest accomplishment.*

Abigail remembered the resentment she felt when she read that card. She understood the sentiment and her grandmother's (failed) attempt to include her mother in this achievement. Except Abigail didn't feel that way.

My mom could've easily been there, if she cared more about life and her kid and taking care of herself than she did about spending every last penny on the internet. I may be her "proudest" accomplishment, but I certainly wasn't her largest love.

She remembered those words and chastised herself for going down the same path now with Jennifer. She *didn't* know the nature of their relationship. Or who Mitch was for the seventy-one years before she met him. Puffing him up to his daughter, Abigail realized, was patronizing.

It was a death benefit, really. The deceased were rarely remembered as they were, but rather as how they should have been. Faults are downplayed while even the mildest accomplishment is polished until it's bright and shiny. It's revisionist history at its best. Abigail knew this.

But she also knew there had been an old man who wasn't getting any younger who seemed to lead a lonely, isolated, angry existence. The letter she'd found in his desk and their short but meaningful conversation about his "first family" had compelled Abigail to act in ways she never had before.

"I—I don't know what to say," Abigail finally offered, clasping her hands together to prevent another bodily outburst. "I didn't live with him, Jennifer. I didn't have to see and experience the hurt and betrayal it sounds like he caused. All I can say is, toward the end? It seemed like he was seeking out moments of joy. He was still a stubborn man, but behind that leathery skin, cloudy eyes and war—well, alcohol-torn—body, he found some gratification. And he didn't find it at the bottom of a bottle. The kids made him happy. Seeing them and becoming involved, however distantly, made him miss his 'first family,' as you put it."

"He didn't smile much," Jennifer said, staring at the rose still on the stage. "But when he did, you could see the pure joy on his face. I wish he would've pursued real happiness, rather than chasing these quick fixes, be that alcohol, other women, or pushing people away in his admirable attempt at pure isolation."

Abigail was optimistic over this brief detour from holding the dead's feet to the fire—an activity she was way too good at herself.

"He had greatness, you know," Abigail offered quietly, almost apologetically. "You're right. He didn't pursue much, but there was something special inside. Buried way inside, but it existed. He the true man that he was existed. Maybe not all the time, but in small, fleeting doses."

"I know he did." Jennifer firmly rubbed the worn leather strap on her purse, making Abigail wonder if its dry, cracked exterior somehow reminded her of her father. "The true Mitch Beaton was down in there. Too bad he was stifled by the real Mitch Beaton."

Abigail's face fell once more. Her sadness was equal parts hers and Jennifer's. She was sad for a missed opportunity for reconnection. And she was sad to hear how she likely sounded to others when this situation was reversed. There were so many times when old resentments compelled Abigail to set the record straight on her own mother, refusing to give anyone a pencil to revise Grace's biography.

Abigail wanted to offer some sort of consolation prize to this woman who came all this way to see a play that vicariously held part of her dad. But Jennifer seemed so sure in her beliefs, so strong in her convictions. Instead, she said the only thing she could think of.

"I hope I didn't overstep my bounds by mailing you that letter."

"No, it was a nice sentiment. Reading that letter and imagining what my father might've looked like, felt like, when he was writing it. That's a memory I'll file in the good column. Plus, since he never sent it, he never had to agonize over how it would've been received."

Abigail tensed.

How it would have been received?

"Can you imagine," she continued, "sending that letter and

then hearing nothing? Days, weeks, nothing? Maybe he'd worry he'd sent it to the wrong address, or that it had gotten lost in the mail, or that I was somehow too sick to respond. His mind could've run rampant with scenarios, not the least of which might've been that I'd chosen not to write back. That he'd poured his heart out to his only child, and I'd deemed it unworthy of a response. Maybe he'd wonder if I'd even read it. Perhaps he'd think I threw it in the trash upon seeing the return address. That sort of thing—the not knowing—could be absolutely torturous to a person."

"Oh, but you would have responded," Abigail exclaimed, her hands making a swift getaway from her body. "You would have . . . right?"

Abigail looked at her hopefully—desperately hopefully— wanting to know that under different circumstances this all could've ended differently. Fences could be mended and grand-daughters could be doted upon. Histories could be rewritten and fates undone, if time were still left and the person hadn't yet shuffled off this mortal coil.

Maybe that would've given him the strength and motivation to fight. To remain on the transplant list or give up the bottle.

But Jennifer was right. The not knowing could be torturous. Maybe one day he would've walked through that door while Abigail was rehearsing a different play and said "Hey. Looka this. You see that? *That's* my grandbaby." He'd hold up an actual photo that was sent to him, flashing a joyous smile that exposed those familiar eye creases. Abigail's body was begging this woman to tell her this new scene would've been so, all the while knowing the answer.

"That's the thing with storylines that never play out," Jennifer said, picking a few specks of confetti off the shoulder-height stage.

"No one knows the ending. Maybe I would have responded, maybe I wouldn't have. We'll never know. That's how life is. You get through it and try to form more good memories than bad."

The woman tossed the shiny dots in her purse. She gave her palms a quick swipe and enveloped Abigail's hands in her own. "Thank you for slightly altering the end of this story," she added before issuing a quick squeeze and walking out of the theater, rose in tow.

At the reception, Abigail's eyes feverishly searched the classroom for that curly bleached-blonde hair, though she knew it was in vain. Instead, she found a room full of chaos. Kids high on fame and way too much sugar bounced off the walls. It was satisfying to see them all so happy, but the noise and bright fluorescent lights were giving her a headache after the long, emotional night.

"You okay?" Nate said as he offered her half of a Snicker-doodle.

"Yeah. This has been quite the experience, hasn't it?" She smiled weakly and rubbed her temples.

"It has been. Why don't we get going? I'm sure the kids won't mind. They're so hyped on sugar I'm pretty sure they can see through time. And those idiot Kraemers didn't even show. I guess they figure the costumes and sets represent enough of their presence," he added, with a dramatic hair toss.

Abigail laughed and patted his shoulder, brushing past him to grab her coat. She was stopped by a nice-looking man who looked eerily familiar.

"Ms. Gardner? Mr. Prichard—er—John Henry's father. Great work you did up there."

Bingo. The man looked just like his son. Or, rather, his son looked just like him.

"Oh, so nice to meet you," she said, extending her hand. "John Henry's come *such* a long way. We are so proud of him."

"We are, too. You should've seen the change in his demeanor. He's even working on a short story of his own. I think it involves an evil force trying to take over the earth and all the good guys banning together to stop it. It's basically a rip off of *Avengers*, or maybe the Bible? You never know with that one."

"Yeah, but isn't that how every great idea begins, from where another's left off?" She gave John Henry's father a knowing wink and excused herself, but she didn't get far.

"Say, this might sound strange," he continued, "but I feel like I know you from somewhere. Perhaps met you before?"

Please tell me he hasn't seen the viral video . . .

They went over neighborhoods, gyms, dry cleaners, to no avail. Eventually they realized they'd both spent time at Poppy Grove.

"That must be it. Though I can't say for sure that I know your mother, I'm sure she's a lovely woman," Abigail said as they parted ways once more. Suddenly, she smelled smoke coming from the attached kitchen and bathroom area. Abigail jogged down the hall and threw open the door to find Quinn puffing away over the small kitchen counter.

"Quinn," she yelled, locking the door behind her. "You can't smoke in here; you're going to get us in trouble."

"Don't worry. I'm blowing it out this open window and I already dismantled the smoke detector." He pointed at the cracked window, then the ceiling and let out a large breath full of carcinogens, as if to prove his point. "I've had a lot of practice on planes. This one's easy compared to some of those bastards."

"What if one of my kids sees? What if someone sees *me* in here? With you. Smoking a cigarette."

"All right, all right, relax." He turned on the faucet and extinguished his cigarette.

"Make sure it's out completely before you put it in the trash," she said while blanketing the room in the Lysol she'd found under the sink. "We don't want any fires starting."

"I will. But c'mon, this night needed a little dirt. A little scandal to muck it up a bit." Abigail shook her head in dismay. Some things never change. Apart from his hair, Quinn Kelly was one of them.

"What?" he shrugged. "It's true. I'm happy for you that it went well, but all this shit about a perfect little play with its perfect little ending and its perfect little dedication."

"Trust me, everything did *not* go perfectly." And that's when it hit her. "Oh. My. God. Speaking of dirt . . . I just ran into Mr. Prichard—one of my kids' fathers."

"Yeah?"

"He said he knew me from somewhere but we couldn't figure out where. Well, I *have* met him before. At Tākō."

Quinn let out an exasperated chuckle that morphed into a belly laugh and, finally, a smoker's cough. Just then there was a knock at the door. He swiftly pulled the butt from the trashcan and tucked it into his pocket. Abigail shot him a death stare before hurrying to the door.

"So sorry, Headmistress, we thought we saw smoke and wanted to block off access . . . for the kids . . . until we figured out what it was." The woman, who occupied the entire door frame, stared at her blankly for a second before glancing at the scene behind the young teacher. Quinn stood in the background, nodding maniacally. "It turns out someone simply left the hot water running. They probably wanted to defrost the ice cream or . . . something."

"Right. Well, Ms. Gardner, I wanted to say congratulations. Your little play. It wasn't . . . terrible."

This may not have been resounding praise, but if it was all the old girl could muster, then so be it. Abigail thanked her for the "compliment" in the same way one might accept an Academy Award: giving all the credit away while denying she had any role in the matter.

33

Breakfast at Tiffany's

he rest of the year was a mix of drama and more drama. There was the natural drama that came with a sixth-grade classroom, and then there was the drama being played out on stage and at festivals. *An R + J Love Story* had garnered regional and then Tri-State attention thanks to its "official" write-up in the *Gazette*. Though it was too late for anyone to see the live version once the Sunday section was published, videos of the play were offered to other schools after Abigail convinced Updike that the recording would be great publicity for EP. She also promised that the headmistress would receive top billing as the play's "executive producer."

Still, the demand for live performances persisted. So the cast spent the spring semester performing at various theater events. Abigail incorporated Mrs. Vangundy, of course, who had a few useful suggestions.

"If you covered the sword in tinfoil, it would look more realistic," she said after seeing the play twice. "Plus, that would mean you could super-glue the blade to the base and no one would know."

There was also the drama with the Boomer Bandit. Apparently spring flowers do, indeed, bring shady prowlers, at least as far as Mathilda was concerned. While winter offers the cover of darkness and the ability to sport a ski mask without anyone giving you much thought, the changing seasons afforded the opportunity of open windows and unlocked doors as independent-living residents shuffled from inside to out.

Mathilda and her team knew this, and soon her trap was sprung. She was almost certain it was an employee at one of the three primary target facilities, so her unit created a fake "resident" who wasn't very good at organizing his many possessions. This crook was smart, though. He never stole anything while on shift. Instead, he took photos of the loot and made sure the man's window was open enough at night for his accomplice to get in and out with ease while the "dummy" slept. Her unit sprang into action after baiting the poor sap for two weeks straight. In the end, she was a little disappointed he wasn't craftier.

"I mean, how many possessions can a guy with no visitors keep accumulating over, like, twelve days?" she'd lamented to Abigail while they took in the annual St. Patrick's Day parade from a window seat at Killian's.

Apparently, the burglar might have been a bit smarter if he'd stayed in school. It was Deacon Ebbisham, who had secured work as part of the custodial crew at Standing Strong before pedaling his pick-pocket talents up and down the senior-living circuit. Abigail hated the idea of Deacon sullying a profession that was so noble for Mitch. It honestly made her heart hurt. Like many un-healed wounds, however, Abigail had to let this go.

By April, she received an offer to start a new program with the National Endowment for the Arts that would allow her to bring her creative drama interpretations to schools across the

Tri-State area. She was saddened to know that, despite a begrudging offer from Updike to revive the art program, she wouldn't be returning to Excelsior Primm. But she was beyond excited to work with other groups of kids who, using their logic and imaginations, could create their own suitable endings. Plus, the amount of material she had to work with was endless. Tragedy was everywhere!

Abigail used her free time during the last few school months to outline the curriculum and plot her course. She'd even decided to honor her OGs by keeping the HEAP train moving. The name would be going with her on her new adventures, complete with a hand-drawn logo that featured two storybook bluebirds hanging a HEAP banner above a stage before curtain time.

She told Nate all about her name deliberation and logo over Americanos one Saturday morning in late May. He was as enthusiastic as she was, suddenly exclaiming, "Get up. I know exactly what we have to do." In a flash he was on his feet, fishing a few errant bills out of his pocket.

"Nate, I've still got a few sips left." Abigail thrust the petite ceramic cup to her lips and gave her mouth a quick swipe as they were off.

"Come on," he said, grabbing her hand and pulling her through the patio area. They hustled down Walnut Street until they got to a corner where Nate asked her to close her eyes.

"This is crazy, what are you *doing*?"

"Shhh. Just walk." He placed both hands over her face and directed her slowly forward.

Abigail tried to get her bearings, but the last two turns had been such a blur that she had no idea where she was heading. She heard someone open a door, then suddenly felt the cool, crisp breeze of air conditioning hit her skin. The space seemed calm, with a faint aroma of flowers dancing in the air. She prayed they weren't in the funeral home on Seventeenth. Nate removed his hands. Abigail opened her eyes, letting out a small gasp.

"Nate, we're in . . . Tiffany's," she finally said, just loud enough to be heard as she took in the grand space.

"I know."

Their relationship had been going strong for six months now. Though they kept it strictly professional at school, the two couldn't keep their hands off each other elsewhere. They had even moved a few possessions into their respective apartments. Abigail kept a bag of toiletries, three pairs of shoes and a dog bed at Nate's. Meanwhile, her own closet was the proud owner of six long-sleeved flannel shirts and a modest electronic drum set.

The pair had grown quite close over this time. Abigail met the rest of Nate's family that Christmas. They'd welcomed her in like one of their own, the way the Kellys had more than twelve years ago. On New Year's Eve, they shared a kiss at Jerry's annual party—one that let her know life could be so much better than it ever had been.

Still, Tiffany's was a startling destination.

"But," Abigail said, unsure how to proceed. She remained firmly planted inside the shiny large door.

"You're starting a new chapter in a few months." Nate narrowed his eyes and scanned the establishment. "You need some new hardware to tag along. Here. Over here." He pulled her to the far back left corner.

"That one," Nate said to a man in a snazzy gray suit and robin-egg-blue tie, pointing to one of the cases.

"Oh, it's beautiful," Abigail fawned, holding her hand out so she could admire it close up.

"It is, right? I knew you'd like it. You'll need a new journal to plot out your next masterpiece."

"Can we get it inscribed?" Abigail asked, petting the Tiffany-blue patent leather.

"Of course. What should it say? Happily Ever After Productions? Nah, too obvious. You'll have plenty of materials with that on them."

Nate took the notebook from the man and opened it. Grabbing the sterling silver pen near the cash register, he scribbled something inside.

You are braver than you believe, stronger than you seem, and smarter than you think.
To Ever Afters . . .Nate.

She turned the notebook to face her, reading the inscription and smiling.

"That's perfect." Abigail held up her hand to toast with a pretend glass of champagne (apparently the real thing was reserved for engagement-ring purchases only). "To ever afters," she said as she moved her "glass" closer to his.

"Wait, wait . . . one more thing," he said, gently holding up his palm as if he could bobble her faux drink. He once again opened the journal. Flipping to the last page, he wrote:

To Charles and Grace Gardner . . . wherever they may be.

Abigail's eyes welled as she read the new addition. The pair toasted, which ended up looking more like a fist bump, as the man at the counter rang up their purchase with an exasperated eye roll.

No, Abigail didn't know where her mom and dad were at this exact moment. Maybe they were looking down from above, doing their own little toast in heaven. Maybe they were reincarnated, running around outside as rambunctious kids or spoiled pets or free birds. Maybe they were simply resting peacefully, oblivious to all of this, on the grounds of Laurel Hill Cemetery. Maybe they were nothing more than the wind, dust and rain that consistently filled Philadelphia. No one knew for certain. While Abigail may not have had this answer, she knew exactly where she and her new notebook were headed first . . . Excelsior Sanctum.

I guess all's well that ends well after all.

To Michael and Gloria Day . . . wherever they may be.

Acknowledgments

For better or for worse, this book would not have been possible without the deeply personal experiences I shared with my parents. Michael and Gloria were two average Joes who worked hard, kept their heads down, and tried to build a little happiness in their corner of the world—but the universe had other plans, and life quickly spiraled after that.

On the good days, I have grace and empathy for all of our situations. On the bad days, I have anger and resentment. No matter what day it is, though, our collective journey was ours and ours alone. Our story inspired this book, and I hope it will inspire others who feel that the universe unfairly targets them from time to time—whether that's true or not.

This book also would not have been possible without the numerous people who acted as my cheerleaders, coaches, and sometimes therapists.

COVID was a mother, but the brightest spot was forming a critique group with three other wonderfully talented ladies as we all worked to perfect our novels and get them out into the world. Angie, Anna, and Tanya—the book I made you suffer through doesn't even resemble the work on these previous pages, and much of that is due to your very wise feedback. Thank you for always having my best interest at heart, and telling me what I needed to hear.

To Caroline Tolley, whom I consider to be the best developmental editor in the business: Your expertise allowed this book to finally break out of its shell and add the finishing touches it so desperately needed. After 3,700 iterations, I didn't think it was possible to come up with any new ideas to strengthen this manuscript, but then I met you. Working with you was a joy, a pleasure, and such an enlightening experience. I look forward to many more projects together.

A big thank-you to my publisher, Brooke Warner, who I'm positive never wants to see another illustrated dog for as long as she lives. I'm grateful you believed in my work in the first place, and I'm appreciative of how patient you were as we navigated through the many, many (many) versions of the dog on the cover. I'm sure you never imagined this two-inch figure would occupy as much time, energy, and brain power as it did, but your engagement in the process spoke volumes about your commitment to your authors and their vision—and to ensuring we are happy with the physical manifestations of our books. Thank you. And sorry.

I guess on that note I should add in Lou, whose formal rescue name was Bindie. That bull terrier was my constant companion in life when I truly, truly felt I had no one. My parents were dead and my love life (and life in general) was a mess, but that 60-pound sack of pure hatred toward anything but me was my ride or die. We saved each other, and she was my rock for many years. I hope I did as much for you as you did for me, Lou. I always knew you'd be in my first book, and I'm so happy I was able to make that happen. You even made the cover (thanks again, Brooke)!

Speaking of messy love lives—I've always believed in the saying, "Someday, someone will walk into your life and make you realize why it never worked out with anyone else." Mike, you did exactly that (although I guess I was the one who technically walked into that bar) on that fateful night in Manhattan. Your daily thoughtfulness always amazes me, as does your love and devotion to your family. On every occasion that demands (suggests?) a card, I always write, "Thank you for making all my dreams come true." I mean it. You were done! You had the suc cessful career, grown kids, and Alec Baldwin good looks every bachelor dreams of. Then you gave it all up to get married again and start a second family, saying you could never take those things away from me. This selfless act shellshocks me to this day. You are the reason I can still believe in happily-ever-afters. Thank you for always supporting me and for offering your recommendations and keen business advice—aka *stop bothering Brooke about the dog*—as this book came to fruition. And to Michael, Kelly, Matthew, and Caylin—thank you for giving me an "instant family" of sorts.

Last but not least, Celine (Cece). It turns out every cliché they say about motherhood is true. You are the air I breathe, the smile on my face, the white hairs on my head, and everything in between. You are magic and love and light, and I know without a doubt that the greatest honor I'll ever have is being your mom. There is no me without you. I hope I make you proud, and I hope one day you read this book and give me your brutally honest feedback. If you're anything like me, I know you will.

ABOUT THE AUTHOR

Courtney Deane has been a writer and pursuer of happily-ever-afters since she can remember. As a full-time freelance writer, her days are spent working for print, digital, and broadcast entities, as well as a variety of PR and marketing clients. She continues her craft by dedicating some space each day to work on her fiction books. After both of her parents died, she worked to turn those tragedies into something beautiful—an effort that inspired her debut novel, *When Happily Ever After Fails*. She holds bachelor's degrees in English and sociology from UC Irvine and a master's in journalism from USC. Deane lives in San Diego with her husband, daughter, and rescue dog—her very own happily-ever-after.

SELECTED TITLES FROM SPARKPRESS

SparkPress is an independent boutique publisher delivering high-quality, entertaining, and engaging content that enhances readers' lives, with a special focus on female-driven work. www.gosparkpress.com

Charming Falls Apart: A Novel, Angela Terry, $16.95, 978-1-68463-049-3. After losing her job and fiancé the day before her thirty-fifth birthday, people-pleaser and rule-follower Allison James decides she needs someone to give her some new life rules—*and fast*. But when she embarks on a self-help mission, she realizes that her old life wasn't as perfect as she thought—and that she needs to start writing her own rules.

That's Not a Thing: A Novel, Jacqueline Friedland. $16.95, 978-1-68463-030-1. When a recently engaged Manhattanite learns that her first great love has been diagnosed with ALS, she is faced with the impossible decision of whether a few final months with her ex might be worth risking her entire future. A fast-paced emotional journey that explores whether it's possible to be equally in love with two men at once.

The Sea of Japan: A Novel, Keita Nagano. $16.95, 978-1-684630-12-7. When thirty-year-old Lindsey, an English teacher from Boston who's been assigned to a tiny Japanese fishing town, is saved from drowning by a local young fisherman, she's drawn into a battle with a neighboring town that has high stakes for everyone—especially her.

The Cast: A Novel, Amy Blumenfeld. $16.95, 978-1-943006-72-4. Twenty-five years after a group of ninth graders produces a *Saturday Night Live*-style video-tape to cheer up their cancer-stricken friend, they reunite to celebrate her good health—but the happy holiday card facades quickly crumble and give way to an unforgettable three days filled with moral dilemmas and life-altering choices.

Bedside Manners: A Novel, Heather Frimmer. $16.95, 978-1-943006-68-7. When Joyce Novak is diagnosed with breast cancer, she and her daughter, Marnie—a medical student who is on the cusp of both beginning a surgical internship and getting married—are forced to face Joyce's mortality together, a journey that changes both their lives in surprising and profound ways.

The Opposite of Never: A Novel, Kathy Mehuron. $16.95, 978-1-943006-50-2. Devastated by the loss of their spouses, Georgia and Kenny think that the best times of their lives are long over until they find each other; meanwhile Kenny's teenage stepdaughter, Zelda, and Georgia's friend's son, Spencer, fall in love at first sight—only to fall prey to and suffer opiate addiction together.